AF573770

A BAD NIGHT'S WORK

We first meet flashy Jack Lovel and quiet, domesticated Alfred Tate on a good night's work—'good' in their terms, since they get away with something over £10,000 in wage packets, and no trouble. It's Lovel who puts the alarm systems out of action, Tate who blows the peters. They work unarmed, and they specialize in careful planning; they are, in their way, craftsmen.

The 'bad' night's work comes when they make the mistake of collaborating with a gang from London, tempted by the huge sum of money involved. Towards the end of the job one thing goes wrong, and then all hell breaks loose. Finally Lovel and Tate are forced to be no less ruthless than the men from London, with shattering consequences.

The authenticity of this excellent crime novel is hardly surprising, since it is written by a man who was himself a safe-breaker for many years. O. J. Currington has now discovered himself to be a first-rate story-teller: a fact which will give the reader as much pleasure as it has given him.

A BAD NIGHT'S WORK

O. J. CURRINGTON

ANDRE DEUTSCH

First published 1974 by
André Deutsch Limited
105 Great Russell Street London WC1

Printed in Great Britain by
Butler and Tanner Ltd
Frome and London

ISBN 0 233 96484 3

TO JEAN

1

JACK LOVEL LEANT AGAINST A PILE OF bricks.

For the umpteenth time he raised a pair of expensive night-glasses to his eyes and scanned the approach road serving a large modern office block some twenty yards to his right.

The rain beat a monotonous tattoo on the metal roof of a nearby shed, and as a sudden gust of wind splattered rain drops onto the lens of the binoculars Lovel crouched over, and withdrawing a dry, clean handkerchief from his inside breast pocket, carefully dried the lens. The rain streamed from his short light raincoat, soaked into his trousers and gradually seeped downwards, a good proportion eventually finding its way into his shoes, and his shoulders were soaking wet.

From the far distance came a rumble of thunder, creeping slowly nearer.

Lovel stood with bowed head, savouring his intense discomfort. The quick lifting of his head coincided exactly with a sudden flash of lightning.

Suddenly tense, all thought of discomfort forgotten, he shrank tight up against the bricks. A car had crept without lights down the approach road, and was even now stopping before the entrance to the premises within yards of where he stood.

Gradually he edged back, feeling with his right hand for the corner of the pile, until with a quick movement he rounded the corner and crouching, watched the policeman who had by now gained entrance to the premises and was moving swiftly and silently up to the office.

The beam from his torch played exploringly over the door. Satisfied, he moved on round the building examining with care each likely means of a break-in.

Lovel watched with relief as finally the policeman regained the car; relief which quickly turned to irritation as a match flared, and in the comfortable interior of the vehicle he could make out the glowing ends of two cigarettes. Gradually he became aware of pain as the sharp edge of a stone he had for some time been kneeling on cut into his knee.

The rain, which had eased with the advance of the thunder, now began to bucket down.

To Jack Lovel the five minutes or so that the two policemen sat smoking and chatting seemed without end.

Then with a blaze of light the headlights came on, and with a wet swishing of tyres the Panda car made its way back onto the main road.

Lovel looked at his watch, the time was exactly twelve thirty-eight a.m.

He had one last job to perform, and then home.

Striding quickly across the yard he knelt before a G.P.O. cover. From his raincoat he brought out two metal keys which he inserted into the appropriate holes and, giving a half turn, lifted the heavy concrete slab. By the light of a small torch he inspected the junction box. Finally satisfied, Lovel replaced the cover.

Alfred Tate watched a swallow effortlessly keeping pace with the car; he glanced at the speedometer and noted that they were travelling at fifty-eight miles an hour.

'Work it out this way,' Lovel was saying. 'There are four hundred and eighty people on the firm's payroll and if they average twenty pounds each, with overtime and bonus that gives them a pay-out of between five and six thousand each week. The cash is collected every Wednesday morning from the bank and delivered by Security Limited. They then make up the wage packets ready for Thursday's pay-out.

The firm's practice is to hand out, each Thursday morning, several black boxes containing wages. These are collected by the foremen of various building sites; the boxes are then handed out by a young wages clerk. Now I very much doubt if he would have the keys to the bulk of the money. The wages left out for early morning payouts will be kept in a strong room. Now, as for the security side, the Old Bill check the place each Wednesday night within minutes either way of twelve-thirty.

'They only check Wednesday nights, by the way. Yesterday afternoon I walked into the place. They were busy paying out; no one took the slightest notice of me. I got right up to the pay office. There were no pressure-pads or tremblers. The outside doors and windows are all wired up, but it shouldn't take more than three-quarters of an hour to fix them. On the footpath about twelve yards from the front door there's a G.P.O. cover; last night I had it up. There are three telephone lines used by the firm.

'None of these are the direct-to-the-police type of alarm so there's no sweat there.

'The best point of entry is by a casement window at the rear. The bars guarding the windows are the hollow type, with an alarm wire running through the centre. I can open those bars with Monodex cutters, fix an extension loop to the alarm wire inside, and then cut the bar out; shouldn't take more than three-quarters of an hour at the outside.'

Easing the car into the kerb Lovel reached into the glove compartment. Selecting a yellow duster he flicked a few particles of dust from his shoes.

'Right, Alfie, here's your list. You want two nail bars, a reamer, two carbon-tipped drills and the necessary detonating wire. You know best what other electrics you'll need. Go to the Home Stores and I'll get the rest of the stuff from Marks and Spencers.'

Jack Lovel watched Alfred mingle with the rest of the pedestrians then, twitching his tie straight, he slipped over to the passenger seat and got out onto the pavement. Lighting a cigarette, he awaited a break in the traffic—then stepped smartly across the road. Entering Marks and

Spencers, he paused and then made directly for the counter marked 'Ladies' Gloves': without hesitation he selected two pairs made from fine, black nylon. From the counter marked 'Lingerie' he bought one pair of black nylon stockings. Crossing the store, he purchased two black medium sized track-suits and two pairs of very large men's socks of a fine material. Tucking the parcels under his arm, he returned to the car. Handing the parcels to Alfred Tate, Lovel started the car and slipped it into the steadily moving stream of traffic.

'You can let me off at the White Horse, and I think you should drop that stuff off,' Alfred said, heaving the parcels onto the back seat.

Taking advantage of a widening of the road, Lovel slowed the car, made a neat three-point turn, and pointed the car back the way they had come. He pressed his foot hard down on the accelerator and the Jaguar leapt forward, forcing Tate back in his seat. Quickly the speed built up to ninety; the speedometer needle then began a slow, wavering dance to the one hundred mark. Alfred stared unhappily through the windscreen at the road rushing rapidly towards him like a fast-moving reel of black ribbon, until a series of bends forced the driver to slow down. Alfred relaxed in his seat and watched Lovel as he fished a packet of cigarettes from his pocket and lit one.

He offered the packet to Alfred who refused. Taking a cigarette from his own packet, he took Jack Lovel's lighter and lit up. The lighter was of solid gold, a Dunhill. Alfred snorted. 'You know, Jack, you're a flash bastard! If it comes on top tonight I don't know how you'll survive nick.'

'I'll leap that hurdle when it comes, if it ever does come. See you tonight, and give my regards to Janet. Tell her I'll slip over one of these nights when you're out.'

Alfred Tate grinned, let himself out of the car and entered the White Horse.

'Morning, Alfie, working hard these days?'

Alfred looked keenly at the landlord.

'Same as usual,' he ordered. The landlord laughed, then taking a whisky glass off the counter pressed it twice to the optic. 'Six bob, Alf.'

Alfred fished a 50p piece from his trouser pocket. Returning the change, the landlord stood smiling at Alfred, who stared unsmiling back.

'Nice morning,' the landlord tried again. Alfred ignored the remark, walked over to the fireplace and began to study an old photograph of a cricket team dated 1936. 'Piss-taking old bastard,' Alfred reflected, 'he knows what my trade is, and I bet he's a would-be grass. Landlords are like bloody old women, just have to gossip. If they can manœuvre a plain-clothes copper into the Lounge Bar when it's empty their day's made. Tell him their life story, and yours too if they know anything. For the privilege of serving drinks after hours they'd grass their own mother. Like taxi drivers, always suckin' up to the law. Christ, I hope nothing goes wrong tonight! I'd pack the game up but I'm in too deep, buyin' the house. Still, if I get nicked, how the hell will Janet manage? Have to sell up and her and Jennie move into a room. I feel bloody awful. Every job I do makes me feel worse, better have another drink.'

The game, Alfie decided, was definitely not what it had once been. His own speciality was blowing peters, or strong rooms. At one time you could forecast when, and how much, money would be in a certain peter at a certain time. Like the job they were doing tonight. However, there were very few of these jobs left. Most firms these days had the money delivered by a security firm on the same day they paid out. No, times were changing, and changing fast. Take alarm systems—today you were up against the best that technicians could devise.

At one time you had to break a wired circuit. Of course you still had to break a circuit to set off an alarm, the trouble was, a good many firms now used the infra-red beam. Lovel knew how to deal with that, but of course it still took time. They still followed a routine which Alfred had used for years. First make an entry, then quickly walk up to the peter they intended to blow, and then out and wait at a vantage point for thirty minutes. If they had set off a straight-through type of alarm they would see the police arrive. This system had saved them on more than one occasion. But there were certain risks which could not be avoided. People who could not sleep, for instance, who might be gazing from a darkened bedroom into the night.

Finishing his drink, Alfred ordered again. Suddenly the room filled with music. An old tune revived from the forties was being played. The effect of the whisky and the soft lilting melody relaxed him. Feeling almost genial now, his good nature asserted itself. 'Have one with me,' he invited the landlord. As another customer approached the bar Alfred bought one for him too.

Later as he approached his home Alfred saw that the garage doors were shut, which meant that Janet was in. He ran a critical eye over the house, noticed two loose ridge-tiles and mentally kicked himself for not having had them fixed.

Walking leisurely round to the back of the house, he let himself in by the kitchen door. Janet was busy squirting a thin jet of icing onto a huge cake. She neither looked up nor paused in her task as the door opened.

'Hallo, Alfie,' she greeted. Alfred approached and stood looking over her shoulder. He watched her write the figure seventeen across the top of the iced cake. Janet finished forming the figure, lifted the icing gun with a flourish and catching a stray wisp of icing on her finger popped it into her mouth.

Alfred put his arm around Janet's shoulder and kissed her. She lifted her head and looked searchingly at him.

'You're going out tonight, Alfie Tate.'

Alfred concentrated his gaze on the iced cake and steeled himself for an unpleasant ten minutes or so.

'I've known for the past few days,' Janet continued. 'You've been edgy and you're always like that when you've got something on. Oh, Alfie, why don't you pack it in? If you would only get a job, we could live like normal people, and if we sold up and moved, we could make a fresh start. You've had a good run, Alfie, so why don't you? I know something bad will happen one day! Besides, it's not right stealing other people's money, and we're no better off.'

'Not right, Janet? My dad worked for forty-six years for one firm and what happened to him? They gave him a slap on the back and a gold watch, after all that time, then told him as he was no longer employed by the firm he would have to leave the house he rented from them. My dad and mum had to move to a flat four storeys up and the effort of climbing those bloody stairs killed him. That's all the thanks he got. He wouldn't keep a pound note if he saw one lying in the street but honesty didn't pay for his funeral. No, it was my money paid for it, and my crooked money supported mum while she still lived. Not the firm who Dad slaved for all his life. They did pay, only they didn't know it. A week after Dad died I blew their peter and got the wages. Anyway the jobs I do are all covered by insurance, and insurance today is nothing but a big swindle from top to bottom. How often have you heard them bleat, there's no sentiment in business, after they've pulled some particularly dirty stroke, fleecing some poor simple bastard out of their life's savings.'

Alfred glared at Janet. She laughed back at him. 'I'll make a cup of tea, then put the candles on the cake. But you know, Alfie, you don't have to convince me. You bring these arguments up to convince yourself.'

She filled the electric kettle, then looked over at Alfred who sat with bowed head, seemingly meditating some problem. She bent over to plug the kettle in. Alfred looked up. The trouble with Janet, he thought, is that you can't make her see reason.

Janet bent further over to straighten a kink in the flex, and Alfred got a glimpse of the creamy white curve of her thighs as her dress rode up at the back.

'She doesn't like tights,' he thought, beginning to take an interest. He admired his wife's trim figure. At thirty-six, Janet's figure would still compare favourably with any young girl's.

Alfred felt a quick surge of desire race through him. 'Christ!' he thought, 'I'm getting stalky, why didn't I do it last night.' He moved over to her and put his arms around her waist, but she sensed his intentions and straightened up.

'No, Alfie! Not now!'

Alfred kissed his wife. She relaxed in his arms.

'We're being silly, Alfie,' she murmured. 'Why can't we wait until we go to bed? Someone may walk in and see us.'

Holding Janet with one arm, Alfred turned the key in the kitchen door with the other.

The electric kettle was not the type which began its warning on a low-pitched note. It emitted a sudden piercing shriek. Janet jumped nervously.

'No, Alfie, not now, darling,' she said, pushing him away.

'Damn and blast that bloody kettle,' Alfred cursed furiously.

Janet giggled. 'You'll have to wash your hands now, before you drink your tea.'

Alfred, his face flushed with the effort and frustration, resumed his seat.

After dropping Alfred off, Lovel spun the E-Type round and drove back to the town centre. Coming to an intersection, he stopped to let across a very small girl in hot pants pushing a smart white perambulator with a very large, new baby inside.

If that baby's hers she ought to get the George Cross, he smiled to himself. As she gained the pavement, he gave a short blast on the horn. The girl smiled at him, Lovel grinned back and winked appreciatively.

Bringing his attention once more back to his driving, Lovel awaited a break in the traffic, then slipped the Jaguar quickly in behind a blue Mini, and proceeded to follow it back to town. There was nothing about the small car that should draw attention, but Jack Lovel grinned to himself as he noticed that the car sported two interior driving mirrors.

Accelerating past the Mini, he caught the next set of traffic lights at amber, but crossed and, without using his indicator, made an abrupt left-hand turn. The Mini stayed tucked in tightly behind him.

For a moment Jack Lovel was tempted to make an emergency stop. That would teach them, he thought. But the thought of the equipment he and Alfred Tate had bought that morning, and the job they were to do that night sobered him.

He cursed himself now, for attracting their attention.

'If they give me a pull, and Alfie finds out, he'll probably put the job off for weeks,' he muttered to himself.

Spotting a small shop, he decided to stop for cigarettes as an excuse. Perhaps they would overtake and ignore him. Putting his near side indicator on, he drew opposite the shop. The Mini pulled smartly in front, its occupants got out simultaneously. The tallest of the two stood immediately in front of the Jaguar. Glancing in the back his eyes immediately took in the parcels.

'Been shopping, eh? By the way, what made you cut us up back there?'

Jack Lovel remained silent.

'What's up, boy,' the detective asked mildly, 'lost your tongue? Have a look in those parcels, Steve.'

'You leave those bloody parcels alone.' Lovel spoke at last. 'There's no law which says you may stop and search me in public.'

'Oh yes there is, boy. We may stop and search you any time we wish! The drugs law provides for that.' The detective grinned at Lovel.

Jack Lovel glared furiously back. 'You know bloody well I never have anything to do with drugs.'

'I didn't say you had. I said the drugs law allows us to stop and search without a warrant, and you never know, there's always the possibility that Alfie Tate may have left the odd stick of gelly tucked away somewhere.'

Steve began to extract the contents of the parcels. 'Quite an interesting little outfit,' he remarked as the tools and clothing were brought to light.

'Better get the Old Man on the radio, Steve, and put

him in the picture, but make sure you've searched everywhere. Jackie boy may still have the gelly parked up somewhere. Now come on, Jack, you can speak. I'm not taking anything down. I don't know if the Old Man will hold you or not, with this stuff it could be a nicking.'

There wouldn't be any nicking. Lovel had no form. They could hold him on suspicion, but then they'd either have to charge him, or let him go.

'There's nothing in my car I can't give a damned good reason for having,' he snapped.

'Well that's all I'm asking,' Norman Bradshaw protested.

'Get stuffed,' Lovel replied.

Steven Finch returned from using the radio. 'What's his excuse, Norman?'

'Get stuffed!'

'What?'

'That's his answer.'

'Well, I can't tell the Old Man that.'

'Now look, Jacky boy,' Detective Sergeant Norman Bradshaw thrust his face close up to Jack Lovel, 'we don't want any trouble from you, and if you have to do a job, make bloody sure it's not on my manor. We're not taking much more from you, and you'd better repeat that to Alfie Tate.'

'Looks like we rattled him that time,' Detective Constable Finch said, watching Lovel drive into a side road and disappear. 'If we could've put our hands on a stick of gelly and a couple of detonators, we could've pulled the perfect stitch-up job.'

2

LOVEL SAT ON A HIGH STOOL IN THE BEST bar of the Regent Hotel, a brandy glass in his right hand. With his left he absently toyed with the gold Dunhill. The taped voice of Frank Sinatra sobbed out a sentimental ballad and, for a while, Lovel seemed to be completely absorbed in the music.

Sitting opposite, also on a high stool, a smartly dressed girl gazed attentively at him.

She took a small sip from a Pimms No. 1 and crossed one very shapely leg over the other.

'Jack, you were telling me, the police stopped you.'

Lovel came back to reality, grinned at the girl. 'You know Sinatra always sends me. Well as I came out of the intersection a blue Mini passed in front. I stuck my foot down and overtook; knew it was the Old Bill, spotted the two driving mirrors so I gave them a chase, just for the gas.'

Suddenly losing interest, Lovel slipped a heavy gold ring from his finger. On the inside he read, 'From Sharon to Jack 1972'. Replacing the ring he twisted it around.

Bending forward, watching, the girl said, 'It's too loose, Jack, shall I have it made smaller? I want you to wear it always,' she continued, looking earnestly up into his eyes.

Jack Lovel gave an involuntary shudder and reached for his drink.

She stood up. 'Back in a minute.'

Lovel watched speculatively as she crossed the lounge, then catching the barman's eye, motioned him over.

'Fancy your chances with her, Jack?' The barman smirked.

'Put a double gin in her Pimms and hurry,' Lovel snapped.

The barman frowned. 'I don't like doing that.'

'Oh for Christ sake! Take a drink out for yourself.'

The barman lifted the Pimms glass and held it to the optic twice.

'Now add a little of whatever you mix with it.' Lovel pulled from his hip pocket a roll of mixed five- and ten-pound notes. Pushing a five-pound note over the counter he ordered a brandy for himself.

'Funny thing is, the harder it is to make a bird the first time, the harder it is to shake 'em off afterwards,' he grinned.

'Must be because you don't give 'em enough the first time,' the barman laughed.

Lovel collected the loose change from the counter and waited impatiently for Sharon to finish the Pimms. Placing an arm around her waist, he escorted her into the adjoining room, and selecting a table, walked over to the bar.

Sharon watched Lovel leaning with one arm on the counter. She admired his tall, well-groomed figure, and felt an urge to run her fingers through his wavy, blond hair. It looked soft and silky.

Lovel placed the two drinks on the table.

Sharon lifted her drink, and sipping, tried hard not to make a gulping noise. She felt relaxed and happy although her head was strangely fuzzy. She had almost seemed to float rather than walk when crossing the lounge.

Jack was talking to her now, his voice seemed to be coming from a long way off. Concentrating hard, she managed to catch, 'So I may trade it in and get a Lamborghini.'

'What's a Lamborghini?' she asked herself. 'Perhaps it would be better,' she heard her own voice reply. She watched her hand reach out for the drink, her fingers closed round the large glass. She looked at Jack and automatically her face broke into a smile. Drinking almost half the

Pimms, she replaced the glass and helped herself to one of Lovel's cigarettes.

Her face felt stiff and unfamiliar.

Jack was talking again. She pulled herself together. He was asking if she would like to go back to the flat and she couldn't decide if she should say 'yes' or 'no'. Well the only thing to do was to have another drink, that would give her time to decide.

'Let's have another drink here,' she said.

'But I've got plenty of drink in the flat,' he objected.

'I want one here,' she said stubbornly.

He collected the glasses and returned to the bar.

Suddenly she felt great, just wonderful. She could see things with great clarity now, and felt there was nothing she couldn't do. She caught the eye of a bald-headed little man sitting opposite and the thought of him with his bald head and fat little body performing, made her giggle.

Placing the two glasses on the table, Lovel eased himself into his seat.

Sharon reached for her glass, drank some Pimms and suddenly decided she must go to the Ladies' Room.

'Excuse me, Jack,' she whispered, standing up. 'I shall have to go somewhere.' Taking a step forward, she swayed as the room seemed to tilt forward and backward. With a great effort she steadied herself, then experimentally took another faltering step. This time she hit the table, the two drinks went over with a crash and the mixture flooded into Jack Lovel's lap.

Lovel looked with dismay as the dark gooey stain spread over his flies and down each leg.

Sharon stood swaying, she looked at the floor, it seemed to be tilting sickeningly up and down. Better ignore the floor, she thought, and looked upwards. The chandelier appeared to be streaking across the ceiling. In desperation she closed her eyes, suddenly the room gave a tremendous heave and, surprised, Sharon found her face buried in the carpet.

She saw a weird mixed-up scene of people, glass doors

and ceiling as she was carried out to the car, and placed in one of the bucket seats of the E-Type.

Lovel grinned down at the newly awakened girl.

Pale-faced and with one leg dangling from the studio couch, she lay regarding him. She felt horrible and she couldn't think what she was doing alone with Lovel, and in a position both suggestive and vulnerable.

Seating himself on the edge of the couch, he gazed at her firm budding breasts. Sharon tried to sit up. Lovel placed the palm of his hand on her forehead and pushed her down again. She struggled a little, but she was feeling sick and confused, and at the same time his hands on her were exciting, so that when he had pinned her down he could feel the quick beating of her heart.

With his right hand he found the zip at the back of her blouse, and with a quick movement unzipped it. Unhooking her brassiere, he removed it and the blouse, and watched the slight rise and fall of her breasts. He ran his hand lightly, caressingly, up the long, torturing sweetness between her thighs, and felt his mind swim as the blood began to pound in his veins.

In one movement he tore off the white panties and the sheer silken tights, and lowering himself, heard her soft groan as she took the sudden, full weight of his body.

Easing her thighs apart, Lovel played, teasing her for long sweet seconds, then with a thrust that was almost savage, he entered.

She came to life with a half stifled scream, her body arching in protest against his roughness, but she was soon overcome by her response to his hunger, allowing her yielding body to be driven deep into the soft couch.

Flushed and panting, Lovel rose to his feet. He stood for a moment looking down at her, then went over to the holdall which was ready packed with tools and protective clothing, and closed it. He then emptied all his pockets of their contents. Next he took a common brand of cigarettes from off the table, wiped the packet carefully, and put it in his trouser pocket with a box of matches. He had on a thin pullover. Pulling this up, he examined each of his shirt buttons and tested them. His trousers fly was of the zip-up type, no worry there.

Taking a single five-pound note he placed this in his trouser pocket with the nylon gloves.

With a last amused glance at the almost unconscious girl Lovel quietly let himself out of the flat.

He drove the E-Type almost to the outskirts of the town. Keeping a watchful eye on the driving mirror, he turned into a small side street with terraced houses on each side of the road. Coming to the last one on his left, he swung the car into a yard and entered a large garage-type building; this had been built almost wholly from raw-looking breeze blocks. A single, bare electric light bulb illuminated the place. Drawing the E-Type close up beside a green Mini Cooper 'S', Lovel climbed out of his car.

He watched approvingly as a cloth-capped little man finished rubbing the small car's bonnet with a large leather.

'The interior's clean, Jack,' the small man greeted him, looking up. 'I've changed the plates to a local number. Got them off a car that was scrapped. I can guarantee there's no prints either inside or out, so there's no sweat if you have to have it away and leave the car. Alfie phoned early this afternoon, promised me two hundred if you have a touch tonight. That O.K. with you, Jack?'

Lovel nodded disinterestedly. 'That all, Eric?' he asked.

'Just said you were to meet as arranged, then rang off. Never does say much over the phone. By the way, I've changed the battery, checked plugs and points. The brakes are maybe just a trifle sharp, apart from that she's in first-class condition and will do the ton if needed. Think you'll cop tonight?'

'Wouldn't be wasting time if we thought otherwise, would we?' Lovel retorted waspishly.

Eric shook his head sadly. 'Don't know how I'd manage, Jack, without you and Alfie. I seem to work like a bloody slave; spend three parts of my life down there.' He pointed to a concrete pit below the Mini. 'Trouble is half of my customers are knockers.'

'You can't be so hard up, Eric! This will be the third time you've touched this year,' replied Lovel, pulling on the nylon gloves and throwing his holdall into the Mini. 'Leave the keys in my car ready for me. There's no point in waking you up at all hours—and if your old woman just happens to know I've been here, tell her to keep her bloody mouth shut.'

'No need to talk like that about my missus!' Eric bristled.

'Well, just as long as you get the message,' Lovel warned. 'I've got long ears, and if I should ever hear of there being a connection between you and me, there'll never be any more easy money from me and Alfie Tate.'

Lovel climbed into the Mini, started the engine and reversed out. Watching his tail light disappear, Eric returned to the garage. 'Big, mouthy bastard!' he muttered.

Lovel mixed in with the stream of traffic heading for the town centre. Eventually arriving at a large car park behind a cinema, he swung the Mini in through the entrance. Proceeding slowly through the centre lane, he made for the exit.

Just before he reached this, a shadow detached itself from a wall. Lovel flicked the side lights once, opened the passenger door and Tate squeezed in.

'Bloody contraption! More room in a coffin,' he complained.

Lovel grinned in the dark.

'Suppose you've spent all day whoring?'

'Don't know what you mean, Alfie,' Lovel replied, following a heavy truck back through the town.

'Knocking some silly bloody bird off! You know damn well what I mean.'

'Did you have it off, Alfie?' Lovel asked, smiling to himself.

'Christ, no! Would I be doing that in the daytime after seventeen years married?'

'Old woman's been playing you up, then; don't like you screwin', Alfie, does she?'

'Oh wrap up!' snarled Tate. 'Clean all the tools?'

'Course,' Lovel replied. 'Removed all traces from the clothing too.' Tate rummaged in the bag.

'At the next pub, pull in,' he ordered.

He withdrew from the holdall the gents' socks. Putting these on his lap, he lit two cigarettes and placed one in Lovel's mouth.

'I went over this afternoon and placed the gelly and detonators at the top of the road where we're parking the car; less chance of getting a pull in the afternoon. So if by chance they do pull us now, we won't have the explosives to answer for.'

'Don't believe in taking chances, Alf.' Lovel laughed as he pulled off the road and into a car-park adjoining a public house. Alfie tossed one pair of socks over to Lovel, who began, still wearing the nylon gloves, to pull them over his shoes.

'That's what done me last time,' Tate said, gesturing at the socks, as they pulled out onto the road again. 'Bloody footprint.'

'What footprint?' Lovel asked.

'Footprint on a peter.'

'What the bloody hell are you on about? Footprint on a peter,' Lovel snapped, anxiously watching a car's headlights, which had gained quickly on them and now held a steady distance behind.

'There was one footprint on top of this peter that I'd been working on, when it came on top. I had to have it away fast, on my toes. The law guessed it was me, although I wasn't seen. Well they came to my house, gave me a spin; took all my shoes away and matched one pair up with that footprint. That and a "verbal", and a few other things they fitted me up with. Put me away. That's what made me take to using socks.'

'Shouldn't go climbing on top of bloody peters,' Lovel answered, his attention mainly concerned with the car following.

Tate glanced over at Lovel in disgust. 'I just said, that footprint wasn't mine.' Seeing Lovel's attention centred on the driving mirror, 'Law?' he asked, conquering an urge to look round.

'Could be,' Lovel answered.

A blue light began to flash on the following car's roof: it picked up speed and began overtaking.

'Looks like we're getting a pull,' Tate said tensely. 'Bloody good thing I planted that gelly this afternoon; slip your gloves off quick.'

He began winding the side window down ready to throw the tools out and into the roadside ditch.

'When they stop, pull round them and keep going,' he whispered urgently to Lovel, 'get them away from the tools: they can't nick us for refusing to stop.'

Lovel nodded his agreement, and sat stoically looking ahead as the police-car drew level, and stayed level for a few seconds: the policeman in the passenger seat stared intently at him.

The warning light on the police-car went, and with a sudden spurt the speed-cops drew ahead and rapidly left the Mini behind.

Neither made any comment for some time, till they neared a cross roads.

'At the cross roads turn left, we'll go in from the village end, could be a police check up there.'

'Thought the job was off for tonight, Alfie.' Lovel laughed with relief.

Tate made no reply. He was forming a mental picture in his mind of the premises.

There was a private road, roughly four hundred yards long, leading to them. At the bottom, immediately in front of the buildings, were large double iron gates, secured by a padlock. Fixed to the gates, and surrounding the premises, enclosing maybe half an acre of ground and various buildings, was Dannette wire, about ten feet in height. This was topped by four strands of barbed wire. The night they had watched the place they had scaled this wire, placing sacks over the barbed obstacle on top.

Tonight they had wire-cutters, which Alfred had brought over with the explosives. He would cut a small hole in the wire, behind a pile of bricks. If they were disturbed and chased they could creep behind these bricks and make their getaway. Anyone pursuing them would have to scale the wire or find the carefully hidden hole. This should give them ample time to get away.

A rough, overgrown field lay behind the enclosed premises. This had been earmarked for future development and had short, white posts dotted here and there, the results of a recent survey. At the extreme end of the field was an overgrown hedge and adjoining ditch full of discarded tyres and tins; several old, abandoned cars had been pushed into the ditch. Immediately behind this hedge lay a road, which served about twenty council garages, which, in turn, served the needs of a council housing estate.

Lovel swung the small car into the road leading to the row of garages, reversed, and parked carefully between a row of council tenants' cars.

Leading the way, Tate made for the gap in the hedge and, groping beneath some brambles, produced a holdall similar to the one Lovel was holding. With a poacher's instinct for secrecy they began following the hedge, making full use of the shadows which it cast; coming to the first corner of the field, Tate stopped. Lovel put down his holdall: unzipping the top, he removed the two track-suits, handed one to Alfred Tate, and then began pulling the other over his thin slacks. This done to his satisfaction, he gave Alfred one of the silk stockings. They adjusted these over their heads, then rolled them neatly up, clear of their faces, so that a quick tug would unroll them, completely hiding their features. Finally they tucked the legs of their track suits into the socks they were already wearing over their shoes.

Lovel was some twenty yards behind Tate, and at times lost sight of him as he merged with the shadows. Heavy clouds obscured the moon, but at times these would clear, and looking up, he would see the moon seemingly racing across a clear patch of sky, to hide herself behind another cloud-bank.

Tate looked back and beckoned Lovel up.

From where they were standing they could easily make out the buildings in the wire-enclosed premises.

Tate reached into his bag and produced a pair of night-glasses. For a good three minutes he studied the office-block and out-buildings, then handing the glasses to Lovel, waited patiently.

Lovel stood for some time, watching as carefully as Tate had done, then handed the binoculars back. 'No signs of movement there,' he said.

They moved on until they came to the pile of bricks which had been neatly stacked the other side of the wire.

For a further five minutes they stood watching the buildings for a sign of movement: finally satisfied, Tate took out the wire-cutters and began work. The cutters easily bit into the soft, malleable steel of the wire, and within a few minutes he had made a hole roughly eighteen inches square.

He took a pair of small walkie-talkie radios out of his bag, gave one to Lovel and slung the other round his neck with the binoculars.

'I'll keep watch from the top of the road, Jack,' he whispered, glancing at his watch. 'The time is now almost nine-thirty. We've got three hours before the law checks. Try and allow me one and a half hours to do my work in before the security check, but don't rush it, we've got all night if necessary.'

Tate crept stealthily round the wire and disappeared from Lovel's view.

As he disappeared, most of Lovel's self-confidence melted away. Suddenly each of the out-buildings seemed to hide some unknown menace. He sat peering intently into the darkness, feeling his knee joints cramp. At one stage, on hearing a dry rustling sound, he held his breath for so long it became an agony. Eventually he had to expel the air from his lungs. It came out with a sudden whoosh, which startled a blackbird in a nearby hedge. The blackbird's shrill warning cry made Lovel jump with alarm.

'I'll watch for another three minutes,' he decided. But

immediately he began to reflect how dangerous his part of the work was.

'O.K. for Alfie,' he thought. 'I have to go in first. If it's a set-up, who's the mug who gets caught? Jack-bloody-Lovel! While I'm watching this job, the Old Bill may well be watching me, could be why that law car didn't stop us; wanted us to walk into the trap. The Old Bill aren't fussy how they handle you these days, jump straight in, lashing out with sticks, some of them with shooters too.' Lovel cringed at the thought of some trigger-happy cop crouching, gun in hand, behind one of the office windows.

He looked again at the luminous hands of his watch. The three minutes he had allowed himself had passed.

Cursing silently, Lovel picked up the bag of tools and carefully eased himself through the wire. Crouched almost double, he made no noise as he approached the two-storey office building. At last he stood before the window.

He could make out an office table, three upright chairs, one swivel-seat chair, and a tall filing cabinet. Taking a sharp wood-chisel, he began removing the putty from around one of the panes. Then, carefully removing the glass intact, he placed it upright against the brick wall.

Reaching inside the window, he felt cautiously around the interior for alarm wires. Finding none, he examined four half-inch bars which guarded the window. Knowing them to be of thin tubular steel, he took a drill from his bag and carefully drilled a hole in the bottom of one of the bars. Then, taking out a set of Monodex steel cutters, he cut easily up the full length of the tube. Lovel could now see the alarm wire which passed through the tube's centre. He took from the bag a small hacksaw, and cut first round the top of the tube, and then round the bottom, so that it came away easily in his hand; guiding the alarm wire through the narrow strip, he placed the tube with the pane of glass, against the brick wall.

With an old cigarette lighter he burnt off part of the insulation from the top of the alarm wire, then from the bottom.

He pulled out a yard of bell wire with a tiny crocodile

clip at each end, and clipped one pair to the now bared wire at the bottom, and one pair to the top. With his pliers he clipped the alarm wire above the bottom crocodile clip, and below the top: he now had a large loop, and at no time during this operation had he stopped the current flowing through the circuit.

He eased himself through the gap he had made, taking care not to become entangled in the loop of wire. One small tug could detach a clip, breaking the circuit and setting off the alarm.

Once inside he made a quick search of the office. As his self-confidence returned, he sat in the swivel chair, gave a shove with one foot, and allowed himself to spin round several times. Grinning to himself, he opened the door leading from the small office to the lobby. He felt around the top and sides of the door for bandit contacts. Finding none, he pulled a small shaded torch from his pocket. A room led off to the left, and the door was ajar. Lovel directed the beam of the torch onto the floor immediately inside the room. The beam showed a plastic mat.

'Pressure pad,' he muttered and, grinning, stepped over it.

The rest of the floor was covered in deep pile carpeting.

A huge walnut desk stood in one corner, and in the middle was a highly-polished mahogany table. This was obviously the Board Room. On the wall facing the door was the portrait of a white haired gentleman with large, flowing moustaches. Lovel moved the portrait to one side, looking for a wall safe. Finding nothing, he swept the shaded light once again round the room and left.

Turning left in the passage, he continued on down until he came to a door marked 'Cashier'.

Just then the radio crackled into life.

He heard Tate's voice coming over the air, enquiring if he were inside yet.

'Yes,' Lovel replied.

'Any problems?' Alfred queried.

'No.'

Lovel switched off the radio and looked apprehensively at the door to the cashier's office.

'I should have brought a brace and bit,' he reflected. 'I could have taken one of the panels out. No good wishing though.'

With a 'here goes' he turned the knob of the door and pushed. He stood stock still for a few seconds, nervously awaiting the sudden crash of alarm bells. Nothing happened. Tentatively he felt round the door, breathed a huge sigh of relief, and entered.

This was it! He played the torch slowly over the room.

In the right-hand corner he saw a large Milner safe.

The safe was operated by a combination and would take longer than an ordinary key-hole model to open.

Playing the light on the far wall, Lovel found what he had been looking for: a large strong room door. This was operated by a key. 'Not the best: but still pretty good,' he thought, critically examining the solid steel door. 'Probably weighs over a ton.'

He played the light over and around the huge door, noticing a wheel fixed to a lever at the top.

Well that's just about all we need, he thought. This'll be an all-night job. Before we can hit that door I'll have to knock out the alarms completely.

As he stood speculating on his next move, the small radio crackled. He could hear Tate's voice very faintly, but he couldn't understand the message. Turning up the volume, he just had time to catch the last part of the message. '. . . small van . . .' and with that two blazing headlights turned into the access road. Instinctively Lovel ducked as the lights flooded the office.

Looking up, he saw the vehicle stop at the main gates.

In two strides he was across the floor of the cashier's office. He raced through the short corridor and squeezed through the gap left by the missing window bar. He sprinted to the pile of bricks and, crawling to the far end of the pile, cautiously looked round.

He saw a man enter through the small gate which was fitted inside one of the two main gates and make for a small brick building; enter and almost immediately re-appear, holding an object in each hand. At first Lovel couldn't make out what they were, but then as the man neared the entrance gate he realized they were red road-lamps. Swinging the van round in a half-circle he returned back up the road.

Lovel, still crouched behind the pile of bricks, watched until the tail lights disappeared.

Standing up, he glanced at his watch, noticed the time was ten forty-five and pressed the 'transmit' button on the radio. Holding the mouthpiece close he spoke: 'I'm outside the building now; hear me O.K.?'

Tate's voice blasted back. 'Were you seen?'

Lovel hastily turned the volume down. 'No,' he replied. 'He came nowhere near this building. Took two road lamps from the shed near the gate and left immediately. But the strong room's wired up, it will take me the best part of an hour to knock the alarm out.'

Tate looked at his watch. 'Carry on; if you're not finished by midnight I'll call you up. Be sure to replace the window-bar and pane, ready for the police check.'

Lovel acknowledged the message, then made his way back to the office building. First he went to the front entrance and noted the exact position of the burglar-alarm in relation to the front door. He then returned to the rear of the building and entered once again through the window. Flashing his torch on the small clips, he gave them a brief examination, then continued through the office and down the passage to the front door.

Shining his torch up, he saw two insulated wires going through the wall. These would connect up to the alarm on the outside. Following the wires with his torch, he saw they were tucked in behind a strip of wood beading. They would eventually lead to the alarm bell, secondary circuit, somewhere inside the building. But where? He followed them to the end of the corridor, over the door to the office where he had entered, and back down the passage on the opposite wall.

'Ah yes,' he muttered. 'Should have guessed.' Into the

cashier's office, and still shining the torch, he followed them to a cream, metal box.

Suddenly Tate's voice came over the air.

'Keep that bloody torch down!' he ordered. 'I can see it from here.'

Lovel pressed the transmitting button, and said: 'Not long now, Alfie.'

'And don't use my name, you bloody idiot!' Tate retorted.

Grinning at Alfie's bad temper, Lovel pulled up a chair, mounted it, and studied the box.

Unscrewing the lid, he could see two large, round batteries. These were the alarm bells' emergency power supply. In the event of the main circuit being broken, this would throw a magnetic contact which would close the open circuit, and off would go the alarm. Usually the box containing the batteries was well hidden; this one however, had been easy to find.

Lovel merely disconnected the batteries, thereby neutralizing the alarm system. He moved over to the strong room door and, with a grin, raised the alarm lever.

If the alarm had been in working order, it would have instantly been put into operation.

Giving it a final tug, he spoke into the radio.

'I've done my job now,' he said, 'the rest is up to you.'

'Come out now,' Tate said, 'but make damn sure you fix that bar and window pane back into position correctly.'

Lovel made his exit, once again through the window. Pushing the loose wire back inside the building, he fixed the metal tube back into position and secured it with putty. He then closed the window and jammed it tight with two small, white-painted wedge-shaped pieces of wood, replaced the pane of glass, and surveyed his handiwork with satisfaction. He finished by giving the window a sharp tug: the small almost invisible wedges held it secure.

Lovel looked at his watch. It was eleven-thirty.

The night had turned chilly. Lovel shivered. 'We've an hour to wait now until the law have checked the place,' he thought, 'then at least two hours keeping watch while

Alfie operates—and that old bastard is bound to take his time.' Still, it didn't matter how long he took, they wouldn't be able to leave for home until five in the morning, when there would be some traffic. Under normal circumstances they wouldn't start for home until six, as anything moving was likely to be stopped by the law in the small hours. But this firm began paying out at six a.m. so they must be home by then.

A slight noise made Lovel jump. Alfred Tate's shadowy form emerged on all fours, crawling through the hedge next to the brick pile.

Placing his bag on the ground, he sat down next to Lovel, and took two cigarettes from his packet. They both cupped their hands over the match to shield it. Lovel lit up, and Tate took a light from Lovel's cigarette, once more shielding the glowing ends. Then he reached into the bag and pulled out a flask with two plastic cups, which he filled.

They both began sipping the hot tea.

'This,' Lovel remarked, 'is the finest tea I've ever tasted, Alfie.'

Tate laughed, drew on his cigarette, and poured the remainder from the flask into the two half-empty cups.

They relaxed, leaning back against the bricks, savouring the first tension-free moments of the evening.

'If tea always tasted as good as this, I'd never touch brandy again,' Lovel said. 'If you get this touch, will you have a holiday, Alfie?'

'Janet wants one, she'd have us go abroad; for myself I'd rather stay at home.'

'There's not much time left, so you'll have to decide pretty fast, if you intend going this year. We're in the middle of August now.'

'What makes you so interested whether I have a holiday or not?' queried Tate.

'I'm on to another job, Alf; more complicated than this, but with probably more in cash value.'

'What do you mean "cash value"? What type of stuff are

you thinking of? Whisky? Snout? If so you can count me out.'

'No, Alfie,' Lovel answered. 'It's platinum. There could be upwards of thirty thousand pounds' worth in that peter.'

'In a bloody peter!' Tate snorted. 'Where's this peter kept, the Bank of England? Because insurance wouldn't cover them for that amount, kept in a normal peter.'

'No, Alf, I know that, but this job's got a very good security system. They've got a security guard in the place all night: but he's bent; wants to see me. The idea is that we should do a tie-up on him.'

'Could be a set-up,' Alfred warned. 'He just might be taking a back-hander from the law.'

'I know,' replied Lovel. 'I've thought of that too; leave it to me.'

'Quiet!' hissed Tate, gripping Lovel's shoulder hard. In the moonlight he had spotted a large dog approaching. As it came nearer it made good use of the short, white, surveyor's posts, which were dotted seemingly haphazardly about the adjacent field.

'Christ!' Lovel giggled, watching the dog's actions. 'How many more? That's six in a row.'

'Just our bloody luck if it begins to bark just as the Old Bill arrives,' Tate said worriedly.

The dog came steadily on: then turned off to the right, following the wire fence as if looking for an opening.

At that precise moment a police car swung into the access road, quickly covered the four hundred yards or so, and pulled up at the gates.

The driver climbed out, flashed a torch on the small gate and unlocked it. He entered, and was almost immediately lost to view as he approached the front entrance to the office-block. Then, coming into view again, he flashed his torch onto a large ventilation shaft and began to inspect it.

Suddenly the dog appeared, loping towards him. It had gained entrance to the premises by some means probably known only to itself.

Stopping a few yards from the policeman, it began to

growl. The policeman flashed his torch on it. 'Come on, boy,' he coaxed, 'here, boy.'

But the dog, lips drawn back in a snarl, went down in a crouching position, and crept in closer. The policeman kept his torch on the animal and began cautiously to move backwards, at the same time scuffing one foot about the ground, hoping to find a stone or brick to use if the animal should suddenly leap into attack. He had already drawn his stick, and his foot came into contact with a small heap of crushed concrete.

The dog advanced slowly, snarling with increasing menace.

Lovel watched the performance with glee.

'Go on, boy, get him!' he whispered. 'Bite him, boy, seize him!'

He nudged Tate in the ribs and rocked backwards and forwards with mirth as the dog snapped at the policeman's legs. 'Dogs only bite bad meat,' he chortled.

Suddenly the policeman bent down, snatched up two rocks and let fly. With the first piece he narrowly missed the dog, which fled, straight for the nearest cover—the stack of bricks Tate and Lovel were hidden behind.

Once more the policeman let fly, this time with success, the hard concrete catching the hound in the rear.

It let out one agonized yelp, then suddenly was scrambling between Tate and Lovel. Tate managed to get in one short, sharp kick as the dog collided with him. Cannoning off him, the dog brushed past Lovel, and instinctively snapped, biting him on the ankle.

The policeman came almost up to the pile of bricks, grinning to himself as he heard the scuffling and yelping. The dog shot out the other end; fortunately, seeing this, the policeman retired, grinning hugely to himself.

Jack Lovel was cursing, hobbling around behind the pile of bricks.

'Bloody thing! Why didn't it bite the copper?' he said.

Tate looked on with amusement.

'Must have decided you were the more rotten meat of the two,' he laughed.

They watched the policeman return to the car.

'Come on! Let's get moving, it's nearly one o'clock,' moaned Lovel.

'I'll give you the down when I'm ready to blow,' said Tate. 'Watch the big house at the top. If the explosion disturbs them, they may ring the police. So they switch a light on, as they obviously won't dial in the dark. The other house isn't on the phone, so should they decide to ring the law they'll have to use the public phone box, a couple of hundred yards down the main road. Now, don't forget! If any of those houses show a light, I want to know at once, and we'll stand clear of the job for half an hour, just in case the Old Bill comes on the creep.'

Lovel took the night-glasses from Tate, picked up his bag and, keeping well hidden by the roadside hedge, made his way to the top, where the firm's private road joined the public highway.

3

ALFRED TATE WAS IN NO HURRY. HE would work slowly and methodically. First he gave the strong room door a brief examination. Then, after he had studied the safe, he took out a steel rule, placed his torch to the best vantage point on the table, and measured the width and breadth of the door: there would be a cavity between the outside and inside plate, to allow for the lock, and free movement of the heavy steel locking bars, two to each side of the door. However, he was more interested in the cubic capacity of the cavity. This would determine the amount of explosive he would need. His aim was to 'blast' the inside plate from the outside plate. When this happened the locking bars would be forced into the unlocked position. It was vital that he use the correct amount of explosive. Too much would wreck the office and probably start a fire, too little would jam the mechanism of the safe.

He took a heavy, two-speed, hand-operated drill, and inserting the bit, tightened it up.

An inch and a half below the combination tumbler he began drilling. The hard carbon-tipped point bit slowly into the lesser hardness of the safe. It was extremely heavy going and after three or four minutes he stopped for a short rest. He was sweating profusely by this time. Wiping his face with a clean handkerchief he resumed work.

The office was centrally heated and Tate was wearing a sweater and track-suit. However, he carried on, and after a further five minutes stopped for another rest. This time he lit a cigarette, smoked half of it and carefully extinguishing the rest, placed the stub in his track-suit pocket.

He resumed drilling until suddenly the bit slipped through the steel plate. Removing the drill, he prodded round inside the hole with a flexible probe. Then he took from a paper bag a rubber finger, cut from a surgical glove. Small holes had been pierced round the open part of the finger, and through these holes had been threaded a very fine thread, leaving two ends: these, when pulled, closed the top of the glove. He prodded the finger into the drilled-out hole.

Turning his attention now to the strong room door, first moving the torch into position, he produced the rule again, and measured the huge steel door. Again he calculated the exact amount of explosive required. Measuring a spot some eighteen inches from the key-hole, he marked the selected spot with the drill. Next he took out a medium sized screwdriver and, first scraping the paint off the flap covering the key-hole, unscrewed the flap and placed it, with its holding screw, on the table. With the reamer he enlarged the key-hole until, as a test for size, his plastic rammer would slide in and out with ease. He then drilled through the door at the spot previously marked. Taking the key-hole flap, he fixed it back into position over the now reamed-out key-hole; inserting a two by five bit, he bored through the flap: the detonating wires would be threaded through the flap which, back into its original position, would stop a great deal of the blast escaping.

By now Tate was bathed in perspiration and had a tremendous thirst. Leaving the office, he flashed his torch on various doors until he found one marked 'Rest Room'. There were several chairs and tables placed strategically about the room. At the far end stood a gas stove, behind which stood a table with cups, mugs and the usual tea-making equipment.

He took a large mug and, filling it with cold water, drank thirstily. Then sauntered back into the cashier's office where he picked up the walkie talkie and pressed the button:

'O.K.?' he spoke into the mouthpiece.

'Yes,' came Lovel's voice in reply.

'About twenty more minutes.'

'Right,' Lovel answered.

Tate replaced the small radio and going to the bag removed a wooden box with a hinged top and switch. Inside there were four small high-voltage batteries, wired together in series. Tate flashed his torch inside, checking the connections. He then took out a plastic box which contained elecric detonators. Each detonator was packed in, and separated by, a good thickness of cotton wool. Tate handled these with respect, he knew they were composed of a highly unstable material and that one of them could easily take a man's hand off if handled carelessly.

These detonators were of strength six, the correct type to use with blasting gelatine.

Placing these with the battery box, on the table, he took one four-ounce stick and a reel of two-strand, plastic-covered copper wire. The key-hole claimed his attention first: no need for a rubber finger here.

Earlier that day he had marked off sixteen equal-sized segments on the wrapper of the four-ounce stick of blasting gelatine. Each of the marking ticks represented one quarter of an ounce.

At the chosen tick, he carefully cut through the stick with a razor-blade.

He removed the glove from his right hand. Now he would have to be extremely careful. Working at a high pitch of nervous tension, it would be easy to leave a finger-print behind.

Keeping his right hand in his trouser pocket he picked up the piece of blasting gelatine with his left, and not until he was in front of the strong room did he remove his hand from his pocket. He squeezed the paper-covered, dull yellow explosive from its container and, with his thumb, worked it steadily into the hole. The first half entered easily; but after this, as the key-hole became more solidly packed, he had to bring the plastic rammer into use. It was a good ten minutes before he finally managed to squeeze the last of the gelatine into the key-hole. Wiping his thumb clean, he pulled on the nylon glove, then carefully slicing another piece of gelatine, he squeezed it into a glove finger and manœuvred the result into the bored-out hole in the strong room door.

Pushing a detonator inside, he pulled the two ends of the string tight, lacing up the finger.

Satisfied that the detonator was firmly secured, he allowed the now live bomb to drop down inside the door until only the two wires from the detonator protruded. Holding these with one hand, he plastered a good amount of putty inside and around the hole until it was completely stopped up. Only an inch of detonating wire remained showing.

Tate performed an identical operation on the safe door, then returned once more to the strong room. Placing the detonator inside, he threaded the two wires leading from it through the bored-out covering key-hole flap, turned the flap until it completely covered the hole, and once more left the detonator wires protruding. Taking up the reel of copper wire, he secured the two ends to the detonator wires; as a precaution against pulling the wires, and so pulling out the detonator, he took a couple of turns round the large wheel which was fixed to the door and used for opening and closing the heavy locking bars.

Next he ran the wires out to the rest room, and tied the ends to a chair.

Unwinding more of the wire, he tied the loose ends again to the chair and, returning once more to the strong room door, he secured these wires to the second detonator. He repeated this action on the third and final detonator.

Collecting all his tools, he placed them outside the door, then drew back the curtains and opened wide the office windows, to allow the blast to escape without breaking the glass. Picking up the tool-bag he returned to the rest room. Gathering the three positive wires, he pared the ends with the razor-blade, then twisted them together and pushed them into the contact socket of the battery box. He repeated this with the three negative wires.

He was ready to blast open the safe and strong room, but first he contacted Jack Lovel, to ask if all was clear.

'Not yet,' Lovel replied, 'there's a car at the top of the road. Not law, a courting couple. Been watching them perform for the last ten minutes. Looks like they're about finished now.'

Tate fumed with impatience. 'For Christ's sake! Why do they have to stop there just now, can't you do something?'

'What the hell do you want me to do,' Lovel grinned into the mouthpiece, 'help him out? He's lit a fag now. By the way he rocked that old car he must have wanted it bad.'

'Wrap up.'

'What?' Lovel asked.

'I said wrap up,' Tate replied, 'call me back when it's clear.'

'Silly old bastard,' chortled Lovel, peering through his night glasses at the two dark figures in the car.

'Gave her something to be going on with. Christ,' he muttered, 'made me feel stalky, watching that performance.'

A cigarette was flicked in a glowing arc, the side lights came on, then the car moved slowly off.

Lovel watched its tail lights disappear. Using his night-glasses he searched the surrounding district.

He was tensed up now, and in his imagination could hear the loud blast; see the lights coming on in the two nearby houses. He knew what the outcome of that would mean: a chase through the night. The police using dogs and he and Alfie going helter skelter, through the hedges, getting torn and scratched, falling into ditches, getting wet, scared stiff and with nothing to show for their pains. It had happened more than once in the past, and once in the dark he had run full tilt into a clothes line. 'Bloody nearly broke my neck,' he reflected. He wanted to put the evil moment off as long as possible; but thinking that another car might appear, he muttered 'here goes'. Speaking to Tate on the radio, he told him that 'the coast was now clear', and sat with shoulders hunched, waiting for the loud crash of the strong room door being blown apart.

Tate had been thinking almost the same thoughts as Lovel. Now, hearing him give the all clear, he picked up the battery box. He put his finger on the on-off switch, and hunched his shoulders. 'I could have muffled the peter,' he thought. With a slight movement of his thumb, he moved the small switch over to the on position.

Instantly there was a tremendous C-R-A-S-H!

Hearing the blast, Lovel cringed: then a sudden surge of anger shot through him. 'What the bloody hell did he use? A bloody atom bomb? It's the same every time! Uses twice as much stuff as he should! Silly old bastard! Never troubles to muffle the sound.'

As no lights appeared in the houses opposite, his next thought was of money.

'I wonder how much is in there?'

Tate reeled backward across the room. But no blast came through at him; it was pure funk that sent him backwards.

He sank down on one of the chairs and, for a few seconds, seemed to shrink in upon himself, all strength drained from him. He sat there for some time with head drooping forward and arms hanging loosely at his sides.

Pulling himself together, he made his way to the cashier's office. At the open door, he flashed his torch towards the strong room. He pulled the rolled-up stocking down and over his face. Breathing through the stocking gave some measure of relief from the fumes.

Tate stood for a while, inspecting the damaged office. Part of the ceiling was down, large flakes of plaster lay scattered over the floor, the table was upended and now lay on its side against the far wall. He flashed his torch again onto the strong room door; it was down, split completely in two halves: one half lay against the vault, the other flat on the floor of the office proper: standing on the nearest half he felt it tilt and sway under him as it balanced unevenly on the large wheel.

He entered the strong room and coughed chokingly in the acrid, gaseous, poisonous haze. Already his head had begun to ache, the pain began in the nape of the neck. Then his brain seemed to swell to an unbearable bursting point; his senses reeled with the pain. And he knew he had to get out fast. But first the money. At the far end of the strong room was a small table and on this were four shallow wooden boxes, containing the wages. The blast had not disturbed them. Quickly he carried the boxes into the office and placed them on the floor. Giving the strong room a cursory glance, he went across to the safe, and took four small, black steel boxes, which he placed with the contents from the strong room. Going to the rest room he gathered up the detonating wires and returned them, with the tools, to the bag. He removed the tea-making utensils from the rest room table, picked up the tablecloth and carried it back into the cashier's office. Spreading it out on the floor, he tipped the wage packets from the wooden boxes into it, placed the steel boxes on top and, gathering the corners of the tablecloth together, slung the bulky package over his shoulder. With his left hand he picked up his bag and the walkie-talkie and left through the front door.

Staggering across the yard with the clumsy load, he dumped it outside the shed which the van driver had used earlier that evening. Inside, among the various tools and paraphernalia, were two rubber-tyred wheelbarrows. A small iron stove was fixed to the back wall.

Pulling the tools and loot into the shed, Tate spoke into the radio directing Jack Lovel to join him. Leaving the door ajar, he sat down on an oxygen-bottle and stared fixedly up the road, watching nothing in particular. He felt washed out; the black silk stocking masking his face was hot and sticky, but he just didn't have the energy left to remove it.

After some five minutes a shadow darkened the door and Lovel stepped inside. The sky had cleared and the almost full moon gave unobscured light.

'Have we had it off?' he questioned, taking in the squashed featureless mass that represented Tate's masked face.

'I think so,' Tate replied, pulling himself together and removing the stocking from his face.

Bending down, Lovel took one end of the tablecloth and tipped its contents out.

'Christ! There's bloody hundreds,' he exclaimed, kicking the pile of wage packets.

Tate rolled the oxygen bottle closer to the heap of brown, square packets and set to work. He slit the tops and tipped the contents on to the spread tablecloth.

Lovel stood beside him watching; he lit two cigarettes, handed one to Tate, then sat down beside him. He waited until there was a sizeable pile, then began counting the notes into small bundles of one hundred.

They worked steadily away at this task for over an hour and a half.

Tate picked up the last packet, slit the top, removed the contents and said, 'According to your count, Jack, this brings the total to six thousand, six hundred and forty-two pounds. There'll be between four and six hundred in silver and copper, I should say.'

Lovel began collecting the empty wage packets, pulled down the stove-flap, and pushed them inside.

He had to force the last few packets, as the stove was jammed tight.

'Like to leave the place clean and tidy,' he smirked. 'Shall I stick a match to it?'

'No,' Tate replied, 'we'll do them a favour. We'll leave it for them to light their fire with in the morning.'

He took from his bag one large, and two small, folded plastic bags. Taking two one hundred pound bundles he handed them to Lovel.

'Give these to Eric when you return the car,' he said.

The remainder he divided evenly between the two bags. Roughly dividing the huge pile of loose change, he did the same with that.

'Take your pick,' he said.

Lovel eyed the bags.

'Take your pick,' he mimicked. 'It's like that television show, only either way I must win. Eeny, meeny, miney, mo,' he began.

'Oh for Christ's sake, don't take all bloody night!' Tate snapped.

Grinning, Lovel reached down and took the bag nearest him. Tate then handed him a piece of red tape which Lovel tied tightly round the neck of his bag.

Securing his own with blue tape, Tate placed both into the one large bag.

He sat down on the oxygen bottle, lit a cigarette, and smoked in silence.

Lovel leaned against the door jamb, looking out. 'Headache?' he asked.

'Had it since I was in the strong room, but it's beginning to wear off now,' Tate replied.

'Do much damage to the office?'

'Enough,' Tate replied disinterestedly.

The moon had gone down and it was pitch dark.

Lovel once more resumed leaning against the door jamb and, staring vacantly into the black void, he noticed the first faint streaks of light.

Hardly had the first finger of light appeared when with a startling suddenness, every bird, and there seemed to be thousands, broke into a crescendo of sound. They at least seemed to be greeting the coming day with joy. Lovel grinned and reflected, 'So am I.' He dreamed away contentedly. 'I haven't got enough for a Lamborghini, but I'll go up to London and buy three more good suits. I can well afford to push the boat out on myself to the tune of two or three hundred smackers. Mr Jack Lovel,' he promised himself, 'is going to have one hell of a ball, and Mr Jack Lovel is not going to allow grass to grow under his feet. That Platinum job comes next.'

Alfred Tate was busy thinking too.

'First I'll put a thousand down on the house. It'll probably cost me a hundred to have the chimney pointed and new ridge-tiles fixed. Say another two hundred for a new super washing-machine for Janet, and then I'll do another two on Janet and Jenny. Let them have what they want up to that amount. The hell with it! Why shouldn't I spend on them? Make a fuss of them? They're all I have in this world. A hundred or a hundred and fifty on each.'

Looking over at Lovel standing over at the door, staring out, he laughed silently. 'He'll be rampaging around like a bloody stallion at stud for the next couple of weeks.' He looked at his watch. 'Come on, Jack, time to go, almost a quarter to five.'

Removing the silk stockings from their heads, they picked up their bags and made their way back to the car.

Arriving silently at the hedge they watched the car and the surrounding area for some ten minutes before deciding it was safe. Then, climbing into the Mini, they returned the way they had come; passed through the silent village, and carried on for half a mile or so, until they came to a large wood.

Tate got out, opened a five-barred gate and, after Lovel had driven the Mini through, re-shut the gate.

Lovel drove the Mini some way into the wood until it was well hidden from the road; he then took a short-handled spade from the back of the car and, choosing a spot near a hawthorn bush, began to dig.

Both he and Tate continued to wear their gloves, and would do so until the car was returned.

When the hole was deep enough Lovel put the two tool-bags and the large plastic bag containing their share of the night's work into it. Finally he threw in the two track-suits, socks and stockings, and replacing part of the soil, scattered the residue about the immediate vicinity. Sprinkling dead leaves over the area, Lovel then climbed into the Mini.

'Be as well to wait a week before we collect the loot, Alfie.'

'Yes,' Tate agreed, 'we'll give it a week to cool off.'

Lovel dropped Tate off within a few hundred yards of his home. He returned the Mini to its owner, paid him the agreed two hundred pounds for his co-operation, and, with a sigh of relief, climbed into his own car.

4

LOVEL HAD THE FLU. FOR THREE WHOLE days he stayed in his flat, never once did he put his head outside the door.

He slept most of the time, for the rest he just moped about, sometimes listening to the radio, at others he would put on his tape recorder and sit listening to his favourite songs. He had a small portable television in his flat, but this saw very little use. He never shaved during this time, neither did he dress, just lounged about wearing his dressing-gown, mostly lying back in the armchair, with one leg hanging over the leather-covered arm, balancing a leather slipper on his big toe.

He would sit for hours thinking, listening to his music and sometimes reflecting with a tinge of self pity how no one ever came to see him. Only his elderly help came in twice to clean the flat up. The second time she came, she brought him a large bunch of purple grapes.

He felt lousy, his head ached in sympathy with the rest of his flu-ridden body. He wandered into the bedroom to lie down, and thought of the tablets he had hidden in the bathroom. Although not a cure, they would make him feel better.

His mind felt too exhausted to decide whether or not he should take the tablets, and pushing the problem aside, wandered onto another track.

The slight urge he had felt for some time to go to the toilet became a sudden pressing need.

He rose from the bed and made his way there. Having

satisfied his needs, he went into the kitchen, and from the small cupboard from below the sink, took out a rubber suction pad with a wooden handle attached. Wetting the suction pad in the sink, Lovel again returned to the bathroom.

The bathroom floor was tiled in diamond shaped, plastic, black and white tiles. He selected the third tile from the far right-hand corner. Pressing the pad until it adhered firmly to the selected tile, he lifted.

The plastic tile had been glued to a piece of wood of the same shape.

Putting down the suction pad, with the tile still attached, he peered into the resulting hole. Inside was a pair of small walkie-talkie radios, several large bundles of treasury notes, and a small bottle.

Lifting the bottle out, he wiped it clean of dust, then poured some of its contents into the palm of his hand: about sixteen small yellow and blue tablets.

Lovel was undecided for a moment as to whether he should take the yellow dexedrine or the 'french blue' tablets. Finally, separating six of the small blue tablets, he crossed to the sink and washed the tablets down with a tooth glass of water.

One of the tablets had deteriorated, and being soft, had partly dissolved in his mouth before he could bring the water into action. The bitter taste made him grimace.

Replacing the tile, he made his way back to the bedroom.

He flopped back onto the pillow and stared up at the ceiling. 'They don't give a damn about me,' he thought bitterly, 'I could die in this bloody place, and no one the wiser for a couple of weeks.'

He watched a fly crawl slowly across the ceiling. A record player in the flat adjoining droned on, and on. For a second Lovel was tempted to bang the wall in protest, the classical music seemed to bore a hole in his brain and he grimaced with distaste.

He watched with interest the fly's antics. First it would wander off in one direction, then another; there seemed no set pattern or purpose to its movements.

In one corner of the room was a tiny spiders' web. He held his breath as the fly, in one of its short flights, narrowly missed the web. He wanted to see it land in the web, but somehow it always seemed to miss the small, obvious trap.

He heard someone knock on the outer door to the flat, but paid no attention. He didn't want to miss the thrill of seeing the fly get caught, if it ever did. Might die of old age, he reflected. I wonder how long they live? Some people believe in reincarnation and that people come back into this world as animals, insects and things. Fancy coming back as a fly, like that one up there, and a bloody great spider sitting in its web waiting to jump on you. Rather come back as a spider.

Suddenly he shot upright in bed. The fly had taken a short flight and landed squarely in the web.

It twisted and turned, desperately trying to disentangle itself from the tiny clinging strands. A spider, large for the size of its web, shot out. For a second it sized up its victim, probably deciding on the type of attack it would launch. It leapt on to the fly. There was a brief, crazy, whirling struggle, then all was still.

Lovel wondered what the outcome would have been had it been a wasp.

Suddenly feeling the effects of the 'french blues', he climbed onto the bed and touched the web; the spider shot out.

'Ha-ha,' laughed Lovel, 'foxed you that time.'

Once again he touched the web. Once again the spider came out. Lovel chortled with glee.

He flicked the Dunhill, and adjusting the flame to high, held it close up to the web.

Quickly the web began to burn. The spider shot out from the dark recess at the back and began to race for dear life across the ceiling. Grinning, Lovel followed just behind with the lighter. He moved the flame in very close, until it almost touched the insect. Feeling the hot flame, the spider made an enormous leap, then quickly spinning a single strand, began to lower itself from the ceiling.

Gloatingly Lovel stood back until the spider was half-way to the floor, then reaching out with the lighter, held it directly below. The spider shot back up the web.

Once more the spider began to descend, but this time with more caution. It almost reached the bed when the waiting Lovel pounced.

The spider burnt up quickly.

Lovel looked guiltily round. The knocking had begun again.

He felt energy flow through his body, and grinned to himself, knowing the french blues were doing their stuff.

Opening the door, he greeted Sharon, then began to sing, softly at first, then louder.

She entered the living room, smiling. 'You seem happy, Jack,' she remarked.

'Why be miserable,' he laughed back.

He tried yodelling, without success. His voice had a tendency to break on the very high notes.

He suddenly felt the urge to be doing something, anything just so long as he was moving about. He got up, went into the bathroom and sluiced his face with cold water. He felt great, just great; yes, it had been the right thing to do, taking those pills.

Rubbing himself dry with the towel, he found he was rubbing twice as hard as was needed. All his actions now were exaggerated. Peering at himself in the mirror, he decided against having a shave. He dressed quickly, almost carelessly. 'Get the hell out of the flat and put myself about,' he reflected, shrugging his shoulders massively. 'I've got energy to burn: God, if I were only to feel like this when we go out on a job.'

His head felt clear; he could think with crystal clarity; in fact, he felt almost superhuman.

Lifting the window, Lovel leaned out. He could see four boys, playing a game that resembled hopscotch, on the asphalt square below. Looking up, one of the boys spotted him and waved.

Grinning, Lovel waved back, then made a rude gesture with two fingers. The boy said something to his pals; they all looked up. Lovel repeated the gesture.

They began to laugh and shout at him.

Still grinning, he withdrew his head. Grabbing a heap of treasury notes, he stuffed them into his hip pocket.

Sharon looked at him with suspicion as he entered the living room. The unshaven, joke-cracking man before her definitely wasn't the Jack Lovel she knew.

Lovel rushed her out to the car.

The boys were still playing. Spotting Lovel, they began to cheer. Lovel waved; they made the rude sign to him, laughingly he returned the gesture.

'He's pissed,' one of them shouted, 'he's pissed, he's pissed,' they all took up the cry.

'I reckon he's a nutter,' one boy shouted above the rest, 'he must be, he don't wobble enough to be drunk.'

Flushing with embarrassment, Sharon scrambled into the car. Lovel climbed in beside her; he was still laughing, seeming to find it a huge joke.

She heard one of the boys exclaim, 'I wouldn't mind his tart for a good . . .' Mercifully, the roar of the engine drowned the rest of the remark.

She sat bold upright, looking furiously ahead, as they drove off.

5

DURING THIS TIME, ALFRED TATE HAD the ridge tiles put on his roof and contracted a firm to re-surface his drive. To pass the time he would have driven round to visit Lovel and discuss business, but in the past when he had called at the flat, it had mostly been empty.

He had been thinking a good deal about the future. They just could not afford to continue doing small jobs, sooner or later they were going to find themselves in lumber. He had to face the fact, if they were to get caught, he could expect anything from seven to ten years.

As a diver in the Royal Navy during the war he had learned how to use explosives and cutting equipment of all types. They would throw that up in a court of law, with the rider that he was highly skilled in the use of those tools. Add to that the fact that Jack Lovel was an electronics engineer, and there you had it, the perfect set-up for successful crime.

Lovel was impatient to go big time. The trouble was not so much finding a job, but the stink a big job would cause. The law in this town were not too bad, but once let him and Lovel pull a big job, something in the region of a hundred-thousand or so, which they could expect from any one of the big banks in the town centre, then the gloves would be off.

The Chief of Police would catch it in the neck from the Watch Committee, and he would then himself begin to put plenty of stick about, with Alfred Tate and Jack Lovel as the targets for that stick.

At the same time if they continued doing small jobs, by the law of averages they must sooner or later get caught. The next one would have to be a big one.

Alfred Tate looked up as he caught the sound of a small engine.

Jennie swung the scooter into the drive, cut the motor and dismounted. She was small, auburn-haired and very pretty. She was in fact the very apple of Alfred Tate's eye. Removing the crash helmet, she swung it carelessly in one hand. Her white teeth gleamed as she smiled. ' Hullo, Dad,' she greeted, 'Mum got lunch ready yet?'

'Yes,' Tate replied, 'she has, and you go easy on that scooter, Jennie. I thought you swung into the drive a trifle fast.'

'Oh, Dad,' she laughed, 'I can handle it easy.'

After lunch Tate helped his wife and daughter into the car, and drove into town.

The police had made no direct contact with him, but he knew they were very interested in his movements. Several of the uniformed coppers he drove past pulled out their walkie-talkies, extended the aerials and began to speak into them. He knew they were making reports on him to headquarters. If he weren't careful these reports would form a pattern.

They were far more subtle now than they had once been. They had to be; a good criminal now—not morally speaking, of course—if arrested, would not fall for the old bluff. He would make no statement and he would keep his mouth shut at all times. The days were finished when the police could pick up two of you, shut you in different cells, and knowing most of the facts concerning the crime, make out two separate statements, each one blaming the other.

They would then confront each separate individual, show him a statement and say, 'Your partner has come clean, but if you'll make a statement involving him, as he's involved you, we'll see you get off light, otherwise we'll make sure you get at least three years.'

If that method failed they would put both of you in the same peter, the cell would be bugged and they would sit back and listen to your conversation. There were of course plenty of mugs who still fell for this stuff, and always would be.

Tate parked the car in the town centre, and went shopping with his wife and daughter.

6

JACK LOVEL AWOKE AT THREE-THIRTY, Thursday afternoon.

He was lying in a strange bed, and was sweating with the effort to contain himself, so great was his need to use the toilet. Opening the bedroom door, he saw a short passage, with a door almost opposite.

Holding himself in desperately, he quickly opened it. Just another bedroom. Groaning with dismay, he made his way down the small passage to another door on his right; mercifully this was the toilet. Lovel made a quick short run for the pan but he was no longer in full control of his bodily functions, and had splashed the floor badly before he made it.

Urinating in the pan, Lovel let out a vast sigh of relief.

'Wonder why I didn't do it in my sleep,' he spoke his thoughts aloud, looking up at the cistern. 'Must have been this that woke me up.'

As the tension began to leave his body, the wet on the floor claimed his attention. 'Have to do something about that,' he worried, then shrugged his shoulders. 'Why worry,' he thought. 'Wherever I am, I won't be here long.' He opened the bedroom door, and acutely aware now of his scanty attire, slipped furtively back into the bedroom.

For the first time since waking up, Lovel took stock of the bedroom. The bed he had slept in was of three-quarter size. The sheets, although not exactly dirty, had been slept in a few times. The whole room had a slightly neglected air. On a cheap dressing-table, hanging grotesquely, partly over the mirror, were a pair of tights. Lovel looked and wondered, he couldn't remember a single instant of the previous night.

Besides the bed was a chair, and over this was folded, surprisingly neatly, his own clothes. It was obvious to him that someone else had placed them there.

He took the trousers from the chair and reached into his pocket; at least some of his money was there. Sitting on the edge of the bed, he began counting.

The sharp twanging sound of a guitar being tuned up caused him to pause in his task.

Shaking his head in puzzlement, he resumed his counting. As the notes were in denominations of five and ten pounds, the job didn't take long.

He could easily have been rolled. Funny how he couldn't remember a thing about last night.

Twang, twang, twang. Someone was again plucking a guitar. He pulled his trousers on, his socks were on the chair; pulling these on he looked under the bed, sure enough his shoes were there.

Half-dressed, he returned once more to the bathroom. His mouth tasted foul, he rinsed it out, deciding against using a dubious looking tooth-brush. With the facilities available, this, he supposed, would have to do. He was normally particular and perhaps a trifle finicky concerning his ablutions.

There was a sudden scream of female laughter, then someone struck up a tune on the guitar. They were playing well, Lovel decided. He returned to the bedroom, quickly finished dressing, and crept downstairs. Immediately facing him at the other end of the short hall was the street door. He could either go straight out, or enter the room from which issued the music.

The knowledge that he had no recollection of where he had left his car decided him.

He listened for a few moments, with his ear to the door. He could hear a jumble of voices from within, but with the noise from the guitar, it was impossible to make any sense from these voices.

Pushing the door open, he entered. There were three men, ages ranging from eighteen to twenty-five, all with very long hair. All wore jeans, one wore a tattered looking blue silk shirt with wide flowing sleeves. He had been playing the guitar when Lovel entered.

Two girls sat side by side on a mattress on the floor.

They had their arms around each other, and had been swaying to the beat of the music.

'How do you feel, Jack?' the guitar player asked.

'Not too bad,' he answered, 'other than my head. I could do with a couple of aspirins or codeine.'

'We can soon fix that,' one of the girls said, leaving the room.

Lovel looked enquiringly over at a blond youth who was sitting with his arms folded on his knees. His head was resting on his folded arms.

The guitar player answered Lovel's unspoken question. 'That's Terry, he's on a come down.'

'A come down?' Lovel queried.

'He's been on the blues for nearly a week. He just can't take any more. You should be on one yourself, after last night, but of course you slept. I've never known anyone sleep after taking the amount of pills you took. Must have been the drink you had with them.'

Lovel eyed suspiciously the three white tablets the girl offered him. The girl laughed, 'They're only codeine.'

Lovel took them, and rapidly swallowed a glass of water. Taking the empty glass from him, the girl resumed her seat.

The guitar player continued, 'Yes, as I was saying, I've never known anyone sleep after the quantity you took last night. You had at least eight blues, four dexies, and four black bombers. On top of that you were drinking whisky like a fish. Then you finished up having a joint.'

'A joint?' Lovel repeated questioningly.

'Yes, a blast-off, you know? A reefer.'

'Christ!' Lovel exclaimed.

'Well it was the joint which finished you off. One minute you were shouting and dancing, the next you were out, like a light. You should never drink alcohol when you're blocking, it can be dangerous. You were blocked, stoned and drunk, all at the same time.

'High,' the other youth chipped in, 'I'd say you were high, you were on a cloud. Man, were you high, oh man.'

'But how did I get here?' Lovel asked. 'I don't remember a thing.'

'Do you remember meeting us in the Gardenia? You know, the small basement club in Church Street.'

'No,' Lovel answered.

'Well, you came in with a girl. We knew you were blocking. One look at your eyes, man, we knew you were on the dubes. At first we thought you were one of us: we knew you weren't fuzz. Terry,' he motioned to the youth slumped over in the chair, 'wanted some bread, so he asked you if you wanted some dubes. He sold you ten french blues. We could see your girl didn't know you were taking them, and as you were drinking so fast I think she put your behaviour down to the fact that you were getting drunk. She began chipping you, and you told her to piss off, so she went, man, just like that.

'Well, we got you and your car back here, just to take care of you, as the fuzz were beginning to buzz about. When we got here, there was a party going; you joined in, and I think you had just about everything going before you passed out.

'Take a seat, man. We'd give you coffee, but we don't have any.'

Lovel turned this over in his mind for a second or two. Did he mean they had just run out or, more likely, they had no money. He knew that most of these people were hard up, ninety per cent of the time. They spent any money that came their way on pills. Food and such other things as most people considered necessities came a very poor second.

'You know,' Lovel said, coming to a sudden decision, 'I had myself quite an evening, and I always like to pay my corner.'

Putting his hand into his pocket he drew out a note;

it happened to be a ten-pound note. Crossing the room, he handed it to one of the girls.

At first she pushed the proffered money away, but he was insistent.

'I want that coffee,' he demanded.

Taking the note and laughing, both girls rose from the mattress.

'But what shall we do with the change?' the very small girl asked.

'You can do what the hell you like,' Lovel replied.

'Come on, Val, let's go before he changes his mind.' The smaller of the two girls laughed up at Lovel.

Watching them go out the door, 'That would have bought a dozen trips,' the guitar player said regretfully. 'Man what a ball we could have had ourselves, what a ball.'

'Tell us some more about what you were telling Tony last night,' the other boy asked Lovel.

Seeing the puzzled frown on Lovel's face, 'Oh,' the boy continued, 'that's Tony,' he nodded in the direction of the guitar player. 'The small girl's name is Sue, and the other Val. My name's Ken. You were telling us how you blow peters, you know, Jack.'

Some of his concern must have shown on Lovel's face.

Tony said, 'There's nothing to worry about, we wouldn't say anything to the fuzz.'

Lovel didn't know what information he had divulged last night; he certainly wasn't adding to it today.

'Oh well, if you'd rather not,' the boy said, 'but,' he added wistfully, 'it's a good way to earn bread, about the biggest job we ever do is a chemist's, for a few thousand dubes, and that if we're lucky. Sometimes we do an odd telephone booth, but they're tricky these days, some of them are wired straight through to the fuzz. How would you knock the alarm out on them?' he asked hopefully.

'Piece of cake,' Lovel replied, 'they can be knocked out in seconds.'

'Would you tell us, Jack?' Ken asked eagerly.

'Yeah, man,' Tony, becoming interested, said. 'If you tell us that, we'll be your friends for life.'

'Would it take us long to knock out a telephone alarm?' Ken asked hopefully.

'It would take me,' Lovel said, grinning, 'about three seconds flat.'

The two girls entered, carrying two plates each. The plates were piled with sausages, eggs and bacon.

Looking at them made Lovel's stomach turn over. He hoped they had not prepared any for him.

He was out of luck however. Placing the plates on the table, Sue returned to the kitchen and came back carrying another. She also brought a large, white jug, filled with steaming coffee.

Val drew five chairs up and all except the youth who still sat with his head pillowed in his arms, sat at the table.

'Come on,' Val commanded him.

Lovel sat before the steaming plate.

'What about these alarms,' Ken said again, 'tell us now, Jack, you did say you would.' Picking up a hot sausage, he bit it almost in two.

'The next time you go to a phone box, look for a flat piece of copper wire, which comes out of the box at the bottom and goes straight to earth; you cut that and the phone is out of action, and that is all there is to it. And another thing if you get lumbered, don't say I told you.'

'I didn't know it was as simple as that,' Tony said. 'We could,' he continued, 'have a couple over tonight, what say, Ken.'

'I'm game,' the boy answered promptly. 'What about Terry?'

'Oh,' Tony answered, 'he won't be any use for a day or two, that's a very big come down he's on.'

Listening to them, Lovel found he was eating. In fact, he had finished the sausages and bacon, only the egg to go. Breaking the lightly fried egg with his knife, he watched the yoke spread in yellow fingers, then gradually turn a sickly light brown as it and the fat on the plate mingled and became one.

He couldn't eat that egg he decided, no, he just could not face that egg.

7

LOVEL WAS ON HIS WAY TO SEE A CERTAIN security guard of British Micro Electronics. The guard was bent, and Lovel had arranged to meet him at a spot in the country where there was no chance of them being seen together. As an added precaution, he drove to Eric's garage, and leaving the E-Type, took an Austin Cambridge in its stead. The car was straight, but he took the precaution of getting Eric to change the number plates, just in case the security guard should remember the number for future reference. The garage where he had the E-Type cleaned would vouch for the fact that he had driven off in it that afternoon. All precautions against facing a Sessions Court judge on a charge of conspiracy.

He drove the slightly battered buff-coloured Austin Cambridge some five or six miles out of the town, till he came to the signpost he was looking for. He turned into the road; a few hundred yards along he pulled up beside a blue Singer Gazelle, which was parked on the wide grass verge.

The driver of the car had been standing beside it smoking a pipe, one elbow resting on the car's roof.

Watching Lovel climb from the Austin Cambridge, he pointed the pipe. 'About time you traded that heap in,' he said with a smile.

Lovel, ignoring the remark, got straight down to business.

'Well?' he asked, 'did you find out?'

The man nodded. 'Yes,' he said, 'a stroke of luck if

you like. They had a stock check last week. I know exactly, in cash value, what there is in that safe.'

'How much?' asked Lovel quickly.

'In platinum, thirty-two thousand pounds. In scrap gold, two thousand four hundred.'

'Thirty-four thousand four hundred,' Lovel said.

'Yes,' the man said, 'that's what there is this week.'

'What do you mean, this week?'

'Well they use it pretty fast, as you can well imagine, a firm that size would, so you can see within a week or two they could be down to half, or even a quarter of that amount. Just now, they're stocked right up. If you're going to do it, this is the week, and it happens to be my week on nights too. Can you do it?'

'Of course we can do it,' Lovel replied.

'Well how much would be my cut out of thirty-four thousand four hundred?'

'Don't be bloody silly, we wouldn't get the full value for knocked-off stuff,' Lovel snorted.

'Well, how much?'

'About half that,' Lovel said.

'Well, my cut out of, say, seventeen thousand. Would I get the same amount as the rest of you?'

'Yes,' Lovel agreed.

'How many of you will there be on this job?'

'Three,' Lovel said, thinking quickly.

'Well then, I can safely expect four thousand pounds.'

'Yes,' Lovel agreed. He added, 'But when you get it, don't go throwing it about. The Old Bill will be watching you for just that, and if they do find out you've been involved, you can expect plenty of stick.'

The security guard laughed.

'It's no laughing matter,' Lovel warned.

'Oh I can take care of my money,' he said confidently. 'The point is, when will you do it?'

'Some time during next week,' Lovel informed him. 'Which will be the best day?'

'Tuesday,' the guard replied. 'Do you still intend to tie me up, and will it be you who does the job?'

'I'm not sure which of us will tie you up.'

'Well you bloody well want to be. I don't want to be slugged over the head by some nutter and half killed. You do the tying up, and don't tie my mouth up too tight, I have trouble breathing through my nose. You better not tie my arms with thin cord, gangrene can set in if the blood is cut off for too long to a person's limbs,' he added nervously.

'Do you still want to go through with it?' demanded Lovel.

'Of course I do.'

'You said that you patrol the grounds at about twelve thirty. Well, as you come out of the front door, we shall take you.'

'Can't you come in? I can let you in if you wish.'

'No,' said Lovel. 'We'll do the job exactly as if we were not doing it with your co-operation. If by any chance we aren't doing the job Tuesday night, I'll contact you.'

'Be sure that you do that then,' warned the guard. 'I'd hate to be sitting there all night waiting. Let me know by Tuesday afternoon, as I shall be working Tuesday night.'

Lovel climbed back into the Austin Cambridge.

'Tuesday night, then,' he called over to the guard.

Now to persuade Alfie, he thought as he drove slowly back to town. And decided to call on him before returning the car.

He was in luck. Alfred was busy re-pointing the garage brickwork.

'See you at my place in half an hour.' Lovel told him and drove off.

He was well aware that if Janet were to see him talking to Alfred, she would worry, and this could put Alfred off doing the job, unless funds were low. He returned the car, collected his own, and drove back to the flat.

Alfred sat in one of the leather-covered armchairs and listened as Lovel outlined what he'd done so far, and his ideas concerning how they should work.

'How do you know this isn't a set-up?' Alfred questioned.

'I have the answer to that,' Lovel said. 'The security guard thinks we're doing the job this Tuesday. I propose we do it Monday night. He won't be expecting us, and neither will the Old Bill if it did just happen to be a set-up. I think the chap is safe enough, he put another little team onto a load of copper from the firm some six months ago. I knew one of the chaps who was in on it. The Old Bill were a bit suspicious, they had the guard down at the station all day, but couldn't shift him. Of course, we'll watch the place for an hour, say from eleven thirty to twelve thirty, that's when the guard comes out to patrol the premises, and that's when we take him.'

'I don't know, Jack, the job sounds good but that means we've done two jobs in less than a week, besides, I was thinking we should be spending our time looking for a big job. We can't go on for ever sticking our necks out for the odd couple of grand. How much would the split be?'

'The stuff,' Lovel answered, 'is valued at thirty-four thousand four hundred pounds. I can get slightly more than half price, cash on the nail and no messing. The security guard has settled for four thousand as his cut, so that we should split something like twelve to fourteen thousand between us.'

'I don't know, Jack,' Tate protested weakly.

'Oh don't be a bloody fool,' Lovel chided him. 'What does it matter if we do two jobs in one week, or two jobs in three months, what's the good of waiting till we're broke? Besides, remember last winter, we were both broke and couldn't find a job to do. We can't afford to let a job like this slip. Well?' He looked at Tate. 'What about it?'

'Count me in,' Tate said, 'I suppose if we have to go, we have to go.'

'You know the place,' Lovel said. 'British Micro Electronics. Do you want to come out with me tonight and get the layout?'

'No need for that,' Tate replied. 'I know the place well; we won't be able to use gelly, the office is practically all glass. The best way is to cut it open with oxy-arc.'

'How many bottles of oxygen will you need?' asked Lovel.

'One,' Tate replied. 'You know where to get that? Under the Upper Road bridge, they've been doing repair work there for the past few weeks. They'll keep the electrodes and the rest of the gear in the small hut. You could look and make sure tonight, if everything's there, we could pick them up on our way out to do the job. Monday morning you'll have to buy a large black cotton sheet from somewhere, but buy it well away from this town.'

8

LOVEL DROVE THE JAGUAR SLOWLY INTO town. He had most of the long Sunday afternoon to while away and nothing to do. He was bored. He thought of going to the pictures, but the idea of sitting there feeling lonely and, worse still, watching people hurrying home, or laughing couples leaving the cinema and walking arm in arm, decided him against it. That, he decided, would make him worse; he always had an attack of loneliness after going to a cinema on his own.

He couldn't pick up a girl and take her out for the evening, he had work to do.

Tomorrow, and tomorrow night, he would be working again. He had a large black cotton sheet to find. Now where the hell would he even begin to look for one?

Alfred had expected him to produce one, just like that, but then Alfie was always expecting him to get things organized. He never did a damn thing to help. 'Expects me to do the lot,' Lovel thought bitterly. 'I have to find the jobs, watch them, supply practically all the tools, and even pick him up and drop him off after the job. I wish someone would do the same for me, by Christ, I do.'

One good thing about its being Sunday, he reflected, as he pulled up in front of a large Greek restaurant, is being able to park where you like and not have some silly bloody traffic warden waiting to pounce.

Traffic wardens, he decided, were like the rest of the uniformed population, too bloody idle to work and not enough nerve to thieve. Hiding behind a uniform gave them what they craved, the authority to order people about. You can't park there, they would snap, you had better move on and be quick about it, or I'll put this sticker on your windscreen. Pasty-faced little men, mostly, probably well under the thumb when at home, and the women traffic wardens, well, he supposed they were well used to chucking their weight about at home; came natural, they'd been doing it all their married lives, dominating some poor bloody cowering, cringing chap, gradually sapping the little spark of manhood he had left, like bloody vampires, then becoming traffic wardens, looking for fresh victims, hatchet-faced old cows, mostly.

Come to think of it, he wished it wasn't Sunday, after all. He'd like one of those women to tell him to move his car just now, and God, he'd singe her ears. And if it was a man he'd let him have it 'right on the bloody hooter'. He spoke the words aloud.

'Pardon, sir?' A waiter, seeing a likely customer alight from his car, had been hovering near the door and overheard Lovel's muttered threat.

'I never spoke,' Lovel said, glancing at the waiter, who ushered him to a small vacant table and placed the menu in his hands.

Lovel studied the menu with seeming knowledge and interest. He knew already what he would order—steak, mushrooms, and chips—but he wasn't going to let it appear that way. Anyway, he *could* be interested in any one of those continental dishes . . . he *could* be, even if he didn't have a clue what most of them were. They were numbered, but what the hell was the use of asking for a meal if the only part of the menu you understood was the number, might as well say anything. The waiter would know that you hadn't the foggiest what to expect, he would go into the chef and say, 'Number six.' The chef would grin and say, 'What, another?' The waiter would say, 'Well what shall I take up?' and still laughing, the chef would reply, 'Oh, some of that left-overs we were going to throw out.'

The waiter at his elbow gave a discreet cough.

Lovel grinned wickedly to himself and ignored him; that's why you're called waiter, pal, you wait on people, so you bloody well wait until I'm good and ready.

He studied the menu for a further couple of minutes, then said, 'Steak, mushrooms and chips.'

'Coffee, sir?' enquired the waiter.

'Yes, now,' answered Lovel.

'How would you like your steak, sir?'

'Medium rare,' Lovel replied.

The waiter was back with the coffee almost immediately. Lovel took out his cigarettes, produced the gold Dunhill, and sat smoking and taking small sips of the hot liquid. He caught his reflection in a long looking-glass on the opposite wall. He looked very well, he decided, but rather pale. Come to think of it he hadn't been feeling too well for the last couple of days, not since he had taken drugs. Well, he firmly resolved, he would never, ever be mug enough to take them again.

That, he decided, was strictly for idiots, prize idiots.

The waiter placed his meal before him. Lovel ate all the mushrooms, most of the steak, but left the chips. He drank one more cup of coffee, paid his bill, restrained his impulse to tip the waiter, and left.

He sat once again in his car, facing the same problem he had faced before going into the restaurant. Where the hell could he go, what could he do with himself?

Starting the car, he made for the town centre. He parked up before a coffee house and entered through the opaque glass swing doors.

The place was practically full, mostly young people sitting at tables with tall glasses in front of them—some with iced tea, some with hot, but all with a slice of lemon perched on the rim of the glass.

He felt slightly better now, having lots of people round him. He knew that almost all these people lived in either rooms or bedsitters, that they mostly came out for the company.

Lovel spent half an hour smoking and sipping his coffee,

then left and returned to his flat. The rest of the afternoon he whiled away, playing records.

Janet Tate rose at seven a.m. on Monday morning and made breakfast for her daughter Jennie and Alfred.

She had hardly spoken to her husband Sunday evening. He was off on one of his so-called jobs. 'The one after this,' he promised, 'will be the last. No more,' but Janet had listened to this kind of talk for almost all her married life. It would never end, Alfred would go on and on, until either he was caught, or he grew too old. It wasn't fair on Jennie, it wasn't fair on herself. Why couldn't she live a normal married life?

Why did she have to put up with the terrible tension and worry, wondering each time Alfred went out if he would come back. If he were caught, she would not stay in this house. She would sell up and move. The *Daily News* would see that everyone knew how they had lived off the proceeds of crime for years. Most of the neighbours were already aware how Alfred obtained his money. She could tell that by the attitude of the other wives if she used the nearby supermarket, which she seldom did now. That was the reason she would take the car and do her shopping in town.

Finishing her breakfast, Jennie covertly watched her parents. She knew there was something in the wind, and she had a pretty shrewd idea what. Her dad was a thief, she had known that for years. The rights and wrongs of how he made his living—well, she supposed that over the years she had become used to the idea. She remembered a time, years ago when she was a little girl, when the police would come to the house, more often than not in the early hours of the morning. She would be wakened by loud voices and the noisy progress as they searched their way slowly through the house. She would sit bolt upright, petrified with fear, listening in the dark until the inevitable happened. The voices would begin to argue outside her door. Her father would begin to protest furiously, and challenge their right to enter her room. Eventually, the door would burst open, the light would switch on, and three or four policemen would enter.

They would immediately begin a systematic search of the room. Only her mother would take notice of her, and understand how frightened she was. White-faced, her mother would come over and give her a squeeze and reassure her. Eventually the police would finish searching the room, and their attention would then be centred on the bed and herself. Always they would make her get up. They would strip the bedclothes completely off, and, on occasion, had wanted to search her. Her father would never allow this, and once, she remembered, a tall policeman had been over-persistent. He had demanded that her mother strip her off, to prove nothing was hidden on her body.

Her mother had refused.

Jennie finished her tea, rose from the table and with a ''Bye Mum, 'bye Dad', picked up her crash helmet and went off to work.

Seconds later, Janet and Alfred heard the phut, phut, phut of the scooter. They listened until it faded away in the distance.

Alfred smiled across the table at Janet, but receiving no encouragement for a friendly chat, went out into the garage.

He was in a huff. Entering the garage, he spotted an empty five-gallon can. He kicked it savagely.

Janet, he decided, was getting worse. She was giving him the silent treatment now; why didn't they just have one damn good row and then be friends.

9

JACK LOVEL HAD NOT BEEN ABLE TO obtain a large black cotton sheet. He had been trying all Monday afternoon, and had left a trail of potential witnesses behind, if he were ever to obtain one, and that one got left behind on the job.

At four in the afternoon he had an idea. He walked into a drapery store and asked for curtain material. He was shown a book of different patterns. Selecting a plain, dark blue material he bought the entire roll. It would have to do. The oxygen bottle and the oxy-arc cutting equipment he would pick up tonight.

The small hut below the bridge had been on a mortice lock. Lovel had gone prepared; he had produced a mortice key, this key had been filed to the shape of a 'T', in other words it was a simple skeleton key. With this, he had opened the door and made sure the equipment they needed was there; he knew that Alfred would also carry gelignite, just in case. He had also obtained a good length of cord for the tie-up, two more black track-suits and a complete set of tools. Further to this, he had added two black balaclava helmets, four packets of 'hilty nails' and a large pair of scissors.

Before going home he left all these with Eric, examined a Rover 2000 to make certain the oxygen bottle would fit inside, and instructed him to have the number plates changed and the car ready by ten-thirty that evening.

He made a late tea, such as it was, in his flat.

At seven-thirty that evening, he walked to a nearby shop, purchased cigarettes and an evening paper.

His eye caught the leading column on the second page. 'Bandits attack Security Van.' He read on.

Early this morning an armoured security van was stopped and attacked at Borwood. The bandits armed with shotguns and a large sledge hammer, stove in the driving side window, after forcing the van to a standstill. Pushing a shotgun through the shattered side window, they forced the driver and his mate to get out. They then turned their attention to a further guard who was locked in the rear of the van. As they could not get at him, they forced the driver back into his seat and thrusting the sawn off barrel of the shotgun in his mouth, threatened that unless the guard in the back opened the rear doors, they would blow the driver's head off.

'I had no option but to open up. I could see they meant business,' the guard told the *Evening News* reporter.

The van was making a delivery of platinum to the Precious Metals Co. Ltd., of North Street, Borwood. It is believed, however, they were after a much larger haul than the ten thousand pounds' worth of platinum that they got. On occasions, the van carries up to half a million pounds' worth of precious metals. The police we were assured, have tightened up security on the method of transporting these precious metals, but they refused to discuss the extra precautions they would put into effect. It is believed the raid was organized and executed by a London gang. The possibility that certain well known local criminals may have been involved, has not been ruled out.

'Well,' Jack Lovel laughed, 'they can't blame that one on us. If they'd done it our way, they would have got the lot. We would have blown the firm's strong room.'

Putting the paper down, he went to the bathroom and washed. It was a hell of a coincidence, he was thinking, a platinum raid at Borwood, hardly three miles from where they'd be operating tonight!

At nine-thirty that evening, Lovel began to prepare himself for the night's work. As he expected to spend quite some time outside the building, keeping watch, he put on a thick string vest under his shirt. The August nights could become very chilly. He looked at his watch, the time was nine forty-five. He was ready to go! He had a vague feeling of having forgotten something, the feeling had been with him for some time, but he just couldn't think what it was. It could be something important, something he would need tonight, in which case he couldn't afford to ignore the nagging little worry in his mind. He wandered into the bathroom, and there it was, lying on the shelf over the sink: the badly fitting gold ring that Sharon had bought him. He picked it up. Should he take the ring or leave it?

It could easily slip off while he was on the job. He was about to replace the ring on the shelf, changed his mind and placed it on his right ring finger, and immediately began to worry it round and round with his thumb, a habit he'd acquired of late.

Lovel left the E-Type with Eric, took the Rover 2000 and picked up the oxy-arc equipment. At eleven p.m. exactly, he drove slowly through the centre lane of parked cars in the public car park. He flicked his side lights on, off, once. A shadow detached itself from a nearby brick wall. The side door of the Rover opened, and without bringing the car to a complete standstill, Alfred Tate slipped smartly in. They were on their way.

Tate pushed the oxygen bottle away from himself and nearer to Jack Lovel.

'Nice bloody thing to cart around, what if we get a pull with this?' meaning the large steel bottle.

'Have you got the gelly and dets with you?' Lovel asked.

' 'Course I have,' Tate replied.

'Well if we get a pull, and they catch us with them, the oxygen bottle won't make much difference. They'd be so busy counting our years in nick that they'd be likely to miss the oxygen bottle.'

'I didn't mean that,' said Tate. 'I mean it juts up where they may see it, and give us a pull. By the way, did you get this bottle from the bridge?'

'Yes,' Lovel replied.

'I meant to warn you against getting one elsewhere, they're all numbered and can be traced back.'

'It's as well I didn't buy one then,' Lovel answered.

'I suppose you got a full one,' Tate remarked, feeling the valve with his gloved hand. He could feel the wire and the small seal securing the valve.

'Is it?' asked Lovel.

'Yes,' replied Tate. 'Did you get the valve key?' he asked.

'No, I don't know anything about these bloody things, what do we do now?' He looked over at Tate who was holding a small, steel, handle-like object up, with a square hole in it.

'Thank Christ for that.' Jack Lovel breathed again.

Lovel stopped the car a few yards from the front entrance. to British Micro Electronics.

While Tate sat inside and kept look-out, he humped the heavy oxygen bottle out of the car and down a small footpath.

He pushed the bottle into a tall privet hedge that followed the high spiked railings for part of their journey around the perimeter of the firm's premises. He repeated the procedure with the rest of their equipment, then drove the car a good quarter of a mile beyond the electronics firm, before they were satisfied they had a good, safe parking spot.

They left the car parked with several others on a small piece of waste ground.

Making their way back to the rear of the premises they sat for a while and smoked in a small shed abutting a narrow path which cut across the middle of some dozen or so allotments.

'Good place to stretch out if we have to make an all

night job of it,' remarked Lovel, squatting down on a heap of sacks.

Alfred pulled a spare pair of large socks over his shoes, and carefully tucked in the bottoms of the track-suit he was wearing.

Lovel did the same, and walked behind Alfred back to the car. Placing the heavy oxygen bottle on his shoulder and also carrying a bag of tools, he led the way while Tate followed with the rest of the equipment, wincing at the heavy crunching sound Lovel made, walking on the rough, freshly clinkered path.

After some thirty yards Lovel stopped and, carefully slipping the bottle from his shoulder, searched for and found the gap in the privet which he knew to be just about there. One of the iron railings had also been bent. Probably the gap had been made and was used by people who worked for the firm and wanted to slip out for cigarettes and suchlike, without going through the main gate.

Lovel manœuvred the bottle through the gap. Inside were stacked some very large wooden crates; he leaned the bottle up against one of these stacks. They both pulled on the woollen balaclava helmets. The bright full, harvest moon shone down on them as they crouched, hidden behind the wooden crates. After a few seconds, Lovel gently nudged Alfred, he then slipped quietly away down the gap between the railings and the crates. Continuing along, every now and then he would peer through a gap and ascertain his position in relation to the main office. Eventually, drawing level, he stopped. One of the rooms was lit up, but without this, the light from the moon was sufficient to see with reasonable clarity.

A light sprung on in the office adjoining that which had already been lighted; it went out almost immediately, and a man appeared in the lighted room.

He stood for a moment or two as if looking out into the night, then took a pipe from his pocket and put it in his mouth.

Lovel had been watching the man intently, trying to

recognize him. When he placed the pipe in his mouth, he relaxed and grinned.

He made his way back to Tate.

Cupping their hands to shield the glare, they lit cigarettes, and sat side by side smoking and holding a whispered conversation for some fifteen minutes. They decided that Lovel should make a complete reconnoitre of the railings surrounding the premises.

After Lovel had crept away, Tate began moving their equipment up to the gap in the boxes where Lovel had watched the guard. The oxygen bottle was just about as much as he could manage. Finally he carried the last item, the roll of curtain material, and placed it with the other stuff. He now sat down and watched the security guard. He knew the man carried a stick, but he would have little chance to use it.

Tate glanced at his watch: the time was ten minutes past midnight. He began to get restless. Lovel should have returned by now. He wished that he had insisted on Jack taking the small walkie-talkie, that way they could have kept in contact. If Lovel were to run into someone at the rear of the premises and get chased, Alfred would be left sitting here watching, probably until the Old Bill picked him up.

Keeping look-out, he decided, was more nerve-racking than actually doing the job. The guard inside the lighted office was bent over, probably reading a crime novel: reading about the impossible antics of some little crook, and the fantastic brilliance of a would-be Sherlock Holmes of a Detective-Superintendent. The crook would inevitably be some shifty-eyed little runt who could never look you squarely in the face, and spoke in an almost impossible-to-understand slang language. The hero of course, that is the policeman, would be a very cultured person with, nine times out of ten, an Oxford or Cambridge accent.

Well, if the guard was reading a crime novel he was himself about to become involved in a crime.

Tate was so intent on watching the guard, and at the

same time busy with his own thoughts, that he didn't hear Lovel approach, and started when he tapped his shoulder.

Lovel whispered, 'When we leave, we'll have to scale the railings at the back. I have put a few sacks over the spikes—they're sharp.'

Jack Lovel lifted the oxygen bottle once more; Tate watched him heft it easily onto his shoulder, and bending down, picked up the heaviest of the tool bags.

Once again they dumped their equipment. Alfred looked up at the steel railings. They were, he guessed, about eight feet high. He glanced once more at the wicked looking spikes. God, he thought, fancy getting one of those through your guts.

'Come on, we haven't all bloody night,' Lovel whispered urgently. 'The guard will be coming out in another ten minutes.'

They crept back to the gap in the boxes.

Lovel glanced at his watch. 'This is it,' he said, and began creeping, keeping to what few shadows there were, up to the front corner of the building.

Tate, watching Lovel's stealthy progress, shuddered.

He didn't care much for violence, even of this nature, when the so-called victim was a partner in the crime. Accidents could easily happen. In pure funk, the man might turn on Lovel—that is, if he got the chance.

Nervously, Tate sat watching, first the barely discernible figure of Lovel, then the guard, who had finished reading his book and was busy putting on his shoes or boots.

Perhaps he wore slippers while in the office.

The guard, who had been in shirt-sleeves, lifted his jacket from the back of a chair and began putting it on. Alfred felt a sudden urge to make water.

The guard almost reached the front door, then returned to the office. 'For Christ sake make your bloody mind up,' Alfred muttered savagely.

He was sweating now.

Lovel, who had been in a crouching position, straightened up. The guard opened a drawer in the office desk and took something out. It was his stick. He opened the main door and stood for a few seconds, looking out into the moonlit night, then he turned left, and shining his torch over the stacked up boxes, slowly made his way across the front of the office block. Just before he reached the corner, his torch shone directly through the gap where Alfred was hidden. Alfred shrank back behind the crates. He saw the beam hesitate on the gap, then pass on. He looked out quickly as the light swept past him. The guard was now at the corner of the building. He turned left again, following the building round. For a second or two he stood, seized with a fit of coughing. Casually he walked on, swinging the stick in one hand, and waving the torch about the premises with the other.

He had taken two steps by the door where Lovel was hidden, when in one huge stride Lovel was behind him.

Tate saw Lovel's arm go up and out, catching the guard securely round the throat. At the same time Lovel's left hand reached for, and took, the stick. The torch, still shining, dropped to the concrete.

There was a brief desperate struggle, with the guard making short gurgling noises as he fought to fill his lungs. Then Lovel whispered reassuringly in the man's ear.

Letting him loose now, Lovel began explaining, and urging the guard back into the building.

The guard bent down to retrieve his stick and torch, but Lovel restrained him. He put his foot on the torch and the light was extinguished. Alfred was up to them now. He could hear Lovel saying, 'There was no other way than this. The police will look for signs of a struggle. They'll find your stick and your broken torch. They'll find plenty of evidence for even them, where the ground has been scuffed up, and, more important still, you'll be able to tell them exactly what happened, without the chance of slipping up.'

'I know, I know,' the guard jerked out at last. 'But you should have warned me. God! What a bloody fright you gave me,' he gasped.

Tate could hear his noisy rasping breathing.

'Christ,' the guard spoke again. 'I bloody near collapsed

with fright. I, yes I have,' he felt his crutch, 'I have, I've wet my bloody self,' he giggled nervously.

'Are you all right now?' Tate spoke.

'I—I think so, but I'm trembling like a bloody leaf, look.' He held his hand out in front of them, it was shaking badly. Lovel laughed.

Alfred had no doubt the man was suffering from shock.

'Once we get inside,' he said, 'we'll make you a cup of tea.'

'Christ, could I do with a cup of tea and a smoke,' the guard answered.

'Come on,' Lovel said, 'we haven't got all bloody night you know.'

They followed the guard inside the office. Crouching down inside, Lovel kept watch on the gate. Tate sat the guard down, and lighting a cigarette, gave it to him. The guard was still shaking badly, his face was ashen. Yes, Tate decided, this was a dodgy game; you could easily have a murder rap hanging over you.

He followed the security guard out to a small kitchen, and lit the gas under a half-filled kettle.

'Christ, I'm cold,' the guard complained.

'How old are you?' asked Tate.

'Fifty-five,' the man answered, and continued, 'I suppose after fifty-five the old ticker does get a bit worn.'

'Think you'll be able to stand up to the law's questioning?' asked Tate.

'Yes, I'll tell them exactly what happened, that I got a good look at you both, but you were wearing balaclavas, so I couldn't recognize any of you. By the way,' he added, 'where's the other chap? Your mate said there were three of you.'

'The other one is outside, keeping watch near the main gate. He's in radio contact with us.'

'Oh,' said the guard, seemingly satisfied, 'but there isn't any real need to have one outside, no one ever comes near the place until six-thirty in the morning.'

Tate made the tea, poured three cups out, and they sat for some ten minutes smoking and drinking from the mugs.

'You won't see me off for my cut?' the man said.

'No, you'll get exactly one quarter of whatever price we get,' Tate assured him, finishing his tea. 'Right. It's time we got down to business. I'll tie you up now, just in case we get disturbed.'

He produced several lengths of thickish manila rope, and tied first his wrists, then elbows and ankles. He finally secured the back rest of the chair to a radiator. He grinned down at the guard.

'Now try and get out,' he challenged.

The man tried, but found that although he was reasonably comfortable while he remained still, to attempt to escape was an extremely painful procedure. Returning to the front office, Tate told Lovel to take their equipment through to the office they were to work in, while he kept watch on the main gate.

After some ten minutes, he heard the noise of a hammer and knew that Jack Lovel would now be knocking the high tensile nails into the wall. It was a good half-hour before Lovel returned to the front office.

'I've left the light on in there, but I'll check from the outside and make sure the place is completely blacked out.'

Tate nodded his agreement. An occasional car would pass by the front gate, but he had seen no foot traffic.

Lovel returned, went back into the now blacked-out office, and this time brought back his walkie-talkie.

Leaving Lovel to continue the watch, Tate left the front office and made his way down the passage. He looked in the kitchen, winked at the guard, and gave the thumbs up signal. The guard grinned back.

Tate entered the office Lovel had taken so much pains in blacking out. Immediately facing him was the window now securely covered by the curtain material. To the left was the safe and two large Chubb filing cabinets. A table took up a good deal of the room's centre, then, to the right, some ten square yards of curtain material covered thick plate glass.

He coupled the pressure gauges to the oxygen bottle. Selecting a hollow carbon electrode, he fitted it into the holder, then plugged his portable transformer into a socket normally used for an electric fire, clipping one lead onto the safe, the other lead being in contact through the holder with the electrode.

He turned on the oxygen which hissed through the hollow electrode.

Tate held the cutting tool in position and struck an arc, which instantly gouged a hole through the outer plate of the safe door. The high pressure blast of oxygen forced the molten metal into the gap between the two door plates. Using a weaving motion, he steadily cut a small square, about an inch below the key-hole. During this operation Tate had been holding a heavy dark glass shield before his face. Now he put the cutting equipment away. The safe was far too hot to touch, so going to the kitchen he took a large pan, filled it with water and poured the contents over the safe door.

He called Lovel in from the front office, directed him to take hold of the safe door handle and apply a steady, continuous pressure. For a second or two he probed inside the small hole he had cut, with his finger. Then, taking out a long steel punch and a small club hammer from the tool bag, and inserting the punch into the hole, he gave it a sharp clout. Nothing happened. Once more he struck the steel punch and this time the handle jerked to the open position as the locking bars sprang back.

Lovel opened the safe door, then returned to the front office.

There were three compartments inside the safe. The top one held ledgers. The second one held a few pounds in weight of small sheets of gold. Immediately behind the gold was the platinum, in the form of wire. It didn't appear to be much, but lifting it up, Tate found it to be extremely heavy for its volume.

Wrapping the precious metals inside a large piece of rag, he placed them carefully inside the tool-bag. Picking the bag up, Tate returned to where Lovel was still keeping watch.

'That's it,' he said in a satisfied manner.

Lovel looked round at him. 'What, already!' he exclaimed.

'As I said,' Tate continued, 'the master criminal strikes again.'

'Where's the gear?' Lovel demanded.

Placing the bag on the floor, Tate produced the rag-covered bundle. They both peered in at the contents. 'Don't look worth a light,' Lovel remarked.

'No, I must say I'd rather have cash,' Tate said.

'Still,' Lovel went on, 'gold is easy to get rid of, so is platinum. I've had two prices offered me in the East End, both were eager to buy, and both are prepared to take any amount.'

With an amount like they'd got, they knew they should have no trouble. The two buyers were part of a syndicate that bought bent gear by the truck-load. As far as cash went, they could put up unlimited ready money.

'Just as well it's not more,' said Tate. 'We'd have to watch them if it was, but they daren't go bent on us for an amount like this. The word soon spreads, and they'd get no more custom. We'll hide the stuff up for a few weeks, and let things cool off. The papers'll quickly let us know how much we're worth, and the London boys will be onto us from reading the papers, so we can just sit back until they come up with the right price. Trouble is, they usually reckon that any team that operates out in the sticks are mugs, so we shall have to straighten them out on that.'

Putting the small parcel back in the tool-bag, Tate left it with Lovel and returned to the kitchen; he spoke to the guard, then put the kettle on, lit a cigarette and placed it between the man's lips.

'After we've had the tea,' Tate told him, 'we'll go. Now, once we get clear of here, you can expect to be sitting there for another half an hour. That's about how long it'll take us to get rid of the loot and get cleaned up. We'll then ring the law, and inform them that they'll find a tie-up here. That's all we need say, they know the drill. It'll then be at least three weeks before we contact you and maybe even a month; don't get impatient, and don't try to contact us.

We won't see you off for your cut. Everything tonight has gone smoothly, the rest is up to you.'

Tate made the tea: he held it to the man's lips, allowing him to sip. He lit another cigarette and held this while the guard had a final smoke. He was now feeling impatient to be gone. Taking a cup of tea to Lovel, he was made aware that Lovel was worrying about the curtain material being left.

'I wore a wig when I bought the stuff,' Lovel told him, 'and I bought it about twenty miles away, but I'd rather we took it with us.'

The rest of the tools and equipment they would leave, as it would be impossible to trace them back.

Finishing their tea, Tate waited, watching the gate while Lovel removed the curtain material, and rolled it; then, as Lovel came in he took from his track-suit pocket a large handkerchief.

Going to the kitchen, he told the guard they were about to leave, gagged him, took one last look around the office where he had been working on the safe, and returned to the front office.

Lovel pulled up his balaclava and began to scratch a spot behind his right ear which had been itching for most of the night. He was pulling the woollen helmet back down over his features when Tate gripped his arm. A car with dipped headlights had stopped immediately before the gates.

As Lovel looked, he could see a dark figure bending over, obviously unlocking them.

'What's the drill now,' he hissed urgently at Alfred, 'do we run for it? I opened a window earlier on in the workshop, we could go through there, or do we stay here and take him?'

'Let's go,' Tate said, 'it just means we shall have to lay up all night.'

Lovel leapt for the roll of curtain material and began to race for the passage door.

'Steady, steady,' Tate whispered, 'one man's not going to take us.' He had the tool-bag in one hand. In the other he carried a short heavy batten. Lovel steadied as Tate called to him, that is, he stopped running, but he now took large rapid strides and Tate had to trot to keep a steady distance behind. They quickly made their way down the passage and into the workshop. Lovel crossed the workshop floor with Tate in close attendance, and came to the window which he had opened earlier in the evening.

They scrambled through the window, and moving quickly, began to cross the yard. The new arrival, who happened to be the manager of British Micro Electronics Ltd, had by this time reached the front door of the office. Opening the door with his key, he knew immediately that something was amiss. There was a thick acrid tang which you could almost taste, hanging heavily in the air, caused by the oxy-arc.

At first he thought an electric fire was burning somewhere on the premises, but not for long. Finding no sign of the guard, he quickly made his way down the passage. As soon as he glimpsed the gagged and bound security guard, he turned and bolted back to the car.

He expected a dark figure to leap out and attack him any second. He raced out of the front door, and yelled to his passenger, another of the firm's employees. The passenger, startled, almost fell from the car, but the manager, still shouting 'get the police, get the police', shot into the driving seat, slammed the door, spun the car round in a very tight turn, his hands grasping both the wheel and the horn ring. In low gear and with horn blaring, he raced for the gate.

Hearing the sudden shouting, banging, and the blare of the car's hooter, Lovel raced for dear life for the tall iron railings.

Tate, tightly gripping the bag containing the loot, followed behind, panting.

Lovel, reaching the railings, hurled the roll of curtain material over the top.

They had come to that position where Lovel had placed the sacks on top of the iron railings, earlier. He was badly shaken, and immediately began to scramble for the top, but halfway up he realized that, unaided, Tate would probably be unable to get over.

Lovel slipped back down and quickly gave Alfred Tate a leg up to the top of the railings.

Tate barely rested on the top. Letting himself drop to the other side immediately, he dropped a good deal further than he expected.

The ground sloped sharply away on the other side, adding almost five feet to the height of the railings. Luckily for him, the ground underneath was liberally strewn with fresh clinkers.

Tate yelled a warning as he hit the ground.

Lovel, in one heave, had gained the top, he had been about to make a clean leap, but hearing the yell and the heavy thud of Tate's body, he changed his mind at the instant he pushed his body from the railings. Grabbing a spike in each hand, he now began an uncontrollable slide down the railings. In that split instant of time he felt the fine weather-worn spike pierce the thin nylon glove on his right hand. At the same instant, the tip of the spike inserted itself firmly between the loose-fitting ring and the finger.

The entire weight of his thirteen and a half stone body came down with a tremendous snatch on the rigidly trapped finger, which was torn completely out of its socket, close up to the knuckle. Not even a stump remained.

A flame of pure pain shot up his arm, enveloping him completely. He never felt his body striking the ground. He was lost in a world of agony. He rolled over and over on the rough clinkers, his face coming into contact with a broken bottle.

The jagged glass bit cruelly. Clutching his hand he continued to roll. Tate had gained his feet, and bending down, was just about to retrieve the precious tool-bag, when he heard Lovel scream.

Looking up, he could make out Lovel, body curled up into a ball, still rolling.

Watching, he saw him stop rolling, and clutching his injured hand to his face, attempt to get on his feet. He managed to get up onto his knees, then fell backward, moaning.

Tate ran over to him and peered down.

Lovel's face was a mask of blood, part caused by the jagged gash on his cheek, but mostly caused by his holding his injured hand to his face as the blood pumped from the torn socket.

Tate couldn't see the damaged hand. He thought Lovel had simply cut his face after making the leap from the railings.

'Get up,' he commanded, 'get up for Christ's sake,' he said, 'we'll have the bloody law here in a few minutes.'

Lovel made no reply. He was too far gone in pain and shock.

Tate reached down and shook him roughly.

This, at last, seemed to get through to him. 'Come on, you bloody coward,' Alfred Tate snarled, 'come on, we've got to get the hell out of here.'

Lovel heard and understood. He got up as far as he was able and began to walk. He was walking on his knees.

'You bloody fool!' Tate snarled at him again, then, noticing for the first time the dark fluid seeping from Lovel's clasped hands, he reached down and suddenly jerked the hands apart. Seeing the empty socket where the finger had been, and the dark blood welling out, Tate recoiled in horror.

'Jesus Christ, Jack,' he said, 'Jesus bloody Christ! Your finger!'

Lovel looked up at Alfred Tate, he seemed to be swimming before his eyes. The pain was still terrific.

'Get up, boy,' Tate said quietly, 'it will be seven years if we're caught here.'

'I can't, I can't, you go, just leave me,' Lovel moaned.

Tate tried to lift him to his feet, but Lovel sank back. He was too heavy for him to carry.

Coming to a sudden decision, 'Get up, you bastard,' he snarled once more, 'get up, you bastard, or I'll smash you.' Tate slapped Lovel, savagely, with the back of his hand across the face, and dragged him up.

The sharp blow had penetrated Lovel's senses at last.

They staggered for some twenty or so paces when the idea hit Tate how Lovel had lost his finger.

Letting him sink once more to the ground, and putting the bag down, which not once had he allowed to leave his grasp, he raced back to the railings. Desperately he pulled himself to the top. The finger was wedged firmly between the spike and the golden ring.

He plucked the gory thing from its trap; but he couldn't ease the ring up and off the railing before his tired arm gave out. He slipped back to the ground, still clutching the finger. But he couldn't leave it lying around, they would still be able to take a print from it.

Tate pushed it into the trouser pocket of his track-suit and raced back to his partner.

Jack Lovel's head had cleared somewhat by this time, although his whole being was centred on the pain which throbbed like molten fire from his damaged hand, and up his arm. He had lost a good deal of blood, and this, combined with shock, had weakened him considerably. Dimly hearing Tate approach, he looked up.

In the bright moonlight Tate saw the pain-dulled eyes watching him. Taking in Jack Lovel's figure, which was now sagging with exhaustion, he almost gave up.

'God! We'll never make it,' he thought.

The sound of a car engine and the scream of its tyres as it turned sharply through the main gate, quickly dispelled his doubts. The scream of tyres spelled prison. Lifting the bag, he put one arm round Lovel, who now began to stagger slowly along. They made their way from the rear of the buildings in a staggering, lurching stumble, slowly covering the waste ground.

Finding a gap in the hedge which separated the waste ground from the group of allotments, Tate allowed Lovel a short rest.

Then he forced him to his feet again; slowly they made their way along the narrow grass footpath which separated the two rows of allotments and reached the small shed they had rested in earlier in the evening. This was it, Alfred

Tate decided, they could go no further. It was a physical impossibility: he was himself in a state of exhaustion through the effort of supporting Lovel's heavy weight.

Allowing him to lean up against the shed, Tate opened the door, then helping Lovel inside, eased him down onto the pile of empty sacks, where he sank wearily down, still clutching the injured hand. For the first time since the accident, Tate spoke to Lovel in a normal manner; until now, he had only spoken to him to exhort by cursing or cajoling him to further effort. He could see the blood was still oozing from the hand, dripping slowly through the tightly clasped fingers of the left hand which he had held over the injury since it happened.

'Let me see the damage, Jack boy,' Tate spoke softly to him. Lovel cautiously unclasped the protecting fingers.

Tate took Lovel's right hand, and by the light of the moon through the open door, examined it.

He could make out the white tape-like threads of torn tendon, hanging loosely from the fingerless knuckle, the blood still steadily oozing out. He would have to apply a tourniquet, he decided.

Glancing at his watch, he noticed the time was three thirty-five a.m.

By this time the police would have road blocks set up at all points leading out of the town, so that there was no hope of their getting home without being stopped.

Lovel had lost a good deal of blood. But one could lose a good deal of blood and still live. To exist through a few hours of pain was far better than to get caught and spend years in prison.

They still stood a very good chance of getting captured if they stopped here. There was also the chance that the police would expect them to have made it back to the transport that was at their disposal, and either to have made a clean getaway, or to be about to do so.

Tate reached into the tool-bag and extracted the piece of rag the precious metals had been wrapped up in. This would have to do for the tourniquet.

Folding the rag, he fixed it into position, just above the

elbow joint, then taking from the bag of tools a pair of pliers, inserted one handle into the loop of the tourniquet and twisted.

He applied pressure until he was satisfied the bleeding had almost stopped.

Jack Lovel had not spoken a word since losing the finger. He just sat and watched Tate with a steady, but disinterested gaze.

Tate now carefully lighted a cigarette.

A foolish thing for a hunted man to do, he knew, but he just had to have one. Lighting the cigarette, he made to place it in Lovel's mouth, but he turned his head away in refusal.

Relaxing somewhat now, Tate sat back smoking and trying to figure out their best route home; wondering, too, if the law had spotted their car. Absent-mindedly he put his right hand into the trouser pocket of his track-suit.

He had almost forgotten the finger which lay there.

Touching the strangely soft, cold object in the warm pocket, he shuddered. What should he do with it? He couldn't throw it away here, and somehow, it didn't seem right to dispose of part of a human being like that. Even were he to dig a hole in one of the allotments and bury it, it didn't seem decent. Removing his hand, he decided to leave the decision until later.

10

ALFRED TATE GLANCED AT HIS WATCH. The time was five forty-five a.m. It would take them fifteen minutes to reach their transport, and there would be plenty of traffic about now.

During the night he had loosened the tourniquet every twenty minutes. Finally, as the bleeding had almost stopped of its own accord, he had dispensed with it altogether. Then, ripping a large portion from the bottom part of his shirt, he had bound this as best he could around Lovel's hand.

Lovel now sat clasping the bulky blood-soaked bandage. He leaned wearily against the rough weather-board side of the hut, his eyes closed as if in sleep.

Tate rose stiffly from his seat, brushed a few rough strands of sacking from his track-suit, and extending a hand, helped Lovel to his feet. They left the hut, Tate steadying Lovel with one hand, and clutching the bag with the other. The morning was bright and sunny, and birds in the hedgerows were singing cheerfully.

They arrived finally at the small hedge which bordered the road; Tate removed his headgear and track-suit, and leaving Lovel in hiding with the bag, crossed the road and made his way back to the car. A few early morning cyclists and a couple of milk-floats passed him on his journey. However, he saw no sign of the police.

His heart began to quicken as he approached the Rover 2000. If the law had spotted the car during their stay in the hut, it would be now they would jump him. Getting into the Rover, he started up and pulled away, breathing a sigh of relief.

Now to pick up Lovel.

He wondered if the police would find any blood-stains, but decided this was highly unlikely as the rusted railings would show only a darker stain where the blood had spurted. The same with the clinker, that was black too, and wouldn't show.

It was a different matter with the ring, and he had forgotten to hide the curtain material.

Arriving back at the spot where Lovel was hidden he picked up the bag, and helped him into the back seat. Lovel thankfully sank down onto the upholstery. Looking round, Tate satisfied himself that Lovel was well hidden, then moved off.

He made a circuitous route of the journey back. There were no incidents, but arriving at Lovel's flat landed Tate with a problem. How to take care of him?

First off, he lit the gas under the kettle, and going to the bedroom, produced a bottle of brandy. He half filled a tooth-glass and gave this neat to Lovel, who almost finished it off in two huge gulps. Seeming to relax somewhat he leaned back on the settee and giving Tate a weak smile said, 'We've made it, then.'

His face was still gory with blood, and he still wore the woollen balaclava.

Winking at him, Tate replied, 'We'll make out yet, Jack.'

He returned to the kitchen and made the tea; handing a cup to Lovel, he slowly sipped his own, pondering the problem of who he would get to take care of him. Tate lit a cigarette. 'Want one?' he asked.

Lovel took the lighted cigarette and sat back in the settee. He was beginning to feel better, even though his hand still throbbed painfully.

'It was that bloody ring, Alf; it was a loose fit and I should've had it made smaller. Just as well she never gave me a good luck charm, might have pulled my bloody head off.' Lovel grinned weakly. 'By the way, Alf, what about that ring, and the finger.' He looked worriedly at Tate.

'I got the finger, Jack, but not the ring. Anyway,' Tate assured, glancing at his watch, 'the law would take about two hours to search and finger-print the place, if they'd found it we'd have known by now.'

Tate rose from his seat and lifted the phone. Dialling a number he spoke for several minutes, finally replacing the receiver he looked with relief at Jack Lovel. 'Well that's fixed. I've got Arthur Penfold to come over, should be here in half an hour.'

'Christ!' Lovel exclaimed, 'he's queer.'

'He's a state registered nurse, and whether he's queer or not don't matter a damn as long as he fixes that.' Tate pointed at Lovel's bandaged hand.

'Give me a leg up, Joe.' Sam Griffin, aged nine years, asked his partner Joe Martin, his senior by some ten months.

'No, I spotted it first.'

'Oh, all right.' Sammy complied, giving the other's lifted leg a heave.

Joe grabbed the wide parallel bar at the top and easily pulled himself up. Taking hold of the ring he prised it off the rusty spike.

Both boys examined the ring with interest.

'That's blood that's dried on it,' said Sammy.

'Yes,' Joseph agreed, 'it is. I wonder how it got up there, and how it got covered in blood?'

'It's a mystery,' Sammy said, 'that's what it could be, Joe, a mystery.'

'It might be one of those black magic rites, you know, what the papers are always on about. That would be a mystery wouldn't it.' He looked up at Sammy.

'Yes,' Sammy agreed, 'that would be a mystery. What are you going to do with it Joe?'

'Keep it,' Joseph said, putting it in his pocket.

'Are you going to wipe the blood off then?'

'No,' Joseph replied, producing the ring again and wrapping it in a grubby handkerchief. 'No,' he repeated, 'that could spoil the spell. Someone went to a lot of trouble to get that blood on there.' He couldn't help a slight shudder as he placed the ring carefully once again in his pocket.

'Look, Joe,' Sammy said, pointing through the railings, 'look, there's something else through there.'

Both boys raced for the gap in the railings, and through the hedge where Jack Lovel and Alfred Tate had made their way, very early that morning.

Griffin reached the bundle of curtain material first. They examined it with curiosity, looking for signs of blood.

'No blood,' said Sammy, disappointed. 'Perhaps it's their tablecloth to cover the altar with, though. What shall we do with them, shall we tell someone, Joe?'

'No,' Joseph said, 'we shan't.'

'Why not?'

'Because I said no,' Joseph said belligerently, 'and another thing, if we tell anyone, they'll want the ring, and it's gold.' He pulled the ring out of his pocket again. They both peered down at it.

'There's writing inside, look,' Sammy said.

'From Sharon to Jack, with love, 1972,' Joseph Martin read aloud. 'Be a right powerful spell on it if she were murdered, Sammy!'

Sammy hefted the roll of curtain material onto his shoulder, and they walked back to the gap in the railings.

Tate finished drinking his tea, and felt in his pocket for cigarettes. Finding them, he began searching for matches. His hand came into contact with the dead finger, caused him to shudder. Hearing a soft tap on the door he rose, and opening it smiled with relief at the male nurse standing there.

Preceding the man into the bedroom, Tate stood looking down at Jack Lovel. His face was flushed and his eyes glittered.

The male nurse pushed his way past Tate.

'Oh duckie, what a torso,' he exclaimed, pulling the bed-clothes back.

'I'm not likely to die, then?' Lovel laughed.

'Not if I can help it, you gorgeous thing.'

Lovel was delighted.

Tate scowled with embarrassment.

Taking Lovel's wrist, the male nurse held it lightly, feeling the pulse. He took his temperature, and finally removed the bandage from the injured hand.

'Made a mess of that, duckie,' he said, liberally pouring powder onto it.

Re-bandaging the injured hand, and looking at Lovel in a speculative way he said, 'Well, ducks, it's going to have to be bottoms up.'

'Oh Christ,' Lovel groaned, 'do I have to have it there?'

Tate cleared his throat, and slipped out of the room.

'What about my arm?' he heard Lovel ask, hopefully.

'No, take off your pyjamas, you won't feel a thing, and anyway you'll get used to them in time.'

Lovel complied; Tate heard a slight 'Ooh' as the needle was pushed home.

The nurse put the syringe away, and seeing him still bent over said, 'All right, duckie, you can put it away now. No need to keep on tempting me.'

Lovel thankfully pulled up his pyjamas.

'Is it giving you pain?'

'Yes,' Lovel answered.

'Take this,' the nurse offered him a tablet and a glass of water. 'I'll see you again this evening.' He winked at Lovel and left the bedroom.

'He'll need looking after, and a course of injections. It's as well you got me to come in; that hand would certainly have become septicaemic. However,' he smiled at Tate, 'he'll be as good as new in a couple of days now.'

'How much?' Tate asked.

'Well you know I take a big risk doing this kind of thing. Should we say a hundred pounds? Would that be too much for you?'

'No,' Tate replied, shortly, 'it wouldn't. You can have that much now and another fifty as soon as the hand's properly healed.'

'Mr Tate, that really is too much.' The nurse watched, rubbing his hands together as Tate counted out the money.

That afternoon, Alfred Tate rang a telephone number in the East End of London.

Yes, a voice the other end of the line said, they had read of the raid, and would be prepared to buy. They knew the prices paid by any of the London dealers, and kept within a shilling or two of the best of them; they would be prepared to deal with him and Lovel, now, and at any time in the future. 'We aren't mugs, boy,' the voice warned, 'and we're sure you aren't, so don't try taking us on. That way we'll all stay healthy.'

They were prepared to take anything provided it was worthwhile—anything from snout to groins, the worthwhile prices being from a few thousand, and without limit, upwards. 'The procedure is this. Bring the stuff with you, and,' he mentioned a certain car park near the Mile End Road, 'at ten-thirty sharp. You'll be picked up there, and brought here. We will weigh out, and you'll be paid cash to the full value, pro-rata, at the price agreed. To safeguard you against the scales being fixed, you can take them away with you. Think the law are on to you?'

'No,' Tate replied, 'we're sure they're not.'

'When we hear from you again then, we shall be waiting as arranged, at ten-thirty sharp.'

Tate rang off.

Next morning Tate turned off the Mile End Road and entered the agreed car park with almost ten minutes to spare. As he drove the car in, a white modern Citroen with two men in it pulled up close beside him. The back door of the Citroen opened level with Tate. Clutching his briefcase with the precious metals, Tate got out of his car and climbed into theirs; immediately the Citroen pulled away, while the man who had been sitting beside the driver had entered Tate's car, and was now following, several vehicles behind.

They made their way down the main road and turned off

into a maze of side streets, eventually stopping before a large block of modern flats. There was no sign of Tate's car. That, he supposed, was a precaution against his having been followed.

They took a lift up to the first floor, where a door opened as they approached one of the small flats. They stepped inside, into a comfortably furnished sitting room.

Two more men were inside; one of them reclining in a large easy chair looked briefly at Tate, then continued to scan a *Playboy* magazine. The other man, who had let them in, shook hands. He was a tall, rather thin, pleasant-faced fellow, very smartly dressed.

Pulling a chair up to the table he motioned Tate to sit down.

'Have a good trip?' he smiled.

'Quite uneventful, if that's what you mean,' Tate replied. 'Still,' he added, 'that's the way I like it, not too much excitement.'

'You boys do a very neat job,' the tall man said, 'but it's a pity about your partner losing a finger.'

Tate looked surprised.

'Oh, we had the information phoned through to us some time ago. Well, let's get down to business. Tom,' he said to the fellow reading *Playboy*, 'fetch the scales, and pour some drinks.'

He set the scales up on the table, then broke off a very small piece of matchstalk and placed it gently in one of the trays. The scales tipped slightly to one side.

Opening the bag, he extracted the metals, and cut a small portion from both the platinum and the gold.

'I'll just run a test on these, won't take me long,' he said and left the room.

The driver came up to the table and peered down at the white and gold metals. 'Funny stuff,' he said, pointing to the platinum wire. 'Don't look worth much.'

They waited in silence for the tall man's return.

They weighed the gold first, and afterwards the platinum, the full value coming to fourteen thousand eight hundred and twelve pounds.

' Satisfied?' he asked.

Tate nodded.

Tom brought in a battered looking attaché case. Opening it Tate saw it was stuffed with currency notes in bundles of five hundred. The tall man quickly counted the agreed amount in front of Tate, while Tom poured another round of drinks, and pushed over a large box of very expensive cigars.

'Fell off a lorry,' he grinned, holding a match to Tate's cigar.

At a nod from the tall man, Tom brought in two more unopened cigar boxes.

'There's one for you, and one for your partner with my compliments.' The tall man smiled, pushing the two boxes and the set of scales into Tate's bag.

'It wouldn't be any use you attempting to contact us here, we've just used this place as a convenience. We use a different place each time, so always use the phone and arrange a meeting. Now,' he continued, 'just to be on the safe side, when you leave, these two will follow you out of London. I am not saying you've been noticed, but there are a few would-be little hard men in this district. They won't try anything on while you have Tom nearby.'

Tom laughed over at Tate and patted his jacket under the armpit.

'Little bloody chancers,' he said, 'mugs and slags.'

The tall man leaned over table. 'Nice to do business with you, Mr Tate,' he said, shaking hands and smiling. 'It's easier to work when there's no suspicion. Give my regards to Mr Lovel.'

Tate left the flat, his bag now heavy with the money, scales and cigars. His car was standing out front and he got in.

The white Citroen stayed with him through London, never more than two vehicles behind. Then, as he passed over a bridge and was approaching some traffic lights, he noticed in his driving mirror the Citroen's headlights flash. They turned off left, and Tate acknowledged the signal by raising his arm.

He grinned with satisfaction to himself, and patted the bag.

Could be my last job, he reflected, yes, that could easily be my last job. A nice holiday now with Janet and Jennie and then settle down in a steady little business. Pulling into a lay-by, he broke open a box of cigars, and after lighting one up, continued his journey, and the same train of thought.

Yes, only mugs kept on and on, and you're no mug, Alfie boy. No, he told himself once more, you're certainly no mug. This little lot proves that, patting the bag once again.

He mentally calculated his share. Take out four thousand for the security guard, that would leave ten thousand eight hundred. The eight hundred, well, he could forget that. With the expenses of the male nurse, and two hundred to Eric for the use of the Rover 2000, plus other expenses, he and Jack would be left with five thousand apiece. Not bad really, but the nearly fifteen thousand had quickly been whittled down to ten! Not bad I suppose, thought Alfred rather glumly. He tucked the car in behind a heavy truck and continued on his way.

At ten-thirty a.m. on the fourth day after the accident Alfred Tate picked Lovel up from his flat.

First they went to an old quarry and collected the bag of money; proceeds of the platinum raid, which Tate had hidden upon his return from London. They then carried on to the wood and retrieved the cash stolen on the previous job. Returning to Lovel's flat, they shared out the proceeds of both crimes.

That evening Lovel drove into the town, but had to return early. He had, in his own words, shot his bolt. He was very tired, and got up late the next morning. It was almost noon when, followed by Sharon Lovelock, he entered the White Horse public house.

There were several people up at the bar drinking. Noticing three of the town's supposed tearaways, he paid little attention to them. He was looking for Alfred Tate, but he wasn't there.

The landlord's wife stood behind the bar wiping glasses. Lovel could see through the public bar into the lounge. He noticed the landlord deep in conversation with a man who looked like a representative of some firm. He had an order book open on the counter before him. Lovel scanned the lounge quickly; still no sign of Alfred. The landlord, finishing his chat with the representative and carrying his half-pint mug, came into the bar, seeing Lovel he stood before him awaiting the order.

'Single brandy, and a Pimms, and two bottles to take away.'

'Bottles of what?' the landlord grunted, holding a glass up to the optic.

'Brandy.' Lovel reached into his hip pocket and pulled out a large bunch of notes. He placed on the counter a new twenty-pound note.

The landlord picked up the treasury note and examined it closely.

Lovel sipped his drink and watched with irritation the landlord's close scrutiny of the money.

'Is it genuine?' he asked.

' 'Course it's bloody well genuine,' Lovel snorted impatiently.

The landlord looked up quickly, his face flushing with annoyance at Lovel's tone.

Before he had chance to answer Lovel reached out quickly and snatched the treasury note from the landlord's grasp. Pulling a huge roll from his pocket once again he flipped the bundle with his thumb, inches from the landlord's face.

'You want to inspect the bloody lot?'

The landlord glared back at Lovel.

'Now drink that and get out. I don't want your bloody type in here.'

'Go on, Fred, chuck him out,' piped up one of the three tearaways, 'chuck him out, but leave the bird.'

'I can handle this,' the landlord said, looking over at the short stocky spokesman of the trio.

'And I can handle his bird,' smirked the tearaway.

'You heard what I said.' The landlord put his face close up to Jack Lovel's. 'I don't want your bloody type in here.'

'What about that type?' Lovel scornfully pointed to the trio. 'Bloody little handbag snatchers and would-be hard cases when they're in a crowd, spending half their lives poncing bloody drinks, the other half grassing each other up to the Old Bill.'

The tearaway moved close up to Jack Lovel. 'You always were a flash bastard, Lovel.' Turning to the landlord he said, 'There's three of us here, if you want him out, we'll do the chucking.'

'Are you leaving?' asked the landlord.

'When I'm good and ready,' Lovel replied, 'but no one's putting me out.'

'We'll see,' said the landlord, and nodded to the tearaway, who reached out and grabbed a handful of Lovel's shirt-front. Pushing him off, Lovel cracked him on the side of the head with a hard left that made him stagger.

The man put his head down and charged in.

Lovel brought his left up, this time splitting the man's lips and jerking his head back. He had almost had enough, but one of his pals shouted, 'Watch his right hand, Ted, he's hurt his right hand, grab it.'

Ted, seeing this was in fact so, grappled with Lovel. He found Lovel's right hand and gave it a savage twist. Lovel felt the pain leap up his arm in surging waves of agony. He lashed out with his foot, catching Ted on the shin. Then, measuring his man, he drove in a powerful left hook. It had all his thirteen and a half stone of bone and muscle behind it.

The blow caught Ted flush on the jaw and he went down. Lovel, almost beserk with pain and fury, didn't hesitate. He put his shoe on Ted's face, and placing all his weight on that foot, twisted. He felt something crunch under his heel.

Taking his shoe away, he saw the blood suddenly gush from Ted's now well broken nose.

He caught a glancing blow from a bottle aimed from

behind. Seizing a bottle himself, he leapt in at the other two.

They had no stomach for more. Leaving their recumbent pal groaning on the floor, they raced for the door.

Sharon hadn't moved off the high stool. She was white-faced, but in full control of herself.

'He,' she said, pointing at the landlord, 'has phoned the police. I heard what he said. Do you want to know?' She looked with indignation at the landlord. 'He said that you came into this bar, and without any provocation whatsoever, attacked one of his customers. He said he had barred you previously for causing trouble. Shall we go, Jack, shall we go before the police get here?'

'No,' Lovel said. 'If we run now they'll only pick me up later, and after all, I was only defending myself.'

'You'll do time for this,' the landlord said. 'I'll see that you do time. I'll make damn sure you do time.'

'You want to hope like hell I don't,' Lovel said savagely. 'If I do time over this little fracas that you started, you're going to be one hell of a sorry man when I come out.'

'I'll tell the police that you're threatening me. I can always get protection.'

'You're going to need more protection than the law can give you, even God won't be able to protect you if I go down,' promised Lovel.

The landlord's wife was on her knees holding a towel to the tearaway's nose. He was groaning and crying. Lovel could hear his sobs.

She had discarded one blood-soaked towel and was busy with another.

The landlord leaned over the bar, looking down. 'Good thing it never happened in the lounge,' he remarked dispassionately. 'Would have ruined the bloody carpet.'

The door swung open and two uniformed policemen entered. They glanced at the blood-soaked form on the ground and exchanged a quick grin.

'Been fighting again has he?' one of the policemen remarked.

No one answered.

'Well, what happened,' the policeman said, 'run into a brick wall did he?'

The landlord lifted the flap on the counter and beckoned the policeman into the now empty lounge bar.

Lovel watched, wooden faced, as the policeman quickly made notes of the landlord's statement.

They returned to the bar.

'Anyone else see what happened?' the policeman asked.

'Yes,' said the salesman, 'I saw how it started. When I saw there was going to be trouble, I came into this bar.'

'Well, who started it?' asked the policeman.

'He did, partly anyway.' The salesman pointed to the tearaway.

'What do you mean, partly?' asked the policeman.

'Well, he offered to throw this gentleman out for the landlord, and that is the result.'

'Did the landlord agree then, that he should throw this gentleman out?'

'Yes,' said the salesman.

'Just as well you never tried it yourself, eh Fred?' the policeman smirked at the landlord.

'Can I have your name and address, sir?' the policeman asked.

Lovel made a note of it, too.

'Better get through on the radio, and see what they have to say about this at the station, and get an ambulance for Eddy boy, here.'

The landlord was having an argument with the salesman. 'I tell you I had nothing to do with starting it. I was not the instigator, and you won't get any more orders from me.'

'Costs me more in buying you bloody drinks to secure an order, than I ever made out of you in commission!' retorted the salesman.

'O.K., you can stop the arguing. That can be done in the proper place, in court. You've both made your statements, and now we shall have to wait and see what this one has to say, when he's in a fit state to make a statement.'

The two policemen escorted Lovel out to the large white

police car and opened the rear door for him. Lovel climbed in.

Sharon came up to the door. 'What shall I do?' she asked.

'Take my car back to the flat,' Lovel said, 'but contact Alfie and tell him what's happened.'

The policeman shut the door with a bang, and the car drove off.

'Tango one,' blared the radio. The policeman sitting beside the driver picked up his mike.

'Tango one to base. Yes,' he answered, 'on the way in now.'

They pulled in behind the police station, and escorting Lovel into the small room, locked him in by himself. The room contained a leather covered mattress, almost chest high, supported on a frame. This, he supposed, was for drunks or medical cases. But he was not in a cell; this was probably the charge room. He began to read some of the scribbling on the walls. 'Jack Bennett is a grass' he read; and 'Billy Davidson, king of the pushers'. There were dozens of these, some in pencil, some deeply etched by a sharp instrument. Another of the pencilled messages caught his eye: this one said, 'I am dying, I need a fix. They won't let me have one, the bastards.'

The door opened and Sergeant Bradshaw came in.

'Hello, Jack,' he greeted, 'been fighting, eh. Alfie should have told you not to go in that pub—'

Hearing the door open, Lovel had hidden his injured hand under the table.

'—Anything you want?' he continued. He seemed quite friendly today. 'Do you want cigarettes? You can have a bottle of beer if you like, anything as long as you pay. I don't think you'll be going home, so what about dinner?'

'What makes you think I won't be going home?' Lovel asked.

'They'll be in shortly to charge you, they're making the charge sheets up now, and I don't think they'll give you bail so that means you'll be held overnight and come before a magistrate in the morning.'

'Bloody set-up,' Lovel snorted. 'What's the charge going to be? I suppose they've rigged that to make it as serious as they can?'

'G.B.H., grievous bodily harm,' the detective laughed. 'Could get six months, Jack,' he added gleefully, 'yes, with a little luck you would be out of our hair for a few months.'

'Bloody travesty of justice, that's what it is,' said Lovel moodily.

The detective left, laughing.

Lovel was charged and bail was refused him. He would be brought before a magistrate in the morning. He was taken through to the cells and locked in.

He sat moodily looking around. Again he saw the scribbling on the walls, but this time he didn't trouble to read them.

Looking up he saw footprints, as though someone had walked across the ceiling upside down.

He picked up an old battered *Time* magazine and began leafing through the dog-eared pages. He felt a growing need to go to the toilet.

Obviously you had to ring here. He pressed the bell. Some ten minutes later the door opened. 'Toilet,' Lovel said.

'Well hurry up,' said a uniformed sergeant, 'you have two visitors.'

Lovel relieved himself while the sergeant watched. He was then taken to the original room.

Tate and Sharon sat on the bench. On the table were two large plastic carrier bags.

'A few things for you, Jack,' Sharon informed him.

Lovel borrowed a pen from Tate and wrote a brief message quickly on an empty cigarette packet he had been saving. The sergeant's back was turned to them. The message read, 'Try and find my ring tonight! They haven't noticed my missing finger as yet, but if they do and they find the ring . . .' He hadn't time to write any more, the sergeant turned round.

Lovel managed to slip the note under the table to Tate.

Sharon handed him a cigarette. He fished the gold

Dunhill from his trouser pocket with his left hand. He kept practically all his possessions in his left pocket now. The sergeant left the room.

'Is your hand playing you up, Jack?' Sharon asked, anxiously peering up into his face.

'No,' Lovel lied. It had been throbbing painfully.

'Your eyes look tired. I suppose that's the result of the drugs.'

She took from one of the bags a packet of codeine tablets.

Lovel slipped them into his pocket.

'So they're holding you tonight for the magistrates in the morning,' Tate said. 'They'll try you there and then, if you agree, but if you wish, you can be tried before a sessions court.'

'What would you suggest?' asked Lovel.

'I'd go for the magistrate. He can only give you up to six months. There's that to consider, plus the fact that if you demand to be tried by jury, the police will ask for a remand in custody. That is, they'll oppose bail being granted, throwing in of course, for good measure, that further more serious charges may be preferred and so hold you in custody for two or three months before you're brought to trial. Then, if you're found guilty, you'd have that sentence to do on top of that which you've already done.'

Lovel stared miserably at Tate. 'Seems like I can't win either way,' he remarked.

'We have a solicitor, he'll be down to see you this afternoon. It's up to you. Think it over, then instruct him accordingly.'

'Time's up.' The police sergeant put his head round the door. Tate and Sharon stood up.

'I shall be in court tomorrow,' Tate said, 'but if there's anything more I can do, let me know.'

Sharon leaned over and kissed Lovel.

He watched them leave the charge room.

'Cheerio, cheerio, Jack,' they both called as they finally left.

The sergeant peered inside the plastic bags.

'Nice to have friends, Jack, when you're in trouble,' he remarked. 'I should search these bags, but I won't. I don't like having to peer and pry into people's things, but I have to do it at times. We get a lot of druggers these days, and if I'm not careful their mates will slip them a handful of tablets. Result is, I go in their cell an hour later and find them stretched out. It's a hospital job then, stomach pump! Makes me look a bloody fool. If it ain't pills it's razor blades. Little buggers will cut lumps out of themselves, given half a chance. Usually go for the wrist; and you get these people, even some doctors writing in the press, demanding drugs to be made legal. They should spend a weekend down here some time, and see what goes on. Bloody madhouse Saturday nights.'

He held the door open to the cell block. 'Want to go anywhere before I lock you up?'

'Not yet,' Lovel replied.

'Tell you what,' the sergeant said magnanimously, 'I'll leave your cell door open, then you can help yourself. How about that?'

'Thanks very much,' Lovel replied gratefully.

'Ring the bell if you want anything.' With that he left, carefully locking the main door of the cell block.

Lovel walked into his cell and sat on the bench-type bed. He began exploring the plastic carrier bags. Inside was fruit, several pieces of chicken, and a salad in a cardboard container; also half a dozen magazines. He took these out and commenced to eat, and read a magazine.

He came to with a start. 'Wakey, wakey,' the sergeant laughed.

Lovel sat up, rubbing his eyes. He had dropped off to sleep.

'Have I been asleep long?' he asked.

'I don't know, but the time is now six-fifteen.'

Lovel calculated he must have slept for some three hours.

'Your solicitor's here to see you.' He led the way into the charge room.

The solicitor, a tall thin man of about forty, shook hands with him. They both sat down.

'Have you made a statement?' he asked.

'No,' Lovel replied.

'Well, could you tell me exactly what happened.'

Lovel related to him faithfully the events leading up to the fight.

'What do you think?' he asked.

'Have you a police record?'

Lovel shook his head.

'Ever been in trouble of any kind?'

'Only motoring offences, speeding and that sort of thing.'

'Well,' the solicitor continued, 'the other chappie has quite a record of violence. We can always bring that up, but of course, if you also had a record, the police would retaliate by reading that out to the court, but you haven't?' He looked meaningly at Lovel.

'I haven't,' Lovel assured him again.

'You wish to be tried before the magistrate, or will you elect to go for trial?'

'I've given it plenty of thought and I think I would rather it were dealt with in the magistrates' court. What do you think of my chances?'

'One can never tell.' The solicitor was non-committal. 'Well, see you tomorrow, and by the way, a Mr Alfred Tate has kindly paid my fee.' He shook hands once more, and left.

Lovel wandered back to his cell of his own accord, and sat on the bed. He picked up a magazine, but found he could not read.

He got up and began pacing. Suddenly he felt very vulnerable; he realized just how lonely he was. He took a good look at the barred window, the heavy steel-lined door with its judas spy hole. He could sense an atmosphere of loneliness and despair pervading the place. He was utterly dejected, realizing now why people slashed their wrists or throats when locked in a place like this. His past life of crime didn't seem so glamorous now, although he could be considered a successful criminal.

Was there such a thing? Jack Lovel began to wonder. On the out, he had a good car, a nice flat, and money to burn, but this did not buy him friendship. There is no friendship when you live a life of crime—crime is a form of moral cannibalism, he truthfully told himself. The true criminal will prey on each and every one. On his friends. On his family, and eventually on himself.

Lovel was escorted the two or three hundred yards to the Guildhall. He was not handcuffed, the charge was not considered serious enough for that indignity to be imposed.

He stood all morning talking to Sharon and Tate in the passage, sometimes peering through the window in the door at the other cases being heard.

At lunch-time they took him down below the courts where he was locked up. His case was the last one that day. It was three-thirty p.m. when he was brought up, on this occasion by two prison officers.

He stepped into the dock.

'Are you Albert Jack Lovel?' he was asked.

'Yes,' he replied.

'You are—' and here they went off, reading out his charge. 'Do you understand?'

'Yes,' he replied again.

'Raise the bible in your right hand.'

'And,' Lovel repeated, 'I swear by Almighty God to tell the truth, the whole truth, and nothing but the truth.'

The whole case took no more than twenty minutes; finally the magistrate summed up.

'Well,' he said, peering over thick-lensed rimless glasses. 'You, I have no doubt, were under extreme provocation. I have heard one witness giving excellent and unbiased evidence to this effect. I have totally disregarded the evidence given by the landlord of the White Horse public house. A good deal of blame attaches to him for your being before me today.

'However, I find that although you were entitled to use force in protecting yourself after being attacked by the complainant, you did use far more force than was necessary, by stamping with your shoe on complainant's face, and thereby causing extensive damage to his nose.

'I find you guilty as charged, and sentence you to twenty-eight days' imprisonment.'

Lovel was ushered down below once more.

He could see the prison officers in the room opposite preparing to leave. One of them made tea, and poured several cups.

Lovel sat on a wooden bench in his cell, and watched as one of them brought a cup of tea in.

'Didn't take long,' the officer said.

'No,' Lovel replied, sipping the tea. 'I was expecting six months if they found me guilty.'

'Oh, well that's not so bad; here's your solicitor and two visitors to see you, better make it snappy though, we'll be going back to the nick soon.'

Lovel stepped out into the passage and walked down to the end, where the solicitor, Tate and Sharon stood.

'Not bad, eh?' The solicitor spoke first.

'Could have been worse,' Lovel answered.

'I was expecting you to get six months, at least,' Tate chipped in.

'How's your finger?' asked Sharon.

'Well, I'll leave now.' The solicitor shook Lovel's hand. 'Won't be long,' he said.

'Have to go now,' called a prison officer.

'Bloody screws,' Tate muttered.

Sharon gave him a long kiss. 'I'll come and see you soon, darling,' she whispered. She was crying. 'I can't help it,' she whispered, 'you have such rotten luck.'

Lovel turned and began walking away.

' 'Bye Jack, write to me,' Sharon called after him.

They made him empty his pockets and placed his possessions in a canvas bag. He signed for them, then was handcuffed to a boy whom he had seen before at the police station.

'How long did you get?' the boy asked.

Lovel told him.

They were driven to the prison in a mini-bus. The small bus stopped outside the huge prison gates. One of the prison officers got out and pressed a bell. The doors swung ponderously open. They drove carefully in. An officer opened the back door of the vehicle.

'Come on, let's have you,' he ordered.

Lovel and the boy staggered out. They were led through a door and into the prison proper, up two flights of ancient stone stairs, to a row of equally ancient cells. The handcuffs were taken off. They sat down. The door of the cell had been left open, and presently a prisoner walked in.

'Bring any burn?'

'What?' Lovel looked questioningly at him.

'Bring any snout in, you know, tobacco.'

'No,' Lovel replied. 'I had cigarettes, but they took them off me.'

'It's his first time in,' the boy told the con.

'Oh! well next time you come in, you want to bring a few ounces with you, stuff it down your shoe, we'll find it. Doing twenty-eight days ain't you? What's that for, debt or something?'

'No, he's in for G.B.H.,' the boy piped up. 'Done three blokes up; put one bloke in hospital seriously ill. Done 'em up real proper.' The boy looked admiringly up at Lovel. 'In the White Horse, reckon there was blood everywhere, he went mad, the screws told me.'

'Christ,' exclaimed the con, looking at Lovel with a new respect.

'Got a fag, Bill?' the boy asked.

'No I bloody well ain't, every time you come through reception, you tap me. Ain't you never got nothing?'

'Righto, bring 'em in,' a voice shouted.

The con led the way, back down the passage and into a room.

'Right, you first,' an officer sitting behind a desk, spoke to Lovel.

'Anything in your pockets?'

'No,' Lovel replied.

'Say sir, when you speak to me.'

'No, sir,' repeated Lovel.

'Strip off, and put that dressing-gown on.'

Lovel complied. Interested, a couple of cons and prison officers stood watching.

'Right, now over there and get weighed.'

He was weighed and measured by a con, and taken to a bath.

Lovel got in, soaped up and began to bath.

'Come on, you gonna take all bloody night.' An officer put his head over the half door.

Lovel scrambled out. His prison clothing was handed him. Pants, vest. Lovel put them on. He felt slightly better, he was no longer naked. 'Socks,' the con said, 'shoes, trousers, shirt, jacket.'

The trousers and jacket were of a rough woollen material, the trousers fitted tightly and were far too short in the leg. He dared not bend down in them, that is, if ever he could.

The jacket was far too big.

'Not bad,' the con said, eyeing him up, 'still you can always change them at exercise time in the morning.'

He was handed a plastic pint mug, a knife, fork and spoon of the same material, a large roll of bedding, and a chamber pot.

Then he was led away with a dozen other similarly laden men, through doors unlocked and carefully locked again behind them.

The journey was a maze of short passages and doors; finally they came to the centre, a large glass-fronted office. A prison officer sat inside.

They were called in one at a time, told how long they were doing, and handed three library books each. These were placed on top of their already huge bundle, together with a cell card, with their sentence, religion and cell number written on it. Lovel was led up a winding, steel staircase, and along a slate-tiled landing with rows of cells on one side and guard rails on the other.

The prison officer stopped before a cell door marked fourteen. Lovel entered. There were two other men inside. The furniture consisted of two bunk beds on one side, and a single bed on the other. Two chairs, a small table and a three-cornered washstand completed the furnishings.

'Top bunk, mate,' one of the occupants told him. Lovel heaved his bedroll and other equipment up onto the high bed.

'Had supper?' the same man asked.

'No,' Lovel replied, 'but I'm not particular.'

The cell door opened. 'Get your mug if you want tea,' he was told.

Lovel held out his plastic pint mug, it was filled by a con, from a large metal can.

The door was once more slammed shut. He sipped his tea. It was hot, extremely weak, and sugarless. He drank some of the tea, and tipped the rest into a bucket handily placed to receive slops, then made his bed.

'Got burn?' he was asked.

'No,' he replied.

'Here, have one of mine.'

The hand-rolled cigarette he was given was hardly thicker than a matchstick.

'This is Frank,' he was told, 'and my name is Joe.'

Joe was busy at the table, splitting matches with a needle. He got three, and sometimes four strikeable splinters from each match.

Lovel heaved himself onto the top bunk and sat with legs dangling down.

Once again he was asked how long he was doing.

'How long are you doing?' he asked Joe.

'Thirty months. I've cracked it now though. Five months left. Frank's got nine months left out of a seven.'

Frank looked up and grinned at Lovel. 'Watcha in for, mate?'

'G.B.H., had a fight in a pub yesterday; kicked a bloke in the face. What did you get yours for?' he asked Frank.

'Screwing, mate. This is my fifth time in, but it will definitely be my last.'

'You hope,' Lovel grinned.

'No, I mean it, unless I get something worthwhile, I'm not doing bird for next to nothing. If I do go next time, it will be on a blag [armed holdup]. Yes,' he continued, 'that's the only game worthwhile these days. They gave me a seven this time, for just over a hundred quid. They say make the sentence fit the crime, but I shall make sure my next crime fits the sentence. If I have to do a ten, then I'm going to make bloody sure it's for something worthwhile. While I was being done this time, there was a geezer up for rape; he'd raped two little girls, both of them under eight. What d'you reckon he got?' Frank looked questioningly up at Jack Lovel.

'Ten, fifteen years!' Lovel hazarded a guess.

'Like hell! He got a two year suspended sentence. The judge said he was a sick man; needed medical treatment. The same judge called me an animal for nicking just over a hundred quid, and sent me down for seven.'

He picked up a magazine and began reading. 'Tasty things, these hot pants, are all the birds wearing them on the out?'

'Not all,' Lovel replied, 'it's mostly the younger birds, but a lot still wear the mini.'

'Wouldn't be the same without the mini,' Joe said pensively, 'hope the mini's still going when I get out. Nice to see a bit of leg,' he added.

Frank got up and made for the bucket. 'I shall have to have another slash, bloody tea runs straight through you.'

Lovel watched as Frank urinated into the bucket.

'Better use the old bucket, mate, and not the piss-pot; they smell like hell after a few days if you keep using them.' He carefully dropped a few pieces of orange peel into the bucket. 'Keeps the smell down a bit,' he informed Lovel.

'By the way, how did you do that?' Joe pointed to Lovel's injured hand.

'Caught it in some machinery,' Lovel lied.

'Took it right off, didn't it? Looks as if it hasn't been done long.'

'Oh, it's been done a few days now, don't worry me none,' Lovel said flippantly, hoping Frank would change the subject. He didn't like being reminded that his right hand was now deformed.

The cell door, opening, stopped any further conversation.

'Slop out,' a voice called.

Joe grabbed the bucket. Frank took two white plastic jugs. He looked at Lovel. 'No need for you to trouble,' he said. 'I'll get enough water for all three of us.'

'I'll have to go somewhere,' Lovel said.

'Oh well, follow me.' Frank grinned, and led the way down the landing, carrying the two jugs. Turning into a recess, 'In there,' Frank nodded to a toilet. Lovel could make out a man's head, sticking up from over the short half door. 'Have to wait till he's finished,' said Frank, filling the two jugs, one with hot, the other with cold water at the two taps in the recess.

Several other men were standing in a queue, waiting their turn to empty plastic chamber pots into a large white sink.

'Christ!' Lovel said, 'a bit bloody primitive, isn't it?'

The smell disgusted him. He saw the fellow in the toilet begin making the obvious movements a person makes after using the lavatory, and before re-dressing. He came out, and Lovel entered.

Taking his trousers down, he carefully examined, then perched himself gingerly on the seat. Hope they don't have crabs here, he thought.

'You get used to the smell after a while,' Frank said, leaning over the small door.

'Hope so,' Lovel muttered, embarrassed at having to relieve himself whilst being watched.

'You won't receive an advance payment as you're only doing twenty-eight days. Now, if you'd been doing say, thirty-one days, you'd have got paid four and six in the morning.'

'Just my bloody luck,' answered Lovel, wondering if Frank was going to stand and watch until he'd finished. He didn't by any means consider himself shy, but he hardly fancied the idea of wiping himself clean while someone watched.

He put the task off, hoping that Frank would go back to the cell.

'No,' Frank continued, 'I don't know how they come to the conclusion that a chap who's doing thirty-one days or over, needs tobacco more than one doing less.'

'Oh, for Christ sake, wrap up and let me finish with at least some privacy,' Lovel thought.

'Nearly finished?' A screw stood beside Frank.

They both watched with interest as Lovel cleaned himself.

'Tight fit,' Frank remarked, as Lovel finally pulled his trousers up. They walked back to the cell together.

Lovel lay awake long after lights out. Twenty-eight days, he reflected, was quite sufficient in this place. He worried about his flat, whether if his landlord were to find out about his having been imprisoned, would he serve notice to quit? But the main and overriding worry was the ring. Would Alfred go tonight, would he find it?

If the police found it, would they be able to trace it back to him? If so, would it be sufficient evidence for them to get a conviction?

He heard Frank get up and noisily use the bucket.

Some time later in the night, he awoke with a start.

Both Frank and Joe were snoring loudly, the noise in the small cell was abominable. Frank would gradually work up to a crescendo, he would then emit a series of choking strangled gasps, turn over, and for a few minutes, breathe quietly in his sleep. Then the performance would start again. Joe woke twice during the night and each time hurled a slipper at the noisy sleeper. Seeing Lovel awake, he rolled two cigarettes, lit them, and getting out of bed, handed one to Lovel.

'Same every bloody night,' he complained bitterly, 'always wakes me up. I got him trained though. You watch this.'

Joe whistled. Frank stopped snoring and turned over. He lay quiet for a few moments, then began to snore.

Joe whistled again. Once more Frank rolled over.

'Like a bloody performing seal, ain't he,' Joe giggled. 'Won't believe it when I tell him in the morning, thinks I'm having him on.'

Lovel was awakened in the morning by the clang, clang, clanging of the huge centre bell.

For some time he lay and watched Frank and Joe bustle about. First making their beds, then tidying the cell.

They were extremely cramped quarters. Cells built to hold one man only, over a hundred years ago, now were made to take three.

'Come on, sport, the screw will be opening up in a minute. You let him catch you in kip, and you're nicked.'

Lovel climbed slowly out of bed, and began to dress.

The door was flung noisily open. An officer put his head in.

'Slop out,' he shouted.

Frank grabbed the water jugs and hurried out.

Joe followed, carrying the bucket.

Lovel finished dressing. He picked up a third jug, which was in a plastic bowl under the washstand, and walked to the recess. Men were hurrying to and fro, each one carrying either a jug or a white plastic chamber pot. Those that were going to the recess carefully held the lids tight on.

He stood behind a long queue, waiting his turn to get hot water. If the smell had been strong the previous night, it was practically unbearable now. Lovel felt his stomach heave.

He could hear the P.O. on the centre calling the different landings to breakfast. Lovel carried his jug of water back to the cell. The other two had gone. He placed the jug inside and went down to breakfast, joining a huge queue. As they came to the hotplate, each one took a cafeteria type tray that had been moulded to accommodate three courses.

The queue filed past the cooks. Each cook in turn would slap something on the tray. First porridge; next a piece of goulash, followed by jam, a small portion of margarine, and finally three rounds of bread.

Lovel returned up the stairs, after being told off for not wearing a tie.

Frank and Joe had had breakfast, and were now busy shaving.

Lovel ate the bread and margarine; he had no stomach for the remainder. He was to find out later that the food was sufficient for the light work they performed. Very few lost weight in prison because the food was practically all carbohydrates.

'You'll have to look slippery, Jack, if you want a shave,' Joe warned. 'The screw will be round any minute now for the razor-blades.'

Lovel poured his now almost cold water in the bowl, lathered up and commenced shaving. Joe was right; he had just begun when an officer put his head round the door. He picked up the two blades lying on the table.

'You gonna take all bloody day?' he shouted. 'Make it sharp, I'll be back in a couple of minutes.'

Lovel hurriedly finished. The officer was already there, waiting. He took the blade.

'First time in the nick,' Frank said to the screw, meaning Lovel.

'You won't have time to drink your tea, if you don't hurry. Be exercise in a minute, and don't forget your tie; get nicked if you don't put it on.'

They were called out to exercise, Lovel still fixing his tie. He spent half an hour walking round the small yard with other prisoners, and returned to his cell.

He sank gratefully down onto a chair.

A cleaner put his head inside. 'All go, ain't it, mate,' he said. 'Come in last night?'

Lovel nodded.

'Got any burn, can you give us a roll-up?'

'No, I bloody well can't. I haven't had one myself since last night. Where the hell do you think I'd get burn from, anyway?' Lovel asked bitterly.

'Thought you might have got some by reception,' the cleaner said. 'A few dog-ends will do,' he added hopefully.

Lovel stood up, ignoring him. His eyes had alighted on

what looked like a piece of poetry pinned up among the bits and pieces on the wall. He went over to have a look, and read:

My parole has been turned down
But then I must have been a clown
To think I even stood a chance
Of ever getting parole
I've worked real hard from morn till night
Once I even stopped a fight
I've tried and tried with all my might
They still refused me parole
'Course I've nothing much outside
They took me for a three year ride
You can be sure my time I'll bide
I'll live without their parole
Now there's two Gods it would appear
One above, and one down here.
One will scorch your bloody soul
And one will turn down your parole
Either way you cannot win
If like me you lead with chin
And always think, the next time in
This time they'll give me parole.

An officer came in. 'You Lovel?' he asked.

'Yes,' Lovel replied.

'You're for Governor's, go down now, you'll see the others waiting, and say sir when you answer.'

'Yes, sir,' Lovel repeated, woodenly.

'Well come on then, don't just stand there—and bang your cell up after you, get everything nicked if you leave it open.'

Lovel joined the other dozen or so waiting outside the governor's office. Eventually his name was called.

'Stand on that mat, and give your full name and number.'

He could still remember his name, but couldn't even make an effort to remember his number. The governor saved him more of the hopeless mental effort by saying,

'You have twenty-eight days.' He looked up at Lovel. 'This is your first time in prison.'

'Yes,' Lovel replied.

'Well,' the governor continued, 'I shall make you a star, and you are allocated for work to the metal shop. Any problems?'

'None,' answered Lovel, noticing that apparently the governor was one of the very rare people in this prison who did not object to being spoken to without the prefix 'sir'.

'That will be all.' Lovel about turned and walked out.

He sat on the chair outside the governor's office again.

He watched enviously as a con sitting next to him surreptitiously took long drags from a very slender roll-up.

'Got a fag?' asked the chap, holding his head low down, and taking another long pull.

'No, haven't had one today, yet,' Lovel replied.

'Here, cop that,' the con said, handing him what remained of the cigarette.

Lovel, too, put his head down, so as not to be observed, and took a long drag. He spluttered and coughed violently.

'What in hell have you got in this?' he gasped.

'Oh, that's black shag,' the con informed him.

Lovel was craving for a smoke. He took another quick, but this time more cautious pull at the powerful tobacco.

'Lasts better than Old Holborn,' the con said.

An officer in a white jacket came up, called a few names out, Lovel's amongst them. 'For doctors,' he informed them.

Lovel, dizzy from the effects of the strong tobacco, rose from his seat.

They followed the male nurse to the hospital block.

'Wait here, and when your name is called, strip off to the waist.'

Hearing his name called, Lovel walked into the small room and stood before the doctor.

'Raise your hands above your head,' he was ordered.

Lovel complied, hoping the doctor would not spot the elastoplast covering his injured hand.

'What's that? Hold your hand out,' the doctor ordered.

Lovel, trying to the last, hopefully held out his left.

'Not that one,' snapped the doctor, 'the right; huh, lost a finger.'

He quickly removed the elastoplast and lint covering.

'Quite recent, too. Where did you go to have this attended?'

Lovel remained silent.

'I said, where did you have that attended?' he asked Lovel.

Lovel still refused to answer.

The doctor tried a new tack.

'Who,' he asked, 'is your doctor?'

'Haven't got one,' Lovel answered.

'See to that,' the doctor ordered the male nurse.

After giving the wound a careful examination, 'Doesn't appear to be infected.' He turned to Lovel again.

'Now look,' he said, 'for your own good, you must tell me where you got this wound attended. We can then check on the type of drugs you were given, and continue giving you them if needed.'

'I don't need any more drugs,' Lovel said.

'Take him away,' the doctor ordered disgustedly.

Lovel had his finger freshly dressed. Except for a faint throbbing, which he had got used to, it hardly bothered him now.

He was taken back to his cell and locked in.

He stood for a while examining what were obviously family photographs. They were all of women and children. None of them were of the owner. He guessed, correctly, that a prisoner was not allowed a photograph of himself.

Lovel was left in his cell until eleven-thirty. Half an hour's exercise followed. Round and round; two separate circles. The stars in the inner circle, convicts that were not first-timers on the outside.

Four or five prison officers stood at vantage points.

Some carried small walkie-talkie sets, these kept them in contact at all times with the centre. Every now and then, a con would fall out to go special sick. Usually the real reason would be that he felt too tired or bored to continue the exercise.

Lovel's afternoon in the metal shop finished uneventfully.

That evening he changed cells and landings.

He was put in with two other prisoners, one a small red-haired fellow in his middle twenties, the other, an extremely tall chap.

Lovel threw his gear onto the top bunk.

'And that's why I'm here.' The small red-haired fellow had been spinning some yarn to his cell mate.

He nodded to Lovel. 'Just in?' he asked.

'No, came in last night,' Lovel replied.

'Same here, I came in yesterday. Where are you from?'

Lovel told him.

'Oh I got done near there. Nice bloody crowd you've got down here; tried to fit me up. I was just telling Lofty here. I'm from the smoke, see; know the Mile End Road,' he asked, 'know the Blind Beggars pub?'

'I've heard of it, must have passed it dozens of times, but never been inside. Fellow got shot there some time ago, didn't he?' Lovel asked.

'That's it. Well I live just behind the place. Well, I'm sent down here to do a job,' Ginger continued, 'and get picked up by the Regional Crime Squad. Done me for carrying a shooter. Got twenty-eight days.'

Lovel nodded.

'Tried to fit me up, the bastards did. You know, for that shot-gun hold-up. Made my bottle twitch I can tell you, when they took my clothes for forensic. Tried to bluff me into thinking they'd found something. I knew the only stuff they could find on my clobber was stuff they'd planted. They even brought one of the Flying Squad boys down to have a look at me, but they were flogging a dead horse, and the only thing they could do me for was possessing a firearm with a barrel that did not exceed a certain length. 'Why would you carry a sawn-off shot-gun?' the old fogey in the chair asked. 'Shoot pheasants your honour, shoot pheasants. I'm a poacher see, and I come down here once in a while for a bit of sport.'

' "But why saw half the barrel off?" he asked me again. "You spoil the gun and it doesn't have half its original range."

' "Well I can conceal it more easily, your honour, and as I shoot from the car, it only has to carry to the other side of the roadside hedge, because that's where the pheasants usually feed."

' "Well I shall give you twenty-one days' imprisonment," he said. "Can't have you Londoners roaming about here carrying guns, bla, bla, bla, and I'm not altogether sure you are telling me the truth, bla, bla."

'The Old Bill were choked. I can tell you. So, here I am, and by the way,' he added, 'that's Lofty,' he pointed to the tall fellow, 'he's in here for drugs. My name's Andy Benett but they all call me Ginger.' He looked up at Lovel.

'Jack . . .' Lovel told him.

'Funny thing,' Ginger said, 'just after the hold-up, damn me if somebody doesn't go and do a platinum job nearby. Done a tie-up on the watchman, then cut the peter open with oxy arc. Tasty little team, whoever they were. Had it off, too. Still, you can't beat the old sawn-off shot-gun for quick cash. Straight in, no messing. You take a bank now,' he said, looking up at Jack Lovel.

Just then the door opened.

'Slop out,' a voice shouted.

'Slopping out, Lofty?' Ginger asked.

'No,' Lofty replied.

'I'm going for hot water,' Lovel said. Grabbing a jug, he made his way to the recess.

'Looks like he's just lost a finger,' Ginger said.

'Yes,' Lofty replied. 'He doesn't know me, but I know him. Works with a fellow called Alfie Tate. Tasty little firm, too.'

'Go on,' said Ginger.

'Yes,' Lofty continued, 'practically every worthwhile job that's ever been done within a thirty mile radius of this town, you could put down to those two. Alfie Tate does the blowing, and Jack Lovel knocks the alarms out. He can even fix the straight-through to the police type of alarms. He's done it a few times.'

'Think they done that platinum job, Lofty?'

'Could have. Alfie Tate knows just about every way there is to open a peter.'

Lovel returned with the hot water.

'Smoke?' Ginger asked, pulling a large two-ounce tin out, stuffed with tobacco.

'Christ!' Lovel exclaimed, 'how the hell did you get that much in?'

'I didn't,' Ginger answered. 'We've got one of the remands straightened. Here, help yourself.' He gave the tin to Lovel. 'Plenty more where that came from.'

Lovel made a decent sized roll-up, obtained a light, and inhaled deeply. He blew the smoke out, and took another long, lingering pull at the cigarette. The room began to tilt sideways, but the feeling was quite pleasant.

He sat on the edge of the bottom bunk, savouring his first really decent smoke for more than twenty-four hours.

'I don't mind giving you a burn,' Ginger said, 'in fact, you can have what you like, but I don't hand it out to the rest of them out there. Bunch of bloody mugs, that's what they are. Live by tapping, and I reckon most of them eat better in nick than they do on the out. I keep Lofty here going, but I don't mind him, he's O.K. Lofty tells me you're a good operator.'

Lovel looked keenly at Lofty.

'I don't think you know me,' Lofty explained, 'but I've seen you about plenty, and I know Alfie Tate's been at it for years. I was telling Ginger, they reckon in the town that you can knock out all types of alarm systems, and there's not much Alfie Tate can't open, one way or another. Even the law admit that.'

'Well,' Lovel said, feeling flattered, and once more on his favourite subject, 'if you ever cop one that's belled up and you can't do it, send for me. Have to be worth while, though,' he added.

'There's always a chance we might do just that, if you're

as good as they say you are,' Ginger replied. 'Still, as I was saying to Lofty while you were out, the old sawn-off shotgun takes a lot of beating. I can be on and off a job in minutes, but your way, you can be on a job all night.'

'Have been, plenty of times,' Lovel agreed.

'That's just it,' Ginger said. 'It's like having a tooth out, you can do it with one quick snatch and have a lot of pain all at once, or you can give it a little tweak every now and again, spread the job and the pain over hours.

'No, we don't work like that. We get a bent car; sometimes two. Car number one takes us to the job. The first minder, that's me, with the shotgun under his jacket, enters the bank. I walk in nice and casual, we always pick our time. The second minder follows, that is, another shotgun man if it's a big bank. We also have a good size chap with a pick-handle. I pull out the shotgun and give them some quick hard chatter.

'Take the one we done at Hammersmith. As I pulled the shooter out, a young clerk standing near made a grab for it. Christ! For a second or two I nearly let him have it. I rammed the gun close up against his head, the bastard. I was all keyed up and I was pulling the trigger when the other minder shouted at me. Brought me round a bit. I just moved the barrel a shade and blasted a bloody great hole in the ceiling. A couple of birds started screaming. For Christ's sake, I thought, why don't we just let the bastards have it. I nearly did with the other barrel, but the manager started throwing the money over. He could see how things were going. The pickaxe-handle man grabbed the money and ran. I waited till they got through the door, then I gives this bloody clerk a good belt with the barrel. Laid him out cold. We had no trouble having it away. Not many people stick their bloody noses in these days. Well, we belts out of the bank, in the car and away. Out of car number one, and two of us get into car number two because they'd be looking for four fellows. The job's over.' He looked up at Lovel. 'Now which is best?' he asked. 'All over in less than ten minutes, from start to finish.'

'Only one thing wrong with that,' Lovel replied. 'The way you operate, you got some of it.'

'Nine grand,' Ginger said.

'Yes, well, we would have taken the lot, and no chance of anyone getting hurt. There would probably have been fifty or sixty thousand in the strong room, and don't forget there are only two of us, to share.'

'Which way would you say is the best, Lofty?' asked Ginger.

'I don't know, I wouldn't have the bottle to do either,' Lofty replied.

The door opened. 'Supper already?' Lovel asked.

They held out their plastic mugs. A con with a large tray of buns handed three into them. The door was slammed shut.

At eleven a.m. the next day Lovel, with half a dozen more, was taken to the bath-house. Six baths half filled with hot water awaited them. Lovel was quickly into the bath, by now having got used to doing most things fast. That is, all except work. He pulled the plug and was out, dressing, whilst most of the others who knew the drill better, took their time.

It was time for exercise. As they would be the last ones to bath before lunch, they wouldn't be rushed.

The officer who had brought them relaxed. He sat in the store room, smoking and talking to his number one, a con who handed out the clean shirts. Another con walked up and down outside the small cubicles which contained a single bath each. He carried a key, and on request would turn on the hot or cold tap from outside the cubicles. For a while he was kept busy. Eventually, as each customer was satisfied with the temperature of his bath water, the attendant wandered off for a smoke.

Lovel dressed quickly and stood outside the cubicle.

The fellow next to him was splashing and singing as he bathed. Suddenly a figure, naked except for a towel round his waist, slipped quietly from a cubicle further up and crept up to Lovel. 'Sex case in there,' he whispered. 'In for a little girl of six, dirty bastard. I'm going to liven him up a bit. Watch this.'

Hardly comprehending, Lovel peered over the half door. The con had placed a key on the screw that turned on the hot water. His hand was now holding the key in readiness.

They watched. The bather was sitting upright in the bath with his back to them, busily soaping under his armpits and over his chest. There was one large, long copper pipe jutting out over the bath, to supply a strong gush of hot or cold water according to which of the two taps was turned on by the key.

They had not long to wait. Having liberally soaped himself with White Windsor, the bather began to bend backwards with the intention of rinsing off the lather. His bare, white back sank slowly below the level of the water pipe. Judging to a nicety, the fellow next to Lovel gave the key a good twist. There was a tremendous jet of steam and boiling water from the pipe.

Lovel saw the bather's head and shoulders completely covered in steam. He heard him give a piercing scream, then saw him project himself from the bath onto the concrete floor.

Lovel was about to run, but the con gripped his elbow. None of the other bathers came from their cubicles, they were in the know.

The officer, hearing the agonized scream, threw his cigarette on the floor, jumped up and ran to the window. He scrambled through the hatch.

'What in the name of Christ happened to him?' he stuttered, peering over the door.

'I don't know, sir; heard the scream and came running out, just about to get dressed. This chap,' pointing to Lovel, 'came after me.'

The officer ran to the hatch and pressed the alarm bell once.

This would bring every officer within hearing distance, and who could be spared, at the double. They would come expecting to find trouble.

Seeing the officer's back turned, the con who had turned

on the tap tossed the key he was still holding into the injured man's bath, winked at Lovel, and said, 'Take your cue from what I say, we'll be all right.'

The officer returned from the hatch. 'How did it happen?' he asked, watching the groaning man. 'His back and neck are one bloody great blister. How did the hot water get turned on? Charlie!' he turned to the attendant. 'Where were you?'

'Up there cleaning the showers out, sir,' Charlie said.

'Well, where's your key?' Charlie showed his key.

'Well, you couldn't have had it all the time, 'cause this bloody tap's been turned on. Turn that bloody hot water off.'

The bath-house gate came open with a crash as the heavy mob burst in. They stood in a group, watching the badly scalded sex case.

He was squatting on the concrete floor, swaying backwards and forwards, whimpering.

One of the officers hurried out of the bathroom. The remaining cons, now dressed, crowded round, curiously watching the injured man.

'Went over the back of his head, too,' one of them remarked.

They debated whether, if a person was scalded on the head, would it leave a permanent bald patch.

'Must do,' one said.

'It wouldn't,' another answered, ' 'cause the roots of the hair are deep in the scalp, and unless they were scalded, a bald patch wouldn't result.'

'Funny how a white man's skin turns red when he gets scalded,' observed another. 'Wonder what colour a spade's skin turns when he cops a good scalding. Hey, Lucas,' the speaker turned to a coloured man, 'what colour does your skin turn if you scald it?'

'My name ain't Lucas,' objected the coloured man.

'Bet he don't feel so bloody sexy now, dirty bastard!' someone remarked, pushing his way through the crowd at the cubicle door.

The officer returned with two of the hospital staff.

'Get these men out of here, and back to their shop,' a P.O., who had followed the two hospital officers, ordered.

At two-thirty p.m. Lovel was brought in from the metal breakdown shop. He had a quick wash and changed. He got into a well-pressed pair of trousers and a jacket that Lofty had given him permission to borrow. He didn't look too bad now, he observed, peering at himself in a mirror, although he had to turn the bottoms of the trousers up, on account of Lofty—whose height was six feet seven inches—being so long in the legs.

'Lovel.' He heard his name being called.

Hurrying out of his cell, he followed several other cons, with an officer in charge, to the visiting room. On the way, they were taken into a small room and searched.

He chose a table in the visiting room, and after ten minutes or so, Sharon entered. She came in with a squabble of mums and kids. They spoke to each other in a self-conscious way, both acutely aware of the prison officer in attendance. He could hear if they spoke in a normal voice, but not if they whispered.

Sharon told him Alfred had been to look for his ring, but had not been able to find it. He had assured Sharon that if the police had found it, and if it were possible for them to trace the ring, they would have done so by now, and Lovel had to be content with this. Sharon had paid his rent for a month, and informed his landlord he was in hospital, recovering from an accident.

They had thirty minutes together, and were informed that time was up. On the way back from the visit, Lovel and the rest were thoroughly searched. He had barely got back to his cell when he was informed that the police were in the prison and would like to interview him.

'You don't have to see them unless you wish to,' he was told.

This posed Lovel a problem. What the hell should he do? They would ask questions, but he need not answer. He supposed it was the ring. He decided to see them. Jack

Lovel was a very worried man as he was led to the interview room.

'Afternoon, Jack.' Sergeant Norman Bradshaw grinned up at him.

He was seated behind a table. Beside him sat Detective Constable Finch. Bradshaw stood up and held out his hand to Lovel, who, ignoring the outstretched hand, sat down, carefully keeping both hands where they had been on entering the room—inside his trouser pockets.

'Lost anything, Jack?' Bradshaw asked, still looking amused.

'What is it you want to see me about?' Lovel demanded; adding, 'I can end this visit any time I want.'

'Several things, Jack, the first one being, what happened to your finger? We're always interested in accidents that are not treated by the proper facilities provided, and yours, Jack, from what we can gather, certainly was not.'

Lovel carefully examined the question for a second or two.

'Go on,' he spoke at last. 'The other things you are interested in, maybe I can help you better there.'

Bradshaw riffled through a bundle of typewritten papers. He pushed over an unopened packet of twenty Players.

Taking one with his left hand, Lovel gratefully lit up.

'We would like to know where you were on the night when Browning & Frost had their strong room and safe blown open and robbed. Also, where you were on the night British Micro Electronics were robbed of certain precious metals.'

'Any more?' asked Lovel, grinning.

'That'll do for the present,' replied Sergeant Bradshaw. 'However, back to the finger you've lost.'

'What finger have I lost?'

'You know bloody well what finger, so don't give me any of your old crap,' snapped Bradshaw irritably.

'Somebody's been feeding you a load of bilge, and you've fallen for it,' Lovel said with a laugh.

'Look, Lovel, we know you've lost a finger from your right hand.'

'You sure of that?' Lovel asked.

' 'Course I'm sure; we were informed by the doctor of this nick. I suppose even he can manage a count of up to five.'

Lovel breathed an inward sigh of relief. So they hadn't found the ring, he was sure of that, now. If they had found the ring, they must have put two and two together. Carry on, Sergeant bloody Bradshaw, he happily told himself, gratefully savouring the cigarette, you have told me a lot more than I had hoped for.

'Well.' Bradshaw was looking at Lovel. 'Have you or haven't you lost a finger?'

'Sorry, Sergeant, can't help you,' Lovel said good-humouredly.

'What are you doing when you've finished this sentence? Going back to it? Because if you do, we're going to nail you, Jack. Oh yes,' he continued, 'we shall, boy; time is on our side, you've only to make one slip. The next job you do could well be your last. I shall have you, Lovel, I shall have you.'

'Not much chance of that,' Lovel retorted. 'You don't have a bloody crystal ball, and that's what you're going to need to catch me,' he continued. 'What chance have you got? You don't know where I'm going, or when. I may do a job the day I get out of this nick, or it could be six months later.' He looked up at the ceiling in seeming despair. 'I sympathize with you poor bastards, I really do. The Watch Committee have got the hump with your chief, and your chief has got the hump with you, so,' he laughed at Bradshaw, 'you cop the bloody needle with me.'

'You know, Lovel, Cassius Clay got beat. They called him "the lip" and like him you've got plenty. When you cop your seven years, we'll see if you spout quite as much then.'

'Get stuffed,' Lovel laughed.

'By the way, Jack, we've heard that you may have been a witness to a certain con who was injured in the bath-house. Like to put the name on the man who did it? Nasty piece of work, you know.'

'Christ! You think I'm a bloody grass?' Lovel snorted.

'Well, I wouldn't say you're a grass, but under the circumstances I thought you might help us. It wasn't a very nice thing to do to the chap, now was it?'

'The bloody man's a sex case, raped a little girl. Christ, she was only a baby!' Lovel answered.

'We're aware of that, but we can't have people taking advantage of him because he's in for sex.'

'You wouldn't think that if it were your daughter he raped,' Lovel challenged.

'Well as it happens, it wasn't my daughter, and the man's sick.'

'Well, it was some poor bastard's daughter, and you'll get no bloody help from me,' Lovel retorted.

The two detectives rose to go. Lovel followed the screw out of the room.

'Sounds like you've been quite a boy, from what those two were saying,' the screw remarked to Lovel. 'Make much out of it?' he asked.

'Made a living, I don't exactly starve,' Lovel answered.

'Oh well, as long as you make it pay, but the majority of the cons we get in this nick don't. Most of them are dossers. Too bloody idle to work, and don't have either the bottle or intelligence to do a worthwhile job. We can pick them out a mile. Always complaining, first about the grub. Out all day in the shops, and as soon as they're banged up at night, they're on the bell. Want to be let out to go to the toilet, want to be let out to go special sick. If we turn on the radio at night to give the cons a little music, what happens, banging on their bloody doors until we have to turn it off. Watch them in the morning, always on Governors. Officer so and so swore at me today, sir; officer so and so wouldn't open my cell door, although I kept ringing my bell for ten minutes. Five minutes after coming off Governors they're busy grassing one of their mates for keeping a spare razor blade in his peter, so that he can have a crafty shave. We know bloody well that the bloke keeps a spare razor blade in his cell, and we also know he ain't likely to cut his throat, or ours. They don't come straight to us and grass. They push a note into the centre box. The P.O. gets hold of it, so we have to nick the bloke with the razor blade. No,' he continued, 'you don't have to watch us screws, it's the cons you have to watch in the nick.'

Lovel got back to his cell just after those in the workshops had come in. Ginger was busy rattling off to Lofty. 'Yer,' he said, 'we came out of this Post Office and jumps into the drag, wallop, so we have it away, it's on top, crash. Well Lacy's driving, Jimmie's holdin' the cash. Sitting in the front seat next to Lacy. And there's Old Bill, sitting right on our bloody tail.

'My bottle's twitching now, I can tell you. Christ, it is. Well, we turns into Mile End Road, and old Lacy is fairly chucking that drag all over the place, but we still can't shake that Old Bill off. So I gets this funny feeling, like I was telling you, although I knew we must shake them off once we hit the heavy traffic.

'So I busts the rear window with the butt, then pokes the shooter through at the Old Bill. I lets them have both barrels. Trouble is with them sawn-off, they don't have much range, even though I use only the best maximum cartridge. Well, I gives it to them, see, it never hurt them, worse luck. I was hoping to blow their bloody heads off. They shears off and nearly rams a lamp-post, but that ain't all, you should'a seen some of the other traffic and pedestrians. They're going up the pavement and scuttling everywhere for cover.

'I curls up in the back, couldn't breathe for laughing. Christ, it looked funny. Jimmie says to Lacy, we've got a bloody nutter as a minder, he'll get us all life yet. Well that pulls me round fast, 'cos I ain't having nobody taking liberties with me, and I gets wild, and this feeling comes over me again. I jams the shooter up against Jimmie's nut and pulls the trigger, but 'course, there's nothing up the spout. Good job there wasn't, else his bloody brains would have gone through the roof of the drag. So Jimmie wouldn't come on any more blags. I never done a job for nearly three months. Then Lacy comes round, says would I like to go to work for this geezer. He sets the jobs up, all we have to do is carry them out. He takes me for an interview. Little chap, but can he talk. I could tell after talking to him for only a couple of minutes that he had a good head on his shoulders. Tells me what I have to do on the jobs. That is, I have to stand shotgun for the rest, while they work. Then, as I was about to go, he threw me an envelope. That should see you over the next week or two, till we are ready to do the next one. When I got outside and opened the envelope there was two hundred quid in it, and well, here I am. The governor sends Lacy down to see me and make sure I get everything I need, while I'm in nick. He won't put his own face on show if he can help it, too clever for that.'

The door was unlocked for tea. They scrambled to join the queue.

Lovel followed as Mason, Rodney and Campbell, three 'special diets' filed slowly by the hot-plate. Campbell was the first to refuse his meal. Faithful to Campbell, faithful to the miserable starving end, Rodney and Mason followed suit.

'Nothing wrong with their guts,' a con remarked as they watched the P.O. cook almost fall over himself in his concern for the trio. 'Can do their thieving, but can't do their bird, bloody slags, that's what they are, bloody slags. Be kicking hell out of their door tonight until they get the radio turned off. Bloody screws are worse than they are, stand for the five card trick, these days. Same if you go sick. Been here six months, went sick once, but never again. Couldn't get near the hospital, it was full up with their sort. The slags what can't do their bird.'

Lovel took his tea to a table. He had been granted the privilege of dining out. Someone—probably one of the centre P.O.'s—had chalked a message on the notice board. The message read: 'Will the person who lost a half ounce packet of Old Holborn at lunch time, please form queue outside the chief's office at tea time.'

After association they were once more locked up, this time for the night.

Lofty told them their cell was in part of what had once been the condemned cell.

'This one,' he told Lovel, 'was the one they took him from.' He was sitting on the edge of his bed talking to Lovel, who sat with his legs dangling off the bunk directly above.

'Go on, Lofty,' Ginger encouraged, beginning to take interest. 'Who told you that?'

'The centre cleaner. He was here when they hung the last one. As I was saying, they took him from this cell, see that,' he pointed to the obviously new brickwork which surrounded the window. 'There was a door there once,' he continued, 'that's the door they led him through, and see that red brick shed,' pointing through the window, 'that's the topping shed.'

'Topping shed?' Lovel questioned.

'Yes, the hanging shed. From the door that was fitted where the window now is, it's about five to six paces to the trap itself.'

'I always thought the condemned man took a regulation thirteen steps to the scaffold,' Lovel said.

'Load of bloody crap,' snorted Lofty. 'They get the job done as quickly as possible, some of the geezers fight like hell. The drill is this. The padre and the governor come in; you've already had your breakfast, that's if you think it's worthwhile. They give you the old chat, say a prayer or two for the benefit of your soul. One of them will give you a cigarette and a light; you have a few good drags at the cigarette, and a sip or two of tea, wondering how much longer you've got left. They are carefully watching the time, without making it obvious to you. You take another pull at the cigarette, and begin once more to sip your tea.

'At a nod from the chief, one of the screws straps your hands behind your back. The door, where the window is now, swings open and the screws close in, and just as you begin to walk, the church clock on the outside chimes the first stroke of eight. You are hustled the five or six short steps in to the topping shed. The hangman's waiting there, just behind the door. Immediately you enter, he places the black mask with the rope attached neatly round your neck. One more step, and the hangman pulls the lever, and by the way, the trap isn't just a small door, practically all the floor opens up. They have a plank for each of the two screws placed across the trap for them to walk on. The time taken is just sufficient, so some of the screws boast, for the first chime of eight to finish ringing, but, if you notice, the church clock outside chimes fast, so I think they are stretching it a bit there.'

'Don't look like a topping shed with all them bikes and building gear standing about, does it?' Ginger exclaimed.

'Wasn't meant to,' Lofty replied. 'They wouldn't expect the condemned man to know what the shed was for, but the last one they hung there would know, he'd know the drill all right,' and he named a man whose trial had made the headlines. 'Reckon he done it?' Lofty looked up at Lovel.

Lovel shook his head. 'I wouldn't know, and according to the evidence that was offered by the prosecution, from what I read of the case, neither did anyone else. They guessed from that evidence, that he was guilty, and from what I can make of it, they hung him on a guess. He was a bad penny too, so that didn't help. The point is, they never proved him guilty. They never had any concrete evidence to do that, but they got a conviction just the same. Which means they don't have to prove you guilty of a crime; you have to prove to a jury that you're not guilty, and that what they boast of in an English court of law, a man is innocent until he's found guilty, is a load of bloody crap.'

'Don't think they're likely to bring the hanging bill back?' Ginger asked.

'I suppose they could,' Lofty answered.

'Christ! Be a bloody turn-up for the book if I were to finish up in here, waiting to be topped. Could happen,' he mused. 'Could be, one day I shall be walking up and down this same cell, waiting to go in there.' He looked through the window-bars at the small, innocent looking red brick building.

11

GINGER HAD A VISIT THE NEXT DAY.

'May have a proposition for you,' he told Lovel.

'What kind of proposition?' Lovel asked.

'Well the firm I work for are interested in a job. I don't know where the job is, even Lacy doesn't know yet. They know you're a bit tasty with alarm systems and the chap you work with is good at opening strong rooms. They also know you had a touch, platinum wasn't it?' Ginger asked.

'If you say so,' Lovel replied.

'Well,' Ginger continued, 'someone would like to visit you. You just send a visiting order to this address and they'll come down. Said I had to look after you too. Here, cop this' he said, tossing over a two-ounce tin of tobacco. 'Plenty more where that came from. Show him, Lofty.'

Lofty pulled his right shoe off. 'Stand in front of the door, Ginger,' he ordered. Ginger stood with a newspaper in his hand, so that if a screw were to peer through the spyhole, all he would see would be Ginger's back.

Using his plastic knife as a lever, Lofty inserted it in the thin rubber covering the heel of his shoe. Watching over his shoulder, Lovel saw the strip of rubber slowly forced up by the knife. The heel had been hollowed out, and inside Lovel could make out part of a folded ten-pound note. Lofty pushed the point of the knife carefully down beside the note and prised up. Out came a small packet of neatly folded tenners. He separated them, revealing five single treasury notes.

'Fifty quid there,' Lofty said proudly. He wedged them back inside the heel.

'Enough there to keep us three in burn for the next three weeks,' Ginger said. 'I get an ounce for every pound. Could get an ounce and a quarter if I wanted to put myself about, but why worry. Let me know when you want more. You can spend your canteen money on soap and toothpaste, anything you want, now.'

Lovel rolled a very fat cigarette. One of the greatest hardships imposed on him, that of not being able to have a smoke when he wanted, had been overcome. He had meant to turn down Ginger's suggestion to send out a visiting order to someone he didn't know, but the present of tobacco put him under a certain amount of obligation.

'Well,' Ginger asked, 'are you sending a v.o. to that address?'

'May as well,' Lovel answered, lighting up. 'Might as well, if they're prepared to come all that way to see me, they must have something sensible to offer.'

Ginger smiled at Lovel. 'I'd like to see you go to work on a place. Hope that if they do have something tasty coming off, they'll use me.'

'I don't want to disappoint you,' Lovel told him, 'but I don't work for wages, I never have, and I never will, and I only ever work with one man.'

Ginger nodded. 'Maybe they would be prepared to cut you and your mate in, equal shares.'

'They'd have to,' Lovel said, 'and the job would have to be big. Still,' he continued, 'I'll send the v.o., you never know.'

A couple of days later, Lovel had a stroke of luck. They had been kept awake for most of the night by a new reception, who had been banging and shouting, and sometimes screaming, from the cell immediately above theirs. The man, quite young, was in the cell on his own. At first Lovel, Ginger and Lofty had tried to pacify him, but this had no effect. Then, in exasperation, they hurled threats, shouting through the bars of the open window, still without success. The chap above raved and ranted all night.

Immediately the lights were switched on in the morning Lovel rang the bell for attention. He wanted badly to go to the toilet. His screw unlocked the door; Lovel heard the sound of breaking glass from above.

'Sounds like he's smashing up,' the screw said to Lovel.

'Pity he doesn't cut his bloody throat, he's kept us awake all night,' Lovel answered, walking to the recess.

He sat, listening to the screws telling the man to open his door, using first a threatening tone of voice, then pleading and cajoling. Evidently he'd barricaded himself in, perhaps by wedging his bed against the door.

As Lovel came from the recess, he could see the two screws pushing and heaving, trying to force the door open. Like all cell doors, it opened inwards. As they heaved against the door with their shoulders, it gave a few inches, then as the pressure was taken off, promptly closed. There were only the two of them on duty this early in the morning.

Catching sight of Lovel, one of them called, asking him to give them a hand. Lovel raced up the flight of stairs.

'The chap in there has slashed himself, he's done both wrists and his throat,' the screw whispered to Lovel. He lifted the flap covering the spyhole, and motioned Lovel to have a look.

'Christ!' Lovel exclaimed, recoiling. Through the spyhole he had seen a sight he was not likely to forget for a while. The cell's occupant had gashed his throat with a piece of glass he had obtained by breaking the window. Both his wrists had been badly slashed too. As he stood facing the door, he looked a ghastly sight, blood-covered, and with eyes that had lost all semblance of sanity. They glared vacantly back at Lovel.

'Come on, help us to force the door, for Christ's sake,' said the screw urgently.

All three of them put their shoulders to the heavy door, and heaved. They managed to force it almost eighteen inches, but immediately they let go, back it sprang. There was the sudden sound of breaking furniture, and a tinkling crunch of more glass being broken.

Desperately they threw themselves at the door. They managed once more to force it a good eighteen inches. Lovel, who was more strategically placed, realized that he could be through the door in a second, if the other two could keep up the pressure.

'I'm going in, hold it,' he shouted. The two screws heaved with all their might. Lovel wriggled quickly through. He took one quick glance at the blood-covered apparition before him, then hauled the heavy steel bed from the door.

Lovel made himself scarce. He descended the stairs and entering his own cell, slammed the door shut.

Lofty and Ginger began eagerly to question him.

'Get remission for that,' Lofty said.

They argued between themselves for some time, how much remission Lovel would get off his sentence.

Lovel didn't have long to wait. On the following Monday he was taken before the governor. 'Not doing long, are you, Lovel,' the governor glanced up from the folder which contained all the prison authorities knew of Jack Lovel.

'Twenty-eight days, sir.'

'Oh, ah, yes. Now this incident which happened early the other morning. Well I would like to take this opportunity of conveying to you my sincere thanks for your prompt, and if I may say so, quite brave action in entering that poor unfortunate man's cell, and under the circumstances . . .'

'Oh for Christ sake,' Lovel thought impatiently, 'am I or am I not getting some time off my sentence?'

'. . . I shall,' the governor continued, 'recommend that you receive ten days' remission of sentence. I think you can take it that you will be going home ten days earlier than you would normally have done. Haven't been in prison before, have you, Lovel?'

'No, sir,' answered Lovel.

'Well, that is all.' The governor smiled up at him as Lovel turned to leave.

Lovel sat in the visiting room. He had sent the v.o. to the address given him by Ginger.

He looked with curiosity as the visitors filed slowly in and began taking seats at the tables facing their husbands, sons and boy friends. Lovel's visitor entered last. He was a nondescript little man, dressed in a dark suit of good quality material. Lovel watched him as his eyes quickly swept the visiting room. The little man's glance finally rested on Lovel, obviously deciding that this must be the person he had come to see, as Lovel was now the only one in the room who did not have a visitor.

Smiling, he walked over with hand extended. Lovel held out his own right hand. He saw the little man's eyes flicker to the gap where his finger had been.

'Hello, Jack,' he greeted, 'sorry to see you in a position like this.' He was talking loudly, obviously for the benefit of the screws.

'How is Aunt Mabel?' Lovel played along with him.

'Oh, she sends her regards, and also says that you must come down to visit us, after your release.'

The little man pulled a chair out and sat down. He was now in a position to watch the screw, who sat some distance behind Lovel. Lovel was positioned so that he could see the second screw directly behind his visitor. They could talk in a low, almost normal manner without fear of their being overheard.

'Well, you must be curious to know what I have come down to see you about,' he said after a pause.

'I can guess it's about a job, but I must tell you this before you go in deeper. I work for no one, and what's more, I only work with one other man. Now, if you have something you consider very good, and it will have to be very good, fire away, but we don't work for wages.'

The small man looked at Lovel keenly for a second or two.

'If you and Alfred Tate were the type to work for wages,' he said, 'I wouldn't be asking your help in doing this job. No, I want two men who are used to working on their own initiative. Any man who works for someone else can't have much of that, can he?' He smiled at Lovel. 'If you agree to come in with me, we'll share equally, that is, half to you and Tate, the other half comes my way. What you do or where you go after the job is your affair.'

'How much would there be in this job?' Lovel asked.

'Half a million, or more.'

'Cash?' Lovel queried.

The little man shook his head. 'No, not cash, but the stuff isn't bulky either.'

'Is it Tom?' [jewellery].

'No, it's a type of metal.'

'Well, that makes it either gold, or better still, platinum, and I have a good market for both,' Lovel said with a laugh.

'I know.'

'Where is it?' Lovel asked, ignoring the hint.

'I can't tell you where it is; you still have Alfred Tate to convince.'

'And me,' Lovel said, looking serious again. 'I'll need more information on this job than you've given me so far. Otherwise you can forget it.'

'I'll give you the details, but I won't tell you where the job is,' said the other. 'As I've told you, it's worth something in excess of half a million pounds. The place is reasonably isolated, but there is a security guard inside the building at night. However, that's our worry, we don't expect you to take care of him. Inside there are two strong rooms, both on a time lock, and they're good. Very good. You wouldn't open these up with a few ounces of gelly. We're only interested in one of the strong rooms. Inside this one is an alarm that works on air pressure.'

'Yes. I know the type,' Lovel chipped in, 'you open the door or make an entry any other way and the air pressure drops. Off goes the alarm, straight through to the Old Bill.'

'Well, that's the way it works up to a certain point,' Lovel's visitor agreed, 'but it doesn't go straight through to the police, it goes through to the security firm who supply the guard. They relay the alarm through to the police. We can fix the guard, can you manage the alarm?'

'Yes, I can knock the alarm out. It would take time but I could do it, but what about the strong room door? If you think blowing is out, what method are you using?'

'The thermic lance; it's fast, and reasonably quiet. However, assuming we use the thermic lance, do either of you know how it works?'

'Yes,' Lovel answered, 'we've had one. Alfred tried it out a few times. He could handle it reasonably well. The trouble is the oxygen bottles, we'd need several.'

'We'd put those in for you, no need to worry your head about equipment. I'd look after those details. On your release I'll show you a detailed plan of the complete building, also the immediate area. Your only job will be the alarm, after you've done that, you're finished. The same with Tate. His job will be to cut the strong room open; no more. You take your half of what's inside, and that'll be that. You can say that your half will amount to a quarter of a million, I guarantee at least that amount. Are you interested?'

'Yes,' said Lovel, 'I am.'

'Now what about your partner?'

Lovel nodded. 'Yes,' he said, 'Alfred may take some talking round.'

'That's why I contacted you instead of Tate. I guessed you would be the one more likely to have a go. If you are prepared to throw in with us, with or without Tate, that'll put him in a spot. He must come in, you see. He'll know that if we're successful your share will be sufficient to keep you comfortably for the rest of your life, without having to involve yourself in further crime. That'll pose him a problem, because without you to handle the alarms, he may as well finish. I think that if you're firm, and let him see that you are in, with or without him, he'll agree.'

Lovel had been helping himself to a packet of cigarettes during the conversation. The man had placed the packet open on the table, when he first sat down. They were the brand Lovel always smoked. Neither of them had made any comment on this, but Lovel got the message. The man had done a great deal of spade work into his character and habits. He was well aware that Lovel had got that message. He looked up. 'Well,' he said, 'that's about all I'm prepared to tell you at this stage. Now you must make up your mind.'

'For that kind of stake,' Lovel replied, 'it's already made up. The answer's yes.'

The little man laughed. 'We'll make quite a team together. Yes, we'll make quite a team.'

Lovel had two more days left to finish his sentence. He walked around the exercise yard with Ginger and Lofty. He tossed the large butt end of the cigarette he had been smoking onto the small, round, carefully tended flower-bed that formed the centre of the exercise yard, and they laughed as they watched Charlie Lane, an old con, step carefully onto the flower bed, pick up the butt end, and, pinching the lighted end out, carefully place the exceptionally large fag-end inside a two-ounce tin. Seldom was he lucky enough to find a cigarette end of that size, although of late he had been keeping close behind the Lovel—Lofty—Ginger trio. His collection of cigarette-ends had been well worthwhile. He had tipped the centre P.O. off about his suspicions concerning these three; undoubtedly they were buying tobacco.

Old Charlie had done a great deal of bird: too much, it had softened his brain. He was now a compulsive grass. He tried not to do it—tried very, very hard—but all to no avail. Any snippet of information he gleaned, all those little suspicions of how some cons came by their extra tobacco, would come spilling out just as soon as he got into conversation with one of the P.O.s. At his own request they had placed him down the choky block [punishment cells], his job being to keep the block clean. This he did, religiously, making an excellent job of it.

He had a heart of gold. During the day he would tap, beg, borrow or steal tobacco, sugar and all the things hard to come by in prison, solely to supply some con or other, who was doing punishment down there. It mattered little to Charlie whether or not he had had a hand in getting the man into trouble by his grassing, he would still keep him supplied. To give the County Prison its due, it was a better friend to old Charlie Lane than the outside public, or rather, than those who dealt out justice on behalf of that public. Almost every time he had finished a term in prison he was fitted out with good quality warm clothing and a good pair of shoes (which he promptly traded for a few bottles of wine). Had the sum of Charlie's depradations been totted up, it would have amounted to less than two hundred pounds, but the prison sentences meted out had been far from miserly. On one occasion, he had received a princely four years for some fifteen shillings' worth of second-hand clothing. In this way the public thirst for justice had been appeased.

Practically all the cons knew old Charlie was a grass. They also understood why and accepted him. Jack Lovel pushed a handful of tobacco into his hand as he followed a stream of cons through A wing and out to his place of work. He had, on occasion, given Charlie the odd five or ten bob 'on the out'. In fact, old Charlie reckoned Jack Lovel as an easy tap.

Lovel settled down to his job; stripping copper cable. Today was Thursday, the eve of his release.

'Out tomorrow then.' Lovel looked up. The screw in charge of the shop stood beside him. Lovel nodded.

'Won't be sorry, hey? Never been in before, have you?'

'No,' Lovel answered, 'this is my first time.'

'Gonna make it your last?'

'I'll do my bloody best to stay out, at least long enough to give you a chance to finish stripping this bloody rubbish,' Lovel snorted.

'Rubbish! Christ, this ain't rubbish,' the screw retorted. 'Number one copper wire, that's what this is. Like gold; worth a fortune, and somebody's making a bloody fortune too, and it ain't the nick. Bloody take-on, that's what it is, bloody take-on. Do you know what the firm who we contract to strip this for, pays?' he looked indignantly at Lovel.

'No idea,' Lovel answered.

'They pay twenty-five pounds per twelve-ton load. Transport it here and pay the prison twenty pound per ten ton to clean it. How about that for a take-on?'

'How much is it worth per hundredweight?' Lovel enquired.

'Well,' the screw continued, 'that same firm pays over thirty pounds per hundredweight for clean number one copper wire like this. As I say, it's either a take-on, or a great big bloody fiddle. Trouble is, us that're in the know can't do a damn thing about it, we are classed the same as civil servants, and so come under the official secrets act. They use this shop as a cheap labour force; onto a good thing, ain't they?'

Jack Lovel woke to the sound of the centre bell very early on Friday morning.

As the door was opened, he shook hands with Lofty and Ginger.

'Cheerio,' he said. He winked at Ginger and grinned. 'See you again before long.' Grabbing his bedroll, he tucked it under his arm. In the other hand he carried his ever-faithful chamber pot.

Lovel was escorted up to reception, offered breakfast, but refused. He did, however, accept a cup of tea. He was told to strip off in a cell. His own clothing was handed in to him, and he was led down to the gate. The screw unlocked a small door set in one of the large studded doors, and Jack Lovel stepped to freedom after spending only eighteen of his twenty-eight days' sentence in prison.

He stood for a second or two, smelling the early morning freshness of the air, then crossed the road to where Sharon was waiting in his car.

Sharon parked the car neatly before a large restaurant. Lovel clambered from the passenger side, and led the way inside.

He ordered eggs and bacon—four eggs and four thick slices of bacon. He managed the lot with no trouble, and several strong, sweet cups of coffee. Forty minutes later they were both in Lovel's flat.

He looked around with appreciation at the fresh curtains up at the windows and the flowers which had been tastefully arranged on the living room table. Then he fetched the suction pad from the kitchen and went briskly into the bathroom. Sharon looked on in surprise, but made no comment. Placing the pad on the third tile from the far right hand corner, he attempted to lift it, but the sucker slipped off. Wetting it slightly under the tap, he tried again, this time with success.

Sharon came in and sank to her knees beside Lovel, and together they peered into the small dark hole.

'What is it, Jack, what on earth have you got in there?'

'Wonga,' Lovel grinned.

'What?' She looked up in puzzlement.

'Put your hand in and take some,' he said.

She stretched out her hand to obey; a huge spider climbed slowly out of the black hole. Sharon shuddered and drew back.

Lovel laughed and reaching in, pulled out a large roll of treasury notes.

'Oh, so that's where you keep it,' she said.

He peeled a small wad off the bundle, replaced the tile, and returned to the sitting room.

Lovel sat in the deep leather-covered armchair; at his right elbow a large brandy, a packet of cigarettes, and his gold Dunhill lighter; on his wrist, two hundred and eighty pounds' worth of Omega faintly and very precisely ticking the first few golden hours of beautiful freedom. He took first a sip of the brandy, then a taste of the freshly made coffee. Leaning back in the armchair, he examined with appreciation the lovely girl, who, with her back towards him, was toying with the very large deep red roses in a bowl on the living room table.

'Like them, Jack?' she asked.

'The best I have ever seen,' Lovel replied with a grin, watching the lovely curves of her thighs disappearing upwards under the extremely short skirt.

'I mean the roses,' she smiled back at his reflection in the mirror.

Lovel winked at her, lit a cigarette, and placed one well-creased trouser-leg over the other.

She laughed mischievously at him, her blue eyes twinkling, her auburn hair full of little golden glints. He took a large swallow from his glass of brandy.

She put the tape recorder on, came over and helped herself to one of his cigarettes, blowing a playful cloud of smoke into his face. Sitting on the arm of his chair, she gently tapped her foot to the rhythm of the never-to-be-forgotten Glen Miller band.

'I like that type of music,' she said. 'Perhaps it doesn't send you, but it certainly does something for you.'

Stubbing her half-smoked cigarette out in the ashtray, she went over to the wall mirror and began to comb her hair. Once again her legs drew his eyes like magnets, and when she raised her arms above her head to stretch luxuriously, he almost groaned with pleasure. The feeling of well-being the brandy had produced was still with him, but now he felt anything but relaxed.

Sharon came back to her perch and began to comb his hair, laughing as she fluffed it up comically, then arranging it in the way she liked best. He noticed she was using his own white metal comb. Every once in a while she took a small sip of his brandy.

Lovel's eyes enjoyed her figure from her trim little ankles upwards. He could see the dimples in her shapely knees through the sheer nylon. He followed the curves of her body upwards, tilting his head to do so: the tantalizing swell of her breasts, their firm softness.

Impulsively, she put her arm round him, drawing his head close into her breast. He could hear the quick tattoo as her heartbeat increased; he savoured the faint perfume that always seemed to cling to her. Then he pulled her down onto his knees, eased her head back and began tenderly kissing her exposed throat and the small lobes of her ears. For almost a full minute their lips were joined, while his right hand gently caressed her knee, and slowly, searchingly, wandered higher.

With a sigh, she relaxed completely, finally surrendering herself. Lovel rose from the chair, the girl in his arms. The bedroom was suddenly too far—the bedroom was a thousand miles away. Down on the soft carpet they went, Lovel gasping and fumbling in his excitement, while Sharon lay passive with her eyes half closed. He felt an electric thrill of pure pleasure as his skin came in contact with the yielding, creamy warmth of her inner thighs. There was no question this time of her resisting. Her body welcomed him deliciously, and soon time had ceased to exist for them as they lay entwined in the middle of his sitting room floor.

12

ALFRED TATE HAD HEARD THROUGH THE grapevine that Jack had gained ten days' remission of sentence. He particularly wanted to gauge Lovel's reaction to his first imprisonment, also to discuss a likely job that could be done sometime in September. He visited Lovel's flat at three-thirty p.m. the day after his release from prison. Sharon had returned to her own home early that morning.

Lovel let Tate into the flat and poured two drinks.

' Glad you called, Alfie,' he said. 'I have to see a chap tomorrow, but I would have been wasting his time if I hadn't seen you first.'

'How did you find your first taste of nick?' Tate laughed.

Lovel grinned back at him. 'I survived.'

'Silly bloody thing to go in the nick for, just the same,' Tate taunted.

'You won't have to line anything up for next month,' Lovel said with a grin, 'or next year, or ever again, Alfie, when I tell you what I've been offered. You remember that when we done the British Micro Electronics there was a shot-gun hold-up on a security van carrying platinum, also soon after that some chap was pulled in for being in possession of a firearm? Well, I happened to share the same peter with him in nick. Name of Ginger. You know how it is in there, Alfie. I had no need to tell anyone who I was, or the type of jobs I done on the out. There were several inside who knew me. As a matter of fact, the third chap in my peter, a fellow called Lofty, only lives a couple of streets from here. I think he talked a good deal to Ginger, who works for an East End firm, he's a minder on the armed hold-ups they seem to specialize in. Ginger was having visits, he had two or three specials in the short time I was inside. I think he mentioned who I was, and that it was rumoured that we were involved in most of the worthwhile jobs that happened in this manor. However it came about, the outcome was that he gave me an address to send a v.o. I sent it, and a man came down; he put a proposition to me concerning a job. Want to hear what it was?' he looked questioningly at Alfred Tate.

'No harm in listening, I suppose,' Tate replied.

Lovel continued. 'They're onto something big, Alfie, real big. This could be our chance to have it off once and for all, then finish. You've said yourself, Alfie, that we can't keep doing small jobs. Sooner or later we're going to come unstuck; sooner or later we'll find ourselves facing a lot of bird. This job they guarantee to be worth half a million . . . What about that, Alfie?'

Jack Lovel leaned forward in the armchair. 'What about that?' he repeated.

'Well, what about it?' Tate said with a touch of sarcasm. 'So the job is worth half a million, so what. What job? Where is it?'

'I don't know where it is, Alfie, they refused to tell me that.'

'Refused to tell you!' Alfred Tate gave a short, hard laugh. 'So they want us to do it for them. So they want us to split the profits I suppose, but they won't tell us where the job is. What's happened to you, Jack, have you gone soft in the head? Christ! You only go inside for a couple of week-ends and you come out with a load of old crap some bloody stir-crazy mug rams down your throat. Don't tell me, let me guess where this job is. Bet it's Threadneedle Street, is that it, Jack?'

Lovel glared back at Alfred. 'No it bloody well ain't Threadneedle Street, and what's more, if you don't want to listen to any more, just say so.'

'It's like this, Jack,' Alfred said. 'I've found a decent

little job for us. With what we've earned on the last two, and this one, we wouldn't need to do another job for some time.'

'And then skint again I suppose,' Lovel said bitterly. 'Always the same, two or three little touches, and we're back on top of the heap. But for how long, Alfie, for how long? Then back at it again. Look at you, Alfie, you're in your forties. Think I want to end up like you, do you?'

'What's wrong with me?' Tate bristled.

'Nothing,' Lovel answered, 'only you've been at it most of your bloody life, and what have you got? Go on, Alfie, what have you bloody well got that a chap who goes to work hasn't?'

'I've got my house,' Tate replied.

'So has the chap next door to you got his house, Alfie, and what's more, it's probably paid for. Go on, Alfie, you were telling me what you've got that no one else has. After all these years on the thieve. After all those jobs, and don't let us ever try kidding ourselves, Alfie, ours is the hardest game in the world. Easy money, Christ, whoever kidded us into that one? That's why I started in this game; I thought it was easy money. Like hell it is. I'm always working. If we're not actually doing the job, I'm watching one. On an average, out of five jobs that I watch, we find only one that's possible to do. Let them who think it's easy try lying out all night; watching through a pair of night-glasses, and the snow gradually covering you up. Frozen to the bloody core. The same every night for a full week. Dark till dawn, and then you find you can't do it after all. So you watch another for a week; blow the peter and find bugger-all inside, like what was happening to us last winter, when we even had to syphon a few gallons of petrol from somebody's car because neither of us had the money to buy juice to get us to the job. No, Alfie, I've had enough. I've done my last small-time job, it's all or nothing now. Either you come in on it, or you don't. Now it's up to you.'

Alfred Tate looked at Jack Lovel in puzzlement. Christ, he thought, what the hell's got into him; two weeks in the nick and he comes out talking of money in telephone number figures.

'Well, you've had your say, Jack,' Tate said at last, 'but I warn you, get mixed up with the mobs, and you're getting mixed up in trouble. Trouble that we may not be capable of handling. We've always known where we stand with each other. I've never seen you off, and I don't think you have me. As you said, I've been at this game a long time. Too long I suppose, but there it is. The past is past. If I have regrets, I'll keep them to myself, but I used to have dealings with the London mobs, years ago. It wasn't so bad then. Not like now. Some of these new chaps will stop at nothing. They've got a price for everything, and that includes murder. The public only think they know, but they don't. The police do, they know. They have an idea of the number of people the bigger gangs bump off in a year. Oh yes, they know, but there's damn all they can do about it. There never is enough evidence. People just go missing. You can read books about Chicago, Dillinger and Legs Diamond. You may think they were hard cases. I can tell you, if they were alive now, and loose in London today among the mobs up there, they'd be eaten alive. Yes, they'd have them for breakfast. I could have you bumped off tomorrow, Jack, for a couple of grand, or the Prime Minister of England for the right price, and that's where money comes in. If there's half a million in this job, wherever it is, greed will creep in. They would probably blow our bloody heads off after we had done the job for them, and take the lot.'

Lovel waited for Tate to finish. 'I suppose there's something in what you say, but we have to take a chance for that sort of money, and we can always take precautions. The stuff they're after is platinum. I was told practically all the details, except where it is. There's a security guard in the place, and there's a time lock on the strong room. We shall have to use a thermic lance to cut through the door. That's your job, by the way. I knock out the alarm system. That's all I do, then I'm finished. They look after the security guard, and they bring in all the equipment.

All you have to do is cut the door open. I'll be quite honest with you, Alfie. They could, if they wanted, bring in a man to do your job. As they must have me to fix the alarms, they would rather have you in on the job too, and keep us together as a team. So there you are. It shouldn't take you more than half an hour to burn your way through that door with the lance, and everything will be there ready for you. All laid out on a plate.'

'How do we split the takings?' Tate asked.

'Fifty-fifty,' Lovel replied. 'They take theirs and scarper; we do the same. When it's finished, they want no more to do with us than we do with them.'

'I still don't like it,' Tate grumbled, 'but if you're going in, that ties my hands. I'll have to go, whether I like it or not.'

'No, Alfie, you don't have to go. No one ever has to go,' Lovel replied.

Alfred Tate sat turning the proposition over in his mind for some time. If he didn't go, and the job was a success, he would be finished without Lovel to knock out the alarms for him. Any future jobs were out. The systems were more sophisticated, far more complex than they had been a few years ago. No, he wouldn't be able to manage them on his own, besides, if they did hit it big and he had decided not to go, he would kick himself for the rest of his life. With that sort of money, Lovel would never be interested in the screwing game again. With that sort of money, a man could retire from crime. He had to go. The chances of a success far outweighed the probability of getting caught.

Lovel sat watching Alfred. He knew he would be counting all the pros and cons in his mind. Whichever weighed the heaviest in the final balance, is what he would plump for.

Tate spoke at last. 'All right, Jack, I'll go,' he said, 'but I'll tell you this. I shall go carrying a gun. With that sort of money at stake, I'll go armed. We don't know damn all about the people we're working with, and I'm not taking any chances. If we do get the stuff, and they try seeing me off, I shall shoot, and what's more, I shall shoot to kill, because I know that if it ever comes to using shooters, they'll play for keeps. However, there's no need to let them know we're going armed; try and put your hands on a couple either of thirty-twos, or thirty-eights.'

Lovel grinned his relief at Tate's decision to go. 'I'll see to them,' he said, 'leave that to me.'

'For platinum we have a good market, Alf. The stuff's as good as cash. A hundred thousand, Christ, what a party I can have with that sort of money; mugs not to have gone for it before, that's what we were, Alf, a couple of mugs. I'll have me a different drum than this,' Lovel made a gesture at his sitting room, 'and Christ, will I liven this town up.'

'We've got to get the bloody stuff first,' Tate warned, bringing him back to earth.

'We'll get it, Alf; we'll get it all right: you cut that door open, and we've got it, and by the way, whilst you're cutting it open, I shall be watching your back. Once we get the stuff, we take our cut and get the hell out of it, but as I said, I shall be watching your back, so don't worry. If there's the slightest sign of trouble coming our way from them, I shall let them have it. Make no mistake about that. Mind you, I don't for one moment expect any. They should be satisfied with their share. There's enough to give everyone a fair crack of the whip.'

After Tate had left, Lovel poured himself another drink, lit a cigarette, and clasping his hands behind his head, leaned back in the armchair. He, too, disliked the idea of working with people he didn't know, but he had one big advantage over Alfred Tate: he had seen the man who was going to organize the whole show, and judged he could make him organize it to his and Alfred Tate's complete satisfaction. If he didn't, Lovel decided, he would bloody soon be put right on the details. Oh yes, as they were the two who were going in, they would have it their way, or else. He and Alfie weren't mugs even though they came from the sticks, and they weren't going to allow any flash bloody London mob to go away with that idea in their heads. He would do as he had promised Alf, that is, he would be watching his back while he was working, and he meant it. If he decided this little mob were going to give him and Alfie trouble, he would get in fast. He'd shoot all right, and he'd shoot to kill, and be damned with the consequences.

The insistent ringing of the doorbell awakened Lovel. He shot up in bed, his sleep-rumpled features creased with annoyance. He glanced at his wrist-watch; two minutes past seven. He hurriedly flung open the door, and glared menacingly down at the man standing before him.

Lovel motioned with his head for his early morning visitor to enter. The little man stared blandly back at Lovel for a moment or two, and followed him into the sitting room.

'Sorry if I woke you, Mr Lovel,' he apologized, 'but this is very urgent business, and I must know this morning how we stand. I take it you have already made contact with your partner. I would like to know his decision regarding the business agreement we discussed last week.' He held up his hand, silencing Lovel, who was about to answer. 'The firm we're concerned with is moving to new, larger and more modern premises next week on account of their rapid rate of expansion. So you see we just don't have time to waste. We shall have to do it not later than the day after tomorrow.'

'Christ!' Lovel exclaimed, 'that's a bit rapid, isn't it?'

'It is, but you see, after that date they will begin moving their stock to the new premises, and you can take it from me, the security on the new building is something fantastic. Now, I have everything prepared and am in a position to go in at this moment if necessary.'

Lovel walked into the kitchen and lit the gas under the kettle.

'Tea or coffee?' he shouted through into the living room.

'Oh, tea, if you don't mind, Mr Lovel.'

'Better begin calling me Jack,' Lovel said with a laugh. 'You're well aware who we are,' he continued, 'but we don't have a clue about you. Things are a little too one-sided in that respect, don't you think?'

'Foster. Geoffrey Foster,' he answered. 'I had no wish to keep my identity secret, or my address either. At present I've taken the lease of a house in this town. It is number two, Lester Way. I would, by the way, appreciate it if you would call round this evening. I have a few things to show you, and I would like to have a few words with your partner.

'I am not known by the police, and I am sure Mr . . . ah, Jack, a man of your intelligence will not allow himself to be followed.'

Lovel brought the teapot in. He poured two cups. 'Help yourself,' he said, pointing to the cream jug and sugar bowl.

'Thank you. I have here a full detailed plan of the building,' he went on, producing a neatly folded plan, properly drawn to scale, which he unfolded on the living room table. They both bent over the large sheet of tracing paper.

'Here is the main office block. The guard uses this room here,' he pointed to a small office, close to the main door. 'We will deal with him first,' he said, straightening up.

'This security guard patrols the building internally, at hourly intervals during the night. The rest of the time he spends in that office with, of course, a phone placed handily beside him. As you see, he has an unobstructed view of the entrance which,' he pointed a finger, 'is a swing bar, manually operated when in use during the day. That,' he said, 'is the small gate house at which all in and outgoing vehicles are checked.'

Lovel looked up from studying the plan. 'How the hell are you going to deal with that guard if he never comes out of the building. Short of shooting the man down through the window, I don't see how you can possibly get in at him.'

'We have a method.' Foster smiled up at Jack Lovel. 'A method which has not failed as yet. We have agreed that you will take care of the alarm system, that's your job and we shan't interfere. We shall take care of the security guard in our own way, and we shall not expect you to concern yourself as to how we overcome this problem. However, I can assure you the security guard will not be harmed; we shall not use violence.

'You will be able to enter the building with safety once we have secured the security guard. The only part of the building which has the alarm system operating are the two strong rooms. They are worked on air pressure, that is, they go off if the door is opened, but close up to the door of the strong room that we are interested in there is the infra-red system which operates the local alarm. Now, Mr Lovel, assuming you knock out the alarm which runs through the telephone system to the security firm, how do you propose to handle the local alarm?'

Lovel grinned. 'To get at the circuit and batteries which control the local alarm, I shall first have to get by the infra-red beams, without breaking those beams.'

'I understand that it's not possible to see an infra-red beam, and of course it will be necessary for you to see them, if you are to by-pass them. How do you propose to do this?'

Lovel grinned back at him. 'We have our methods, Mr Foster,' he laughed, 'we have our methods.'

'Well I suppose you know your job,' Geoffrey Foster said grudgingly. 'If you could convey all this to Alfred Tate and induce him to come with you this evening, what time would be acceptable?' He looked questioningly at Lovel.

'Seven-thirty,' Lovel said, 'and Alfred Tate will be with me.'

13

ALFRED TATE DROVE JACK LOVEL TO their rendezvous with Foster. He swung the Cortina into the drive of 2 Lester Way, and carefully parked so that the car would not be visible from the road.

The front door of the house opened on their approach and they entered the large, old-fashioned hall. Neither of them recognized the man who held the door open.

He led them into the sitting room, where Foster greeted them and then got down to business.

'I take it you are in full agreement with the details we thrashed out this morning?'

Tate nodded. 'Providing the two fellows who fix the security guard can be relied on, I mean they're not likely to go off half-cocked and do something bloody silly. I suppose they'll be carrying shooters on this job?'

Foster smiled. 'My men always carry shooters. I've found that if one goes in fully prepared and ready to meet trouble more than half-way, then one is less likely to be troubled. People these days have a vast respect for the twin barrels of a sawn-off shot-gun.'

'We never carry firearms on a job,' Tate said. 'Never have. Been screwing for more than sixteen years, and never been in a corner where a shot-gun would have helped. Don't like the damned things, and don't believe in them, either.'

'I have a spare one here.' Foster pulled open a drawer attached to the table, and extracted a heavy looking ·38 revolver. 'Nice weapon,' he said turning the gun over in his hand. 'Perhaps you would like to carry it with you on this job? Perhaps it would be a better guarantee of fair play concerning the share out than my word?'

He placed the revolver on the table before Lovel.

'No,' Lovel replied. 'As you've just been told, we've never carried firearms.'

Cautiously, using the knuckles of his hand, Jack Lovel pushed the revolver back across the polished table.

Smiling, Foster placed it back into the drawer and produced a small cardboard box, from which he took two domino-shaped ingots. 'This,' he said, holding one of the small ingots up between finger and thumb, 'is the stuff we are going for. It's industrial platinum. This stuff is heavier than lead. The amount in weight, that would be of the value of half a million pounds, will not be so very bulky. You'll be able to transport your half in the back of a car. I want no part of other metals or stones, which could be difficult to place.

'What you take other than the platinum is up to you. It is none of my business where you sell your half; if you wish me to place it for you at some later date, then I'll do so. But I should warn you to be extremely careful who you deal with as regards selling. I know the people you're likely to deal with. I know them well, and although under normal circumstances they're quite safe, two hundred and fifty thousand pounds' worth of platinum could hardly be classed as normal.'

Geoffrey Foster leaned back in his chair.

'My men,' he continued, 'will drive up to the firm's main gate at exactly nine-thirty tomorrow evening.'

He rose from the table, and left the room.

Jack Lovel winked at Tate, who frowned back.

'What do you make of things now?' Lovel asked. 'Think we should still go through with it; think we should carry guns?'

'I'll carry one, Jack,' answered Tate.

Foster re-entered the room with three other men. The first was the man who had opened the door to them. He was a tall, well-built man of some thirty-five years, with a receding hair line, and slightly bulging eyes. Stripped down, he would show a very powerful physique. Jack Lovel guessed that this was the strong-arm man of the trio.

The man behind him was also of a largish build. Not as powerful-looking as the first, he was certainly no weakling. Lovel noticed his extremely small hands. He also noted the unsightly blue tattoo markings on the finger knuckles of both hands. H.A.T.E. had been tattooed on the right fingers, L.O.V.E. on the fingers of the left hand. Both Tate and Lovel instantly recognized them as the work of some prison artist, using either Indian or marking ink, and an ordinary darning needle. The third man was Ginger, Lovel's cell mate.

He grinned over at Lovel. 'Watcha,' he greeted. 'Got out yesterday.'

Ginger looked by far the least sinister of the three. His features were split into a huge good-natured grin. Lovel knew by experience that Ginger would give you his last fag; that he would never dream of grassing you up; that he would gladly die before he grassed. He was the epitome of the underworld's code of honour. He also knew that of the three who had just followed Foster into the room, Ginger was by far the most deadly.

Ginger ran a hand through his hair and, still grinning, said, 'Nothing to worry about, chaps, you've got me as a minder. Ginger Benett, the best in the game.'

Geoffrey Foster spoke to his team. 'Those two men,' he said, pointing to Lovel and Tate, 'will be in complete charge of the job, after you have dealt with the security guard. You all have your own special job to do. Just do that, and allow the others to do theirs without interference or unnecessary orders. Now, if you will follow me,' he led the way from the sitting room through the passage and into a large kitchen, which smelt strongly of recent frying. Opening a door, he switched on a light, revealing a set of stone steps. They followed him down the extremely steep steps, and came into a large cellar with a work-bench at one end. Fixed to this was a vice, and various tools were littered about the bench. Close to the door was a wooden chair that had lost its back. A single, bare, high-powered bulb dangled from the high, whitewashed ceiling.

Foster took them over to a row of six oxygen bottles, lined up neatly against the wall.

'I hope the protective suit meets with your approval,' he said. 'Of course, all this equipment will be placed ready for you, close up to the strong room door.'

Tate took in the thick white jacket which he knew would be made of an asbestos-based material, the large helmet and visor, and a pair of long grey gauntlets. There was also a pair of protective trousers.

He examined the thermic lance. This consisted of a holder, with a hollow tube at one end. Into this tube the rods would be screwed. Stacked on the bench were some twenty of these. They were four-feet lengths of tubing, similar to ordinary household conduit piping, and filled with three-eighth mild steel rods. A set of high-pressure gauges to which was attached some twenty feet of high-pressure rubber pipe, completed the outfit.

'How many bottles will you require to be coupled up ready for your use?' asked Foster.

'Three will be enough,' Tate answered, 'although to be on the safe side you may as well bring the six. Burning through the steel door will be no trouble, but it would be a different matter if we were cutting through the concrete wall of the strong room.'

'Well now, you've examined the equipment you are to use, are you satisfied?'

Tate nodded.

They ascended the cellar steps and followed Foster into a different room, more comfortably furnished than the sitting room had been.

'Drinks all round, chaps?' Ginger asked. He poured six good shots of whisky, added a splash of soda to each, and served them out.

'Here's to success,' said Foster, 'and may none of us here tonight have need, ever again, to venture his liberty for the sake of money.'

They all downed their drinks in reply to the toast,

except Alfred Tate, who seemed to ignore the salute, and coughed. 'Well,' he said, glancing at his watch, 'if that's all we need to know, we may as well be on our way.'

Foster nodded. 'There is no reason why I should detain you any longer. Tomorrow night then, at nine-thirty. I take it you will already be concealed and watching the place by the time my men arrive. They will come in a white Zephyr, similar to the ones used by the police in that area. The equipment will follow some twenty minutes later in a van. Now, if by chance you wish to contact me, here is my telephone number.' He handed a piece of folded notepaper to Lovel. They shook hands all round and left the premises.

'Whew!' Tate exclaimed, mopping his brow as they headed back towards Lovel's flat. 'I can't admit to being over keen on your friends, Jack.'

Lovel laughed. 'We'll use them as they'll use us, to the best of our, and their, advantage, and when this is all over, Alfie, and you're sitting in the living room of your nice new twelve-thousand-pound house, you are going to bless the day that Jack Lovel got bird.'

Tate snorted his reply. 'I've said before and I'll say again, we'll have to watch that little mob.'

'Well, if it makes you feel better, Alfie, I shall pick up the two shooters tomorrow morning. Now there's no need to drive right up to my place, drop me off here.'

Alfred Tate parked his car in the garage after dropping Jack Lovel off. He was happy to get home: to be once more surrounded by familiar objects and faces. He smiled as Janet handed him a cup of coffee, but then he forgot her and everything else as he began to brood on the dangers ahead.

This job didn't feel right; probably, he reflected, it was because they had become entangled with one of the London mobs. He felt completely out of his depth. If anything went wrong, they could get ten years.

His stomach turned over at the thought of what tomorrow night had in store for him. He glanced around the small, comfortable and satisfying familiar sitting room.

He almost groaned aloud with dismay at the thought of how quickly his surroundings could change. Why hadn't he been firm? Why hadn't he told Jack Lovel straight out that he wanted no part in this one? He could, within not so many hours from now, be sitting in a police cell waiting to be charged. Awaiting a possible ten years, or even more, for the size of this job would warrant plenty of bird. Ten years? For half a million quid they could hand out twenty bloody years, or possibly more.

He suddenly realized why the younger generation of thieves carried guns. It was the bird they were dishing out. The judges were giving from ten to twenty years these days, as they once gave out a three or five year sentence. You might just as well carry a gun, and use it. They couldn't take more than life, and that's what they took when they gave a man more than twelve years, because you would be dead after serving that amount of bird. Dead from the neck up, at least. Look at the train robbers. Thirty years, thirty bloody years, Alfred savagely reflected. For what? he asked himself. For money, that's what. The same people would calmly sit in judgment upon some animal of a sex fiend who had destroyed the mind of some innocent little child, and sentence him to a year or maybe eighteen months' imprisonment. He would be out after a year or so, and rampaging around the countryside leaving a trail of ruined little mites in his wake. Would that matter a damn to them? Oh no, but touch their money, and hear them scream.

Oh, they'd scream loud enough then, oh yes.

Janet resignedly replaced Alfred's cold cup of coffee with a hot, fresh one. He would be going on another job in a day or two she knew. She had no need to be told.

Jack Lovel swung the car, a large grey Austin, into the car park and proceeded slowly up the centre lane of neatly parked vehicles. Just before reaching the exit, his side lights blinked once. A figure detached itself from the dark shadows of a brick wall. Lovel, without stopping the car, reached over and opened the front passenger door. Alfred Tate slipped quickly into the waiting seat.

'Five minutes late,' he snapped. 'Why the bloody hell can't you be on time?'

'Traffic hold-up,' Lovel answered, grinning to himself. Going to be our lucky night, he thought. Alfie's really got it on him this evening.

Lovel put his gloved hand into the glove compartment and took out a snub-nosed revolver. 'Watch it,' he warned, 'it's loaded, and if you pull the trigger it goes bang.'

'Have you got one?' Tate asked, ignoring Lovel's weak joke.

Jack Lovel patted his breast pocket. 'Both the same, both ·32's. They're small, but still big enough to kill, and if I do have to use mine, I'll play for keeps. Now once they've taken that guard,' Lovel continued, 'I shall of course go in and knock the alarms out. After that it's your turn. You get that suit on and cut the door open with the lance. Then we'll put the others in to fetch the platinum out. That'll keep their hands occupied and ours free. While you're cutting the strong room door open I'll be watching your back. If by chance they intend any funny stuff it'll come immediately you've opened that door and are still muffled in the asbestos suit. I want you to know I'll be standing nearby all the time. I don't expect trouble from them. In fact, I'm fairly sure there won't be any. I suppose we'll hide our share of the loot in the old chalk quarry.'

Tate nodded his agreement. 'The law won't dream it's us,' Lovel continued. 'By the way, I gave that security guard from British Micro Electronics a thousand quid, on account.'

'What did he say, did you tell him how much he was getting?' Tate asked.

'No,' Lovel replied. 'I didn't tell him anything, just said it was on account and to be careful how he used it. He seemed relieved he'd got some of the money he had coming. Well, Alfred,' Lovel mused, 'this could well be the last job we do together; yes, it could be our last job,' he repeated, almost sadly.

'Christ! I hope so,' Alfred fervently replied. 'Whichever way it goes, I think I shall pack it in.'

'What line will you go in for, then?' Lovel asked.

'Well, if we get nothing tonight, I think I'll invest what money I've got in a shop. Been thinking of it for some time. Yes, either way the job goes tonight, it'll definitely be my last job. No need for me to go screwing any more, not even tonight, really.'

'What sort of shop are you thinking of, Alf?'

'Oh, just a small grocery type, nothing big like a supermarket. A quiet life, that's what I'm aiming for. I've had my fun; too much fun. It hasn't been an easy game.'

'I suppose you'll stock the shop up with a load of bent gear, Alf?'

'Christ, no! I won't ever touch another thing bent as long as I live, and if anyone ever comes in with a load of bent gear to sell me, I shall without any hesitation boot them from one end of my shop to the other. No, I'm finished after tonight, Jack. I won't even fiddle my income tax returns.'

'You know, Alfie, you almost have me believing you, but somehow I can't ever see us finishing. It seems as if we've always been screwing; always going out to do a job. Somehow it seems as if we always will. Christ! No more laying out all night watching a job, frozen bloody stiff. No more blowing peters and finding damn-all inside. Nor having the Old Bill spin your drum. Life wouldn't seem the same somehow, Alf. It seems unbelievable.'

Tate nodded his agreement. He couldn't picture a life without the constant niggling worry of being caught, with no shadowy fear of imprisonment forever haunting his mind. No, miracles just didn't happen.

Somehow neither of them thought they would get the platinum. There was too much money involved. That sort of money would never come their way. Two hundred and fifty thousand between them! No, things like that just didn't happen. Maybe it could happen to other people, but not them. They were both confident of their ability to do their part of the job, but their minds refused to allow them to believe they would then become rich men.

Lovel swung the car into a small street at the north end of the market town and parked it on a large patch of grass adjoining a housing estate.

After a walk of some four hundred yards they reached the low wall which surrounded the premises of Richard Goldbergh, Industrial Diamonds and Precious Metals Ltd.

'Not long now, Alf, before we see how this little team operate,' Lovel whispered, glancing at his watch for the tenth time.

Alfred Tate sat peering furtively over the wall. He felt the old familiar urge to urinate as his stomach contracted with apprehension, and Lovel grinned at the sight of his kneeling figure attempting to pass water. Even so, he understood; he felt the same urge, but controlled it. He could see the security guard sitting in the office, where he had an unobstructed view of the front entrance. This had a single black and white bar which would open at a touch.

Blazing headlights suddenly swung into the access road. The guard looked up from the book he had been reading and peered out into the night.

The large white Zephyr entered the road hammerhead directly in front of the firm's entrance and came to a crunching stop on the loose gravel.

Two men got out, one of them wearing a police inspector's uniform, the other that of a police sergeant. Lovel recognized them as Tracy and Tom, who had been at the meeting with Foster the previous day.

The guard stood up. Shielding his eyes, he peered out at the two uniformed figures. The 'sergeant' shone the torch he was carrying onto his companion, and they walked straight to the window through which the guard was peering. Lovel and Tate heard the 'senior' of the two call out to the security guard, asking him whether he had seen anything suspicious.

The security guard didn't answer their enquiry. He immediately made his way to the front door which he opened, and beckoned the two figures inside. For perhaps ten seconds, he and the two 'policemen' were concealed from view. Then the latter entered the office, and Tate and Lovel could see that the guard had already been overpowered.

Lovel moved quickly across the yard and joined Tom and Tracy; the security guard made no attempt to escape, but sensibly allowed himself to be propelled down a passage and into a small office. There they quickly and expertly tied him to a chair.

Lovel didn't waste time after the guard was tied up. Going to the small manhole cover, which he had first located on the blueprint that Smith had shown him, he inserted a key and lifted.

Shading his torch, he peered down at the bunch of insulated telephone wires. He got down on his knees, looking for the two alarm wires which he knew would be somewhere among the complicated maze.

His job now was first to locate the two alarm wires, and join them up without earthing them. If he allowed contact with earth to be made, the alarm would come into operation. With rubber-gloved hands he separated the two white alarm wires and carefully traced them back to their terminal points. He now took from his pocket a short insulated length of bell wire, with tiny but powerfully sprung special needle-pointed crocodile clips at each end. Once more making certain that he was onto the right terminal point, he fixed the crocodile clip into position. He traced the other alarm wire to its terminal and secured the second crocodile clip onto it. He had now shorted the alarm system's circuit. Taking a pair of insulated side cutters from his track suit pocket, he severed the two wires immediately behind the two terminals. The circuit was still alive from the junction box to the exchange. It had not been broken, only shorted. There was no contact now between the strong room they were about to rob and the exchange. Like any normal telephone system, the complicated alarm still had to be earthed before it could operate.

Lovel straightened up from his task, replaced the manhole cover and went over to Tate.

'Manage it?' Alfred asked.

Lovel nodded, grinning down at him. 'Ever known me not to?' he asked.

'I suppose we still wait and make sure?' Tate said.

'Yes,' Lovel agreed. 'We'll give it twenty minutes, then I'll go down to the strong room and fix the local alarm.'

They watched two men carry the last of the oxygen bottles in and stand them just inside the door of the building. Finished, they drove off to park the van which had been used to bring the heavy equipment. As this van was of no further use, and could not be traced back, they would leave it behind after the raid.

Lovel wandered behind the building, lit a cigarette and stood smoking for some five minutes.

Ginger Benett sat with a heavy pair of night-glasses slung round his neck and his short-barrelled shot-gun propped up beside him.

He had carefully chosen this vantage point, from which he was able to see the top of the approach road two hundred yards from the firm's main gate.

He spoke into a small walkie-talkie radio, to check that it was working efficiently, then placed it beside him.

Jack Lovel picked up a holdall which he had left with Alfred whilst he fixed the telephone alarm, and extracted a polaroid camera. Carrying this and a small battery-operated infra red lamp, he made his way to a lift shaft inside the building that jutted out into the passage. Opening a door by the side of the lift, he exposed to view a short flight of stairs. Bringing the camera into play he took two exposures. He examined the result. Nothing. Descending the few steps he faced right. Raising the camera he took two exposures of the strong room door and the immediate area.

Once again he examined the result. Both exposures showed a pencil thin beam which passed directly across the front of the strong room. It was about two foot from the floor and very close to the exterior wall and door. Producing his torch, Lovel flashed the beam onto the wall at his left. He could just make out the tiny point of the photo-electric cell, which he knew the infra red beam to be directed at. Placing his torch in a fixed position so that it shone directly onto the photo-electric cell, and switching on the infra red lamp which he had been carrying, Lovel carefully manœuvred it into position directly before the photo-electric cell, extending the legs of the tripod stand to which he had fixed the lamp, to the required height.

Finally satisfied, he straightened up and, bringing a small table from an adjoining room, put it directly over the infra-red lamp on the tripod. Then he returned to the front office and put his head inside the door where the guard sat bolt upright, securely tied to a chair. He had been gagged, and a blindfold tied round his head.

Lovel called Tom and Tracy, who had been keeping watch through the front office window, and they followed him down to the strong room, each carrying an oxygen bottle. He warned them against moving the table. Switching a large battery lamp on, Tracy illuminated the area Alfred Tate would need to work in.

Lovel then went back to Tate and, after giving him time to smoke a final cigarette, accompanied him to the strong room.

Everything was now in readiness for Tate to start work. A rod had already been placed in the thermic holder, and the three bottles were coupled from one to another and onto the lance.

Lovel told Tom—the strong-arm man—to go up and keep in radio contact with Ginger from the front office.

Tate pulled on the baggy grey trousers and the jacket. A blow-lamp was already alight, standing on the floor.

Tate pulled on his gloves and picking up the thermic lance, held the tip of the rod in the flame. He watched the rod change from red to white hot. He nodded to Tracy who was standing by the oxygen bottles. Immediately he turned the key which was secured to each bottle.

Tate placed the mask over his head and holding the tip of the rod a few seconds longer in the flame, began turning the oxygen screw of the holder, simultaneously lifting the lance away from the blow-lamp. There was a loud roar, and a thick jet of flame began to extend from the end of the rod. Tate slowly fed more oxygen through. Gradually the flame began to lengthen and broaden.

Tate pushed the now loudly roaring jet of super-heated flame close up to the door. Already, almost a quarter of the rod-packed tube had burned away. He watched through his visor as the hard thick metal of the strong room door began to melt. Molten streams of metal began to run away from the lance-tip. He was now having to push hard upon the lance to keep it steady against the widening hole. He expended the first rod. Turning the oxygen off, he quickly fitted another, and holding the tip against the white-hot metal of the strong room door, once again began to feed oxygen through. Again the flame appeared at the end of the lance and Tate continued.

He used four more of the rods before he was finally satisfied that the hole he had burned would be sufficiently large. Turning off the lance he put it near the bottles of oxygen. They would have no further use for it now. Then he got out of the protective clothing and sat down in a corner well away from the door, which was still throwing out a considerable amount of heat. He lit a cigarette, and tiredly watched Lovel and Tracy fetch buckets of water and throw them over the super-heated door.

Before they had finally cooled it down sufficiently to enter. Tate had smoked two cigarettes and was half-way through a third.

Finally Lovel told Tracy to go into the strong room with the large lamp. After a while the man began pushing small sealed boxes through the hole in the door. They were extremely heavy.

Lovel took the last of the boxes and burst the seal with a small case-opener. The box was packed with small domino-shaped platinum ingots. They counted sixteen boxes.

'Eight each,' Lovel said.

Tracy nodded his agreement.

14

MEANWHILE, THE SECURITY GUARD HAD been putting a continuous steady pressure on the cord binding his wrists. At the same time, he had been clenching and unclenching his fists. He had felt only a very slight slackening of the cord, so little in fact that he had almost given up, but not quite. Suddenly he felt the cord slacken; he stopped instantly. If they were to catch him untied . . . Fear welled up in him at the memory of his brief struggle. One of them had caught his neck in the crook of an arm and damn near choked him. Whoever had owned that arm was a very powerful man.

He could make it, he decided, he could be free in minutes if he chose. After all, they were still busy in the basement. He could still hear them working.

If he were to free himself and make a bolt for it, what then? One of them might be stationed at the door, but he was sure he could outsprint the average man. He was fit, and also, once he had cleared the firm's premises, he would soon be lost in the dark. Everything was in his favour. All he had to do was extricate himself from the now slackened cord, creep to the front door as quietly as possible, and run like hell. His only danger lay in that man guarding the entrance, if there was one. He didn't want to finish up getting himself coshed. Not bloody likely. Stanley Eves didn't believe in all this dead hero tripe. Not with a wife and three kids to look after. But if he did escape and raise the alarm, it would certainly be a feather in his cap, besides there was always the chance of something from the insurance firm.

Quickly removing the cord binding his ankles, he stood up and flexed his muscles. Hardly any stiffness. Then he crept quietly on the balls of his feet along the passage to the front door. It was ajar. Cautiously he peered round, and instantly spotted the man Lovel had ordered outside to stay in radio contact with Ginger. He was squatting down below the front office window, smoking and holding a murmured conversation over the walkie-talkie with Ginger. Now that the final moment of decision had come the guard had second thoughts about the advisability of making an escape. His mind kept repeating the phrase 'dead heroes, dead heroes'. Christ, how I wish I had stayed where I was, he thought. Suddenly, being bound, gagged and blindfolded in the chair seemed a very haven of safety. Out there could be death. If that chap he had seen was armed, sudden death he thought, sudden bloody death. His legs turned weak at the thought. What the hell was he to do now? Jesus Christ! What a mug: it ain't my money, why the hell am I sticking my silly bloody neck out?

The sound of footsteps coming up from the basement decided him. He leapt out into the yard and was half-way to the exit before the guard was on his feet. From the corner of his eye he saw the man's arm whip forward; a small walkie-talkie radio hurtled past his ear.

He ducked under the single wooden bar guarding the exit, and with arms pumping and flashing legs, began racing up the narrow approach road. He had made it! But Ginger had seen the figure hurtle across the yard. He had seen the walkie-talkie thrown at the flying figure, and heard the angry shout.

He needed no second bidding. Mentally calculating the distance between himself and the fast-approaching security guard, he waited until the man was almost level. Then, holding the shot-gun like a club he took a swing at his head with the butt. But the security guard saw it coming and ducked under it.

Nervous fear made him laugh. The guard's high-pitched

shriek of laughter infuriated Ginger almost to madness. Reversing the sawn-off shot-gun he took quick aim and fired.

The thunder of the huge maxim cartridge exploding rang out into the still night. The guard took the charge of heavy shot mostly in the fleshy part of his buttocks. Some pentrated his legs, and some his spine. Stark terror made him continue running. His back, buttocks and legs seemed to be a mass of flame. He didn't know he was slowing down; by now he had shut his eyes, attempting to shut out the fear and pain.

Even through the mists of pain and the noisy drumming of his fear-crazed heart, he heard the pounding footsteps as his pursuer rapidly gained. He knew instinctively that he was listening to the fast approaching footsteps of death. His mouth opened wide. He could hear his own great gulps of agony. He sucked in huge lungfuls of air.

The cold barrel of the deadly shot-gun touched the nape of his neck. The blast from point-blank range lifted the top of his head completely off.

Ginger Benett almost fell over the corpse as it slumped suddenly down in front of him. He inspected with interest the bloody mess that had once been a human being's head. Seizing a shoe in both hands he tugged and pulled until he had the body on the brink of the roadside ditch, then with a thrust of his foot, sent the body rolling down out of sight.

Lovel almost dropped the box he was carrying as the sound of the shot reached him. With the box in his arms he raced for the door.

Another shot echoed through the night.

'The security guard broke free, sounds like Ginger's just finished him off,' said Tracy grimly.

Tate hurriedly placed the box he had been carrying on the ground. 'Get the cars, for Christ sake get the cars. We've got to get out of here.'

'Get the bloody loot up first,' Lovel snapped, 'that's what we came for.'

They raced back down the basement steps and quickly

hauled up the eight remaining boxes of platinum. Then Lovel ran off to fetch their car while Tate strode quickly up the approach road.

He had to know what they were up against. Perhaps the security guard had only been wounded. He hoped so. What a mess, what a bloody stinking mess. He had known all along something like this would happen. Shot-gun mad, crazy bastards. Jesus, how he wished he hadn't got himself involved with this bunch of lunatics.

He could see Ginger squatting on his haunches, the shot-gun resting across his knees, smoking a cigarette as cool as you like.

He grinned up at Tate.

'Where is he?' Tate snarled down at him.

Ginger casually motioned with his thumb to the ditch immediately behind him. 'In there, won't be doing any more running.'

Tate stepped into the short grass bordering the road. Shielding his torch, he looked down at the body. It was twisted into an impossible position, with one leg tucked under the buttocks and the other leg sticking straight up, resting on the steep slope of the ditch.

It was the head, or what remained of it, that held Alfred Tate's gaze.

'Fixed him good, won't be any more trouble,' Ginger grunted.

Tate strode over to him. 'You bloody animal,' he growled. 'You bloody raving lunatic.'

Ginger straightened up with a jerk. Tossing the partly smoked cigarette down, he brought the shot-gun up on a level with Tate's throat. 'Call me that again,' he said quietly. 'Go on, just once more.'

Tate backed away from the muzzle, and without another word, walked quickly back to the car. He could feel the ·32 bulging heavily in his inside breast pocket. For a second, as he had turned away from Ginger, he had almost used it.

Tate and Lovel quickly loaded their share of the platinum into the Austin; they watched as the other three bundled the last box into the white Zephyr. Lovel glanced at his watch, it was one-thirty a.m.

'Well,' he exclaimed, 'are you moving off now, or waiting?'

'Waiting for what?' asked Tracy.

'Be just as well to hide up somewhere until some traffic gets about,' Lovel explained.

'Not bloody likely, not with him lying up there in that ditch; we're getting to hell out of here. Once we're home we're clean. They won't have a clue who done this. They'll never dream of you two either, not in a million years. No, none of us have a thing to worry about. You take your cut and sit on it for a month or two, pal. We'll look after ourselves.'

Tracy climbed into the Zephyr, with Ginger in the back, while Tom sat beside Tracy.

Winding down the rear window Ginger called nonchalantly to Tate and Lovel, 'Be seeing you in the Bahamas some day.'

Tracy travelled the quarter mile distance of the firm's private road without lights. Reaching the top, he switched them on and turned right onto the deserted public highway. This was perhaps the most dangerous part of the night's operation. He watched a white cat streak across the road, barely missing the Zephyr's front wheels as it quickly picked up speed. The driver held the car to a steady fifty miles per hour; just about right. Not so fast that they would draw unwelcome attention, but fast enough to make short work of the eighteen-mile journey from the market town to Foster's rented house. Clearing the small town, they lit cigarettes and relaxed.

'Swung at him with the butt first,' Ginger began. 'Should have stopped, he should, when he saw me leap out at him with the gun. I would just have marched him back and tied him up.'

'Yer,' Tracy agreed, 'all he would likely have got then would have been a bloody good belt in the mouth. Been having his breakfast with the old woman and kids in the morning.'

Ginger waited till Tracy had finished, then continued. 'Well as I was saying,' he wound the side window down slightly, pushed the cigarette stub out and watched the burst of sparks as it hit the road and rapidly dwindled into the distance. 'I swung at him and missed, bloody near fell over with the swing,' he gave a short laugh. 'If it had connected he wouldn't have needed shooting. He laughed at me. Yer, he started laughing like a bloody maniac. I wasn't standing for that.' Ginger smiled to himself as he remembered the rage he had felt. 'Don't know why, but Christ, I got mad. I said to myself then, if that won't stop you, try laughing at this. So I ups with the shooter and wham! I'm using the best Maxim cartridges, but the bastard kept running; made him jump though, I can tell you. Christ, for a moment I thought he was going to take off. I started after him and he began to slow down. You should have heard the funny noises that fellow was making just before I reached him. His legs were pumping up and down, but he wasn't getting anywhere, and all the time he was making these funny slobbering and choking noises. I think he must have known I was going to do him. I don't know why, but you know something?' Ginger stared intently at the backs of the two men sitting in the front seats, 'I felt sorry for that guy,' he continued. 'Yer, I know it sounds funny, but I did, and I just wanted to put him out of his misery. I done him a favour, the poor bastard. I couldn't let him live like that, all shot up, could I, Tracy, could I for Christ's sake?'

'Hold it,' Tracy snapped. 'See that, what we just passed?'

'No, I wasn't looking,' Ginger replied.

'There was a car parked in the side road. Here it comes.' Tracy adjusted the driving mirror to gain a better view.

Ginger twisted round. 'I've got him, Tracy.' The car behind switched on its headlights. It was a good distance away.

'Put your foot down for Christ sake.' The big man sitting in the front seat beside Tracy spoke for the first time.

'Hold on a bit, let's see if it tries to catch us up first. We're doing nearly ninety now,' Tracy replied. 'Could be a courting couple,' he added hopefully.

'Could be, but I bet it's the Old Bill,' Ginger said, grabbing the shot-gun.

'Don't go using that,' the big man said, turning in his seat and seeing Ginger peering through the window with the shot-gun held at the ready, 'you've got us in enough bloody trouble tonight already.'

'I'll be the judge of whether I use it or not,' Ginger retorted angrily.

The car behind was beginning to gain. Tracy put his foot down a shade harder and watched the speedometer climb to, then pass, the ninety mark.

'Give it the gas, Tracy, they're still gaining,' Ginger called excitedly.

Tracy pressed still harder on the accelerator but the headlights behind were still gaining.

Tracy pushed the speed up to, and over, the one hundred.

'It's no use,' he said, watching the road, and his driving mirror. 'It's the law and they're definitely going to give us a pull. They'll have buzzed through by now, and as we come to that junction before we hit the town, we're going to run into a road block. I'm turning off to the right at the first chance, so hold your hats on.'

Tracy quickly slowed the car to a more reasonable speed. As he anticipated, the headlights picked out one of the many side roads leading off to the right. With a further rapid deceleration he took the corner, still slightly too fast. The front wheel struck the grass verge, making the car roll. Tracy fought it back under control, and once more slammed his foot down on the accelerator. Ginger watched as the twin headlights of the following car swept round the corner. He blinked as they caught him unexpected, blinding him. Holding his head down he shielded his eyes.

Tracy threw the Zephyr crazily round a sharp right hand bend.

'Give it the bloody stick, Tracy, for Christ's sake,' Ginger called excitedly, 'they're gaining.'

He was about to say more as Tracy took another sharp bend, the fast cornering catching Ginger by surprise. He was hurled up against the opposite side of the speeding car, the shot-gun rattled to the floor.

A blue light began to flash on the roof of the following police car, and it had gained appreciably; in fact, each time they took a corner it crept further up on them.

'It's no use, Tracy,' Ginger called, 'they've got us licked.

Tracy heard the back window go as Ginger pushed the butt of the shot-gun through. A second later there was an almighty bang, quickly followed by another. In the confined space of the Zephyr the two detonations were stupendous, deafening the car's three occupants.

Tracy came to a straight stretch of road. He rammed his toe hard down.

The Zephyr leapt forward. Ginger watched as the police car began to lag.

'That's done it,' he called, 'they got that bloody message all right.'

The police had got the message. The shot-gun pellets had pitted their windscreen making it difficult for the driver to see.

Tracy hauled the Zephyr round another tight bend. This was their chance, they could still make it. Straightening up, he pushed it to the limit down a half mile stretch of straight road. Grasping the wheel he watched intently the black ribbon flowing towards him.

Ginger was chattering excitedly in the back, but Tracy wasn't listening. All his attention was centred on speed. So intent was he, he was up to and past the road sign before his eyes could flash the message to his brain. He hit the sharp hairpin bend at almost ninety miles an hour. His headlights suddenly ran out of road. For a split second he glimpsed a ditch and on the other side a large straggling hedge.

The Zephyr went out of control as the nearside front wheel struck the high verge. Like a projectile the car leapt into the air. Landing with a sickening crunch, it spun crazily completely round before rolling over. Over and over the big car rolled, tearing off a door and flinging Ginger clear. But as the car made its final plunging roll the big man who had been sitting beside Tracy in the front passenger seat came down with all his weight on to his head, which had been flung hard back on his shoulders.

There was a sharp crack as his neck was cleanly broken.

Except for some severe bruising neither of the car's other two occupants was injured.

Ginger scrambled from the ditch into which he had been flung. Grabbing Tracy he pulled him clear. Together they hauled on the big man's heavy dead body, eventually succeeding in extracting it from the jumbled wreckage of the car's interior. Pulling it roughly on to the grass they wasted little enough time, a brief glance at the crumpled remains was enough. The two struck off across the field in which the battered wreck of their car had finished.

They fell through a hedge a few yards distant and sat down, panting.

Rounding the hairpin bend, the police car's headlights picked out the skid marks and broken glass.

Ginger and Tracy watched silently as the police car came to a stop.

They watched as the two policemen cautiously made their way through thc gap in the hedge the wrecked car had made, then at a steady trot headed across the fields.

Meanwhile Tate and Lovel had arrived safely at the old disused chalk quarry. Concealing the boxes of platinum, they sat side by side, smoking. Neither of them referred to the night's events.

Lovel glanced again at his watch. A further half an hour before they could safely leave, he decided. Somehow he didn't want to go. He felt safe here. No one could see them whilst they stayed in this old quarry. Well, they had overstepped the mark this time. There would be hell to pay over this night's work.

Were only he and Tate involved, well that would be different; he could rely on Alfie: but those others, they were an unknown quantity. If the police got wind of them and pulled them in, what would happen? Would they prove as tough then as they acted, or were they all front?

Alfred Tate wanted to get home; just let him get home, he would feel better once he could talk to Janet, sane, ordinary, honest Janet. God, his eyes were open now. How right she was. How right she had always been. Something terrible will happen one of these days, she'd said, well, now it had. Why hadn't he taken notice of her, why hadn't he called it quits after the last job? He was a thief, but, oh Christ, he wasn't a murderer. He was now though, all because of that ginger-headed little bastard. He could break him in two. Alfred ground his teeth in rage. Even had the front to push that gun in my throat. Thought he'd make me back down. I could have had that bloody gun out of his hands before he could blink. Should have, he reflected savagely, should have, and shot him, the murderous little bastard. Why did he have to kill that poor bloody watchman? The man was only doing his job. Could have stopped him easy, didn't have to shoot. Probably got a wife and kids at home. Tate groaned out loud. Jack Lovel looked sharply at him, but held his peace. He felt very much the same.

15

JACK LOVEL WAS LYING ON HIS BACK looking up at the ceiling. He had heard nothing from Alfred Tate for some two days. He didn't want to hear. Any news would mean trouble. At the jarring sound of the doorbell, he walked quietly through the living room and opened the door. Lovel stood staring silently at Tate, then motioned him to enter and followed him into the sitting room.

'Trouble?' Lovel asked, looking at Tate's white, set face.

Tate nodded. 'Read the papers?'

Lovel shook his head. 'No,' he replied, 'I don't have to, I can imagine the kind of write-up we've been getting.'

'You don't know then?' Tate asked.

'Know what, for Christ sake? Don't talk in silly bloody riddles. What don't I know?'

Tate ignored Lovel's irritated outburst; he understood.

'The police have recovered half of the platinum; one of them was killed in a crash. Evidently, after they left us, the law got on to them, there was a chase and I think it was the larger of the three who got killed. The other two got clear away.'

'Well, that's down to them, just their bloody hard luck,' Lovel replied. 'So they got sweet F.A., so what? We still have ours.'

'I've had a phone call from Foster, received it this morning. He wants half of ours; says he'll sell the stuff for us, then give us half.'

'Like hell he will,' Lovel snorted. 'Like bloody hell he will. We'll sell our own gear, and as for him getting half, he's got no chance. Not of mine anyway. You should have told him that.' Lovel glared down at Tate.

'I did, I told him what he could do. Didn't make any bones about it either. He gave us both an ultimatum. Either we come to terms with him in the next twenty-four hours, or he'll get rough. Says he's got two men to pay.'

'What does he mean by getting rough?' Lovel asked. 'Thinking of bumping us off, or something?'

'Could be,' Tate replied, 'but I've had all afternoon to think about it, and there's no doubt in my mind how Geoff Foster will go about getting his hands on our share. He knows we've hidden the platinum and the obvious thing to do is to pick one of us up and make him talk. The man has never been born yet who wouldn't talk under torture. He may hold out for a while, but he'll talk in the end, and the way I see it it's better to spill the beans first, rather than finish up ruined in health and still having to give them the information.'

'You're not thinking of just handing over our share to them? There's two of us. We're not giving way just because three flash bloody so-called big-time mobsters start putting the threateners on us. Do what you like with yours, Alfie, but they won't get mine.'

'They won't get mine either, Jack, but we've got to be prepared. As I said, the obvious thing for them to do is to pick one of us up, at gun-point. When you answered the doorbell to my ring, that could have been them. They could either have carted you off, or worked you over in here. My bet is they'd have taken you to that house in Lester Way where they'll stay while the police are convinced that whoever is responsible for what happened last night is a London team. That little mob will stay put. Yes, if they do pick one of us up, and I'm sure they will, you or me can expect to finish up in the cellar of that house, and the bet is, whichever one they select will not come out alive.'

'And what's the answer to that little riddle?' Lovel asked.

'Bump them off; hit them before they have a chance to get one of us?'

'There's that way, Jack,' Tate admitted, 'but if we tried that, we'd have to do it today, and we could well come unstuck. You could take your share and light out; you're single, with no ties.'

Tate took a shoe off, holding it upside down. 'Or else,' he said 'I could hollow that heel out and get two ounces of blasting gelatine inside. With a very small transistor battery, a detonator, and the necessary springs and what have you. Screw the heel firmly back on, and there you have it. A booby trap, and it would work.'

'I must be thick, I don't follow you,' Lovel said, puzzled.

'Well, Jack, if they pick you up, they're going to ask you where we've hidden the platinum and they're going to give you a chance to talk before they begin to work you over, and that's what you do, talk. Remember what that cellar contained. A work-bench with a vice, and an old chair with the back broken off. You sit in that chair and talk, making sure the chair is near the door, well away from the vice. You could tell them that we expected them to try bumping one or the other of us off, to frighten the one left into talking. If they grab you, say it was my idea and that in the event of my death I had left instructions for you to sell my share and hand the proceeds over to my wife, Janet. Take your shoe off, show them the head of the large screw I shall place in the heel to hold it secure. Say to them, "There's the instructions where to find mine, and Alfred Tate's is in the heel of his shoe; may as well tell you before you work me over, as after." Give them that reason for parting with the information without first being tortured. They'll understand.

'Now when they take that shoe off they're going to put it into the vice. Stands to reason.' Lovel nodded. 'And,' continued Tate, 'one of them will begin to work on the heel screw, and with any luck, that little ginger bastard who will be holding the gun on you, is going to become curious. There's a good chance he'll hover near Tracy to watch that heel come off. Now you bend down and begin tying your shoelace. The heel will spring up as the last thread of that screw leaves it, and you must be prepared; don't let the noise put you off, jump in right away. Grab that gun or anything else that comes to hand and let whoever is left standing have it. Make sure you finish them off: remember you're dealing with animals.'

'You haven't mentioned Geoff Foster. Where,' Lovel asked, 'is he going to be during all this?'

'My bet is he'll be upstairs,' Tate replied. 'I don't think he'll be down in the cellar knowing one of us is about to be tortured, too messy for him to be directly involved, but there's two cartridges in that shot-gun. I'll have the shoes ready tonight,' he promised.

'The sooner the better,' Lovel replied, 'but, Christ! I don't fancy walking on two ounces of blasting gelatine: you use only one ounce of that stuff to blow a peter.'

Alfred Tate had worked patiently. The heel of Jack Lovel's shoe had been neatly hollowed out, the cavity base lined with a thin copper plate ready tapped for screwing into place. From the centre of the plate obtruded a sleeve. Within the cavity also lay a tiny battery to which two wires had been soldered, one to the positive, one to the negative contact. Over the metal sleeve a spring had been slipped, with a rubber tube containing an electric detonator. The spring had to be compressed until it equalled in size the rubber covering cylinder, the compression held in place by a temporary thread, thus permitting the rubber cylinder to travel upward with the spring's action once it was released. A hole had been drilled through the shoe's heel, and through this a knitting needle had been passed directly over the spring to retain it in place. The rigid rubber cylinder had been pierced and a terminal wire tied to it, forming a small coil around the top of the rubber cylinder with the thick wire from the detonator. Around the cylinder was packed the blasting gelatine. As the rubber cylinder was projected upwards by the spring's expansion, it would take with it the battery wire; contact with the coil would be automatic.

Tate screwed the heel into place with one large screw through the centre and for added safety four smaller screws around the outside. Finally he removed the needle and plugged the small holes. He was already wearing a shoe which had received similar treatment.

Tate put the shoe in the boot of his car. The time was then six-fifteen. He heard the telephone ring as he walked to his back door. Picking it up he heard the voice of Geoffrey Foster.

'Mr Tate, I must warn you my men are beginning to get very impatient. You must realize that we put a good deal more into the partnership than you, in fact, we lost a man. Under these circumstances I hope, for your own sake, you will be reasonable and allow us to share what's left. These men you were working with last night can be very dangerous, as you will have no doubt realized.'

'What do you suggest we do?' Tate asked.

'I suggest that you hand the complete proceeds over to me for disposal. We will then share out. Half to you and your partner, half to myself.'

'In other words you want the lot.' Tate gave a short, hard laugh over the phone. 'We had an agreement that immediately this job was completed, you would go your way, we would go ours. If it had been us who had the accident we would have sucked our lemon, now you suck yours.' Tate slammed the phone back on the hook and returned to the car. He caught a glimpse of his wife's white, anxious face pressed to the window as he pulled onto the road.

Lovel took the shoe which Tate handed him, and examined the heel.

'You have yours on?' he asked. Looking up, Tate nodded. 'Well, stamp your foot, stamp on the heel hard, hard as you can. No, not in here, out in the kitchen and for Christ sake keep well away from me.'

Tate complied. He left the soft, thick pile carpet in the living room, and standing on the firm plastic tiles of the kitchen, brought the heel of his right foot crashing down. Lovel winced.

'Wish I had your faith,' he remarked, slipping his own shoe on. He walked gingerly round the living room, carefully putting his weight on the toe. 'If they're coming, let's hope it's soon, before this bloody contraption goes off.' He shuddered at the thought. 'Enough in there to take my leg off,' he mused, looking down at his right shoe. 'Enough in there to put me right out in orbit, for Christ sake.'

'Somehow I don't think we shall have long to wait,' Tate said, glancing at his watch. 'It's about time I got going.'

Immediately Tate left, Lovel took the shoe off. He would wear it only if he had to answer the doorbell.

16

JENNIFER TATE SAID GOOD-NIGHT TO her friends, and kicked the small engine of her scooter into life. She made her way carefully through the town. Within ten minutes she had cleared the town centre and entered Elm Tree Avenue. The badly lit road was deserted. There was seldom much traffic after six thirty when the half dozen small factories turned out.

Pedestrians were almost non-existent in Elm Tree Avenue at any time.

Jennie had traversed almost half the lonely road. She could see the well-lit junction at the bottom, and her home was barely fifty yards to the right of the junction.

She heard the car coming from behind. Drawing level, it slowed. Glancing at the car Jennie could make out two youngish-looking men.

The driver began edging the car in nearer.

Jennie wobbled as she tried to keep the scooter from touching the high concrete kerb and away from the encroaching car.

The driver pulled relentlessly in. Jennie felt the car brush her arm. She slammed her brakes on as the front wheel struck the kerb. She fell towards the car first, and bouncing back, left the scooter and landed spreadeagled on the concrete pavement, grazing her chin, hands, and knees.

Instantly the car stopped. The two men leapt out. As Jennie rose to her knees, the largest of the two grabbed her savagely by the hair, hauling her to her feet. Jennie screamed. The man holding her hair, wrenched hard, backward. The short scream changed into a half stifled sob, and she felt herself bundled into the car and thrust onto the back seat. She fought desperately, trying to ward off the assault, hearing the harsh panting breaths of her attacker, until she could resist no longer. Suddenly all strength deserted her. She felt the flimsy blouse she was wearing ripped away from her body. A hand was thrust roughly up between her thighs. She lay naked from the waist down, too terrified to move now as she watched the figure, crouching above her fumble impatiently with his trousers.

Leaning over the front seat, with growing excitement Ginger watched the white heaving buttocks as Lacy savagely raped the girl. The soft subdued, partly muffled moans she made as the man thrust into her caused him to chatter with excitement.

Suddenly Lacy rolled off from the now supine girl. Looking up he beckoned, inviting Ginger to take his turn, but—strangely—Ginger refused. Together they watched as slowly, realizing the ordeal was over, the girl began to gather the remains of her clothing.

As the two men moved off in the car, they saw Jennie down on all fours. 'He should get the message now,' Ginger laughed.

Jennie covered the remaining distance to her home in a stumbling half-run half-walk. She looked down all the way; just followed the pavement. Instinct made her turn in the correct direction at the junction. At one stage of her tormented journey she stumbled into a lamp-post. It would normally have been a painful collision, but she felt no pain. Jennie was beyond physical pain. Shock had flooded her nervous system to such an extent that she was now completely numb to all feeling.

She found the back door, the door by which she always entered her home, and pounded with her small fists.

Janet opened the door. She almost screamed but controlled herself, and putting her arm around Jennie half lifted and half pulled her into the kitchen.

Alfred Tate's face went stark white at the sight of his girl. He stood immobilized for seconds.

The scooter, he thought, that bloody scooter. She's come off it.

Janet answered his unspoken question. 'She's fallen off the scooter, oh my God.' She still had both arms around the now wildly sobbing Jennie.

Jennie was shaking her head. 'No,' she sobbed, 'no, it wasn't the scooter. Two men in a car.'

Janet eased her gently into Alfred's armchair.

Her stricken face looked up at them.

'Are you sure, darling, are you sure?' she asked.

Jennie nodded. 'It was two men attacked me.'

'My God! Get the police. Get the police while I bathe Jennie's face! Alfred, hurry. Get the police and a doctor.'

Tate stood rooted to the spot. So this was their way of getting at him. Through his daughter.

They both watched, deeply concerned as, white-faced she lay with her head back, resting with one of her mother's coats around her, her bandaged hands resting on the arms of the easy chair.

At a nod from Janet, Tate followed her into the other room. She glared at him. 'I've never asked you before what you did, or where you went,' she said, 'but I'm demanding to know the reason for this. You knew those men, Alfred,' she accused. 'I want to know everything.'

Tate had no alternative. He told her everything from beginning to end.

Janet stared incredulously for long seconds. 'You realize I shall have to take Jennie away,' she said finally. 'I shall have to. I daren't allow her to stay here.'

Tate closed the door of the garage. He worked steadily through the night. In a large square tin he had placed four four-ounce sticks of blasting gelatine, a battery and a trembler contact. He secured the lid and fixed a powerful magnet to it. For safety of handling he had made the trembler movement so stiff that it would need a severe shock to move to contact. There was no room in his mind for doubt. He would go after those bastards, until either they got him, or he finished them off. He would kill them all. What's more, he wouldn't wait until tomorrow or the next day. It would be today! Tate clenched his fists in fury. 'Christ! they'll suffer for this day's work,' he muttered. 'Quarter to five in the morning, time to go.'

He pushed the car backwards and on to the road so as not to waken his family, then drove carefully through the deserted streets, the bomb resting beside him. As an extra precaution he had placed a neatly folded sack beneath it, to absorb any small jolt.

Entering the street to the rear of Lester Way, he carried the large square box: slowly and carefully he scaled the low brick wall which enclosed the premises.

Crouching down among the weeds in the overgrown garden he watched the house for movement. After a few minutes, and satisfied that all was clear, he cautiously followed the wall down to the side of the garage. It took only seconds for Tate to unlock the Yale on the garage door by slipping a thin piece of perspex between the door jamb and the lock.

Fetching the bomb, he reached under the chassis of the Rover 2000 which was parked inside. The magnet attached to the bomb was attracted and secured itself firmly to the sump of the Rover. Tate gave it a gentle tug but the bomb stayed firm.

Locking the garage door firmly behind him, Tate crept quietly away.

'I have a few things in the town to attend to this morning,' Foster told Tracy the following morning as the two men sat at the kitchen table. 'While I'm about it I'll get groceries, enough to last for a few days. By the way, if there's a phone call from Alfred Tate while I'm away, tell him I'll ring him back. Let him sweat for a while.' He looked meaningly at Tracy, who laughed.

'Should have got the message by now, boss.'

'Yes and as he's not the violent type there's only one thing left for him to do.'

'Pay up,' Tracy answered, laughing. 'You don't think Tate or Lovel are likely to come gunning for us?'

'Not the slightest.'

Nevertheless Foster lifted the bonnet of the Rover and carefully examined the plug leads. Alfred Tate was a blower and good at his trade, so he had heard. They usually fixed the detonator wires to the plug leads, he reflected, pushing the bonnet down and making it secure.

Reversing carefully from the garage, he turned the car.

There was a sharp dip at the bottom of the drive. Tate had noticed this when he and Lovel had paid a visit a few days previously. He had expected the explosion to happen there, and under normal circumstances it would probably have done so, but as Foster drove slowly down the drive a small van backed in, using the driveway as a turning point. This forced Foster to slow almost to a stop, so that there was hardly any jar as the Rover negotiated the sharp ridge.

Foster followed the van to the town centre, travelling at a slow speed. His intention was to make two phone calls, one of them to his wife. He made certain that those who worked for him never got to know his home address—they didn't even know he was a married man with three children, for in his private life Foster put up a very respectable front. He had not one item on his clothing or in his possessions that could be used to trace him back to his family, and should anything ever happen to him his family would be well provided for. He had made certain of that.

He was reflecting on his next move, if Tate refused to be intimidated by the assault upon his daughter, although not for one moment did he think he would ignore that assault. No, he would do the only thing a family-loving man possibly could do: pay up.

Foster was hardly ever wrong in his assessment of a human being's reactions. That was why he had always managed to keep a jump ahead of the rest.

He swung the Rover into the narrow side street leading to the public car park. Half-way down he met an awkwardly parked car. To get past, he had to mount the pavement. His nearside wheel hit the kerb with a hard jolt.

But Foster never felt that small shock. His whole being was centred on a far bigger one.

The explosion caused by the blasting gelatine lifted the front of the Rover completely off the ground and hurled it hard up against a low brick wall. For almost a minute Foster lay in a crumpled heap, wedged between the two front seats and the dashboard. As he gradually regained his senses he could hear the far-away murmur of voices. Suddenly he was gripped by strong hands which tugged and heaved until he was clear of the car.

Alfred Tate rang the doorbell to Lovel's flat at five forty-five a.m. Within seconds the door was opened. Knowing Lovel would be standing to one side of the slightly opened door, suspicious and ready for any eventuality, Tate quickly identified himself. Following Lovel inside he seated himself in an armchair and wearily passed a hand over his face. Lovel watched Tate questioningly.

'Well,' he demanded, 'what's wrong now?'

'Just about everything,' Tate replied. He told Lovel of the assault on Jennie. Lovel stood meditating for some time. 'What are we going to do about it?'

'Nothing,' Tate replied.

'Nothing,' Lovel repeated incredulously, 'nothing?'

'No,' Tate said. 'I've already done it.' He told how he had booby-trapped the Rover.

'Should have shot the bastards,' Lovel said bitterly. 'Should have shot all bloody three of them. Only half done the job, Alfie. If you'd called here first we'd have gone round and sorted all three of them out. You'll probably only kill one of them with that bomb, we'll still have the other two to deal with. We still have time. We could go up there now and finish all three off.'

'Maybe we should, Jack, could be you're right. I don't know, but whatever happens won't matter much now. Janet's taken Jennie away this morning and she won't be coming back. I might have been able to persuade her to stay but how can I? It's not safe any more, anything might happen.'

Tate rose from the chair. 'Going already?' Lovel asked.

Tate nodded dumbly and made for the door. Lovel watched silently as he left.

17

FOSTER WATCHED THE TWO DETECTIVES, guided by a pretty young nurse, approach. He had already decided to act the part of a person suffering from amnesia.

'Hello, old chap.' Sergeant Bradshaw bent over him. 'Had a little accident have we?' he asked. 'Not too much damage though, I hope.' He turned and smiled at the young nurse, ignoring the doctor who had quietly approached. 'Small fracture you say?' he spoke to her.

'Yes,' she answered, 'and several broken ribs.' Sergeant Bradshaw nodded. The doctor frowned.

'Your name, what's your name, old chap?' he asked, peering intently down at Foster's bandage-swathed features. 'Come on, everybody knows their name,' he demanded.

Foster smiled blandly back up at the detective. He put on a puzzled expression. 'My name,' he answered. 'Well, my name is . . .'

'Yes, yes,' Sergeant Bradshaw said excitedly, 'yes, come on, what is it?'

'It's . . . it's . . . I don't know, I don't know. Somehow I don't seem to remember.'

'Damn it, I thought he had it then, Steve.' Bradshaw spoke to D.C. Finch.

'Come on, man, try harder. You can't forget your own name. Where do you live, do you remember, where do you live?' He spoke each word singly and slowly.

Foster closed his eyes for a second or two and appeared

to withdraw inside himself. A single tear slowly trickled down his cheek.

Bradshaw shook his head and tried again.

'What happened to your car, what caused the explosion?'

The nurse bent over the patient. 'Now come along, the detective hasn't all day to waste,' she said importantly.

'That's enough,' the doctor snapped.

'But I was only asking him a few questions, we must know who he is and how the accident happened,' protested the detective.

'That's all for now.' The doctor stood firm. 'He may have visitors, but he must not be upset. I must ask you to leave. There will be no more questioning, not today anyway.'

Geoffrey Foster watched the two detectives, accompanied by the nurse and the doctor, leave the ward.

The ward contained only six beds, all occupied by accident cases. Next to the window was a telephone on a small trolley. Catching the attention of a young patient who was limping around on a plastered leg, he asked for the use of the telephone. He took the proffered phone from the youth and inserted a few coins, dialled his number at Lester Way. Ginger answered, and Foster told him where he was, and asked him to come immediately. Except for a dull throbbing in his head the damage wasn't so bad, considering. A slight fracture of the skull he had heard the doctor say. But it would be at least a week before he could move about in reasonable comfort, and he just did not have that amount of time to waste. He had badly underestimated Alfred Tate.

Ginger sat for some ten minutes outside the hospital, suspicious; knowing the police could well be watching him.

At last he went in and, entering the ward, he spotted Foster. Ginger grinned to himself. 'Take some of the bloody starch out of you, you bouncy little bastard.' Almost as if he could read his thoughts Geoffrey Foster scowled up at Ginger's face and motioned him to lean close over.

'You know what to do,' he whispered, 'get Alfred Tate, now.'

'Now?' Ginger asked, surprised.

'I mean tonight! You must get him tonight. I shall discharge myself tomorrow, but I want Alfred Tate killed first. He must be killed before I leave this hospital.'

Ginger nodded down at him. 'Read all about it,' he whispered.

'Tomorrow we will take care of Jack Lovel. A little work-over down the cellar and he should be only too willing to co-operate.'

'Now you're talking boss; now you're talking. Action is what we want. Let's get the loot and get the hell out of this place. Cash it in. I want my cut. I'm not used to hanging around waiting for my bit after a job. Leave it to me. I'll fix him tonight. I'll fix Alfie Tate; both barrels.'

'Don't come near this place again,' Geoffrey Foster warned. 'Remember I shall discharge myself early tomorrow morning. I have a slight fracture of the skull, several broken ribs and severe bruising; however, nothing really serious. See you tomorrow.' He grimaced as sudden pain seared through his head.

Alfred Tate surveyed his desolate kitchen. Already it had a different atmosphere. All life and laughter had fled the place. He had neglected to stoke up the small patent kitchen stove, and already the place had become chilly.

He strode over to the window and stood staring out at the small kitchen garden. It badly needed digging. He'd have to do it soon before the weeds got out of hand. It was a job he usually tackled at week-ends, but what the hell. Useless even to contemplate. No point in digging the garden now. Tate placed both hands in his trouser pockets. His gaze rested on the far right concrete garden post. He had buried Jack Lovel's finger there. Christ! that seems like a life-time ago. That should have been my last job, he reflected. It should have been. He had determined then never to go on another. Against his own better judgment he had allowed others to change his mind, and this was the result.

This, he decided, was the culmination of all those risks

he had taken. Everything he valued was gone. Jennie mauled by those bloody animals. The security guard murdered. Oh, why the hell hadn't he just handed over his share of the loot? He would at least have had his family.

He would get them back though; of course they would come back: couldn't leave him like this, not after being together all these years.

He had been a thief yes, but hadn't he always looked after them? They had had damned nearly everything. They couldn't have had the better things in life if he hadn't put himself about, now could they, he asked himself. I put myself on offer for them, he thought bitterly. Could have got twenty years at any time. Now when something goes wrong, I'm deserted. We've had good times. Janet never talked of leaving then. She never mentioned morals, rights or wrongs when we had the good times, only when danger threatened. I'm finished. Should have gone with Janet and Jennie. Sold the house and moved right out of it.

Tate stared out into the fast-gathering gloom. Turning round he filled the electric kettle and plugged it in. Even that small act brought back memories. Its warning shriek interrupting his love-making with Janet now seemed a lifetime ago.

It brought a grim smile to his face.

He wandered into the sitting room. The wedding portrait of a young couple standing outside a village church caught his eye. He and Janet on their wedding day. Janet looked very much like Jennie now, and certainly no older.

She was laughing up at him, dressed in her white bridal gown. He could make out small pieces of confetti clinging to her veil. He and Janet had grown older, but the photographer had captured their youth and held it; never to grow old.

Tate switched on the sitting room light and drew the curtains. The kettle sent out its piercing shriek. Tate lifted the photograph and carried it into the kitchen. He switched the kettle off, and putting tea in the pot, poured in the boiling water.

Closing the kitchen curtains he sat for a while listening to the silence that now reigned all about him.

Tate poured himself a cup of tea, his eyes went back to the wedding photograph and he became lost in memories.

The doorbell's loud shrill brought him reluctantly back to the present. Almost in a trance he gazed once more into the blue of Janet's eyes.

Again the doorbell sent out its shrill demand. Alfred rose from the table. For a second he glanced round the kitchen, bewildered; opening the door to the hall he switched the light on and took three paces towards the front door before he stopped in mid-stride. He could see the twin black circles of a shotgun protruding through the letter flap.

He heard the first blast. The heavy slugs tore into his stomach, mincing and shredding the soft intestines, and hurling him violently backwards. So great was the blast at that short range that he was lifted completely off his feet.

Tate never heard the second explosion, which peppered his chest and face.

He was floating in a soft hazy world of his own, staring up at the light bulb. It didn't seem to be a white light that was glowing up there. It was a swirling, misty blue, slowly darkening. He was still thinking, but very slowly. Blood welled suddenly from his mouth. A long violent shudder shook the dying man's frame, then his body twitched and Alfred Tate finally left this world.

Ginger stood for a second or two watching Tate's last movements. Then he prepared to leave.

On his way through the kitchen his glance rested on the wedding portrait. Curious, he bent down to study it. Must be his, he thought. The fixed gaze seemed to pierce his very brain. Picking the portrait up, he hesitated for a second, then let it drop to the floor.

Ginger placed the shot-gun on the kitchen table. He looked enquiringly at Tracy, who was staring worriedly at him. 'What's up?' Ginger asked.

'Did you?' Tracy questioned.

' 'Course I did, both barrels. Lifted him clean off his feet; never knew what hit him. Got him through the letter flap in the front door. Second one I've had like that. Always works.'

'Well, he's dead,' Tracy stated.

' 'Course he's bloody well dead, you'd be too if you copped both barrels up the gut.'

'No, I mean the governor. Came over the radio not more than ten minutes ago. Said unidentified man whose car mysteriously exploded this morning died suddenly in hospital. Gave the cause of death as unexpected brain haemorrhage. He was known to have had a visitor, and the police have appealed for that visitor to come forward.'

'Christ! that's me,' Ginger exclaimed. 'Knew I shouldn't have gone near that bloody hospital.'

'Well,' Tracy reassured, 'the description wasn't too good. They're looking for a blond man of about twenty-two years. Medium build.'

'Well the builds' right, but then Christ, whoever gave the description is colour blind.'

'You're not medium build, you're short, and you're twenty-seven or eight,' Tracy answered. 'The point is,' he continued, 'what do we do now? That's what I keep asking myself. Three men dead and we haven't made a brass farthing so far. Think we should call it a day and pull out, Ginge? While the going's good? Christ help us if the Old Bill get on to us now. We'll break all bloody records for porridge.'

'You must be joking! Pull out now? Not bloody likely. We get that platinum first. There's only one man between that and us. Besides that, he's the only one who could give evidence against us. We put a grip on Jack Lovel, bring him in here, and perform on him. That's what we do. Geoff Foster's dead. So what? We can still operate without him.'

Tracy nodded his agreement. 'Suppose you're right. We'll have to go all the way now. What about Lovel? We're going to finish him off?'

'Have to,' Ginger answered. 'Can't let him go, after we take the stuff from him. Scream his bloody head off, or come looking for us, and I don't rate him as a mug. No, we bring him in here, work him over down the cellar, then knock him off.'

Jack Lovel answered the door to his flat. He had already decided that if they were coming to fetch him he would go without fuss and rely on Alfie's method to defend himself. But it was Sergeant Bradshaw and D. C. Finch who were standing before him at the partly open door.

Lovel led the way into the sitting room.

'We haven't come to question you, we just want your co-operation in a small matter. It is purely voluntary on your part,' said Bradshaw. 'There's been an accident and we'd like you to come with us to the morgue. Now I don't want you to get wrong ideas, Jack. You may if you wish drive down in your own car, or accompany us in ours.'

Lovel looked suspiciously at the two plain-clothes detectives. Immediately Bradshaw had mentioned the morgue his mind had jumped to the booby trap Tate had placed under Foster's car that morning. So it had worked after all. Wonder how many it got? They can't tie me or Alfie in with it. They can think what they like, but they can't prove it.

'What the hell would I want down the morgue?' he queried.

'As I said, there's been a small accident,' repeated Sergeant Bradshaw.

'Small accident! Sounds to me like a bloody big accident if I have to go down to the morgue,' Lovel snorted.

'Well, will you come?'

'If it makes you feel better.' Lovel grinned.

Bradshaw led the way out to his own car; he held the door open for Lovel.

'Not giving me much bloody choice are you?' Lovel grumbled, getting in the front passenger seat.

They drew to a halt inside the hospital grounds.

Bradshaw led the way to the morgue. An attendant

opened the door and stepped to one side for the party to enter. Evidently things had been prepared for them. The outline of a body showed through a covering shroud.

Bradshaw stepped up to the slab, waited until Lovel was standing beside him, and whipped back the covering.

He peered intently up at Lovel's face. Jack Lovel stood frozen to the spot. 'Alfie!' he said. 'Jesus Christ! Alfie!'

Stupefied, he stared down at the familiar, now almost unrecognizable dead face of Alfred Tate. The body was just as it had been brought in. Lovel saw the blue puncture marks peppering the throat where the heavy shot-gun slugs had entered. Two had pierced the right cheek and there was a tiny dribble of dried blood below each. He saw the still dampish huge blood clot which had issued from the mouth and had spread in a thick dark red mass just below the chin and neck.

Tate's eyes were wide open, staring up at the powerful, fluorescent light.

Lovel's face went a ghastly grey for a few seconds, then slowly a high flush spread over his features.

'Who done that?' he asked tensely.

'You don't know?'

'Been shot, ain't he?'

'Did you know Alfie's wife and daughter have disappeared?' Bradshaw asked, as he pulled the sheet once more over Tate's features.

'No, why should they leave? Anything happened to them?'

'We don't know yet. When did you last see Alfred Tate alive?'

'When he came to my flat this morning,' Lovel answered.

'Well, that'll be all for the present. I think you must know something about this. I'm not saying you're involved. I'm not saying you weren't surprised, but you must know what led up to Alfred Tate's murder. There's not much point in taking you down to the station. That would be a waste of our time, if you don't wish to tell us anything, you won't. I'm advising you to think things over for a while and decide. If you've been involved in anything with Alfred Tate, remember, it could be your turn next.'

Lovel followed the two detectives out to the car.

'Want us to take you home, Jack, or drop you off somewhere.'

'Drop me off in the town,' Lovel said in a very subdued voice. 'Anywhere I can get a drink.'

Bradshaw dropped Lovel off in the town centre, drove into the police car park, and with Stephen Finch, made his way to the C.I.D. room.

Chief Inspector Roper was at his desk. He looked up as the two detectives entered. 'How did he take it?' he asked.

'He didn't know. I would swear to that,' Bradshaw replied. 'There was surprise written all over his face. Shook him rigid.'

'Did you bring him in?'

'No, not much point in that. Would only mean holding him for a few hours; we're bound to let him go then, and I'm sure we'd get nothing out of Lovel.'

'Well, you have a nice little trip in front of you. We've located Alfred Tate's wife and daughter. They're at a place called Knightswood, near Glasgow. You'll go up there. Fly, tonight.'

'Tonight!' Bradshaw exclaimed.

'Yes, tonight. We've everything arranged. You personally will break the news to her, and get what information you can. By the way, Alfred Tate was shot at eight-fifteen this evening. We have the time exactly, verified by the man who found him, his next-door neighbour. He also heard the killer's car drive away, but didn't see him.'

18

'I WANT TO GO HOME, MUM,' JENNIE TATE complained to her mother. 'We shouldn't have left Dad on his own. I don't care what happened to me, we shouldn't have left him.'

Janet Tate stood looking out of the front window of her sister's bungalow. 'We shall stay here another week or so at least,' she replied.

'Shall we go home then? I don't mind staying another couple of weeks just so long as I know we are going back. We are going back, Mum, aren't we? I mean, you're not leaving Dad for good? After all, you haven't a reason. I mean, it wasn't his fault what happened to me, besides, he's always treated you well. He's treated us both well, Mum, hasn't he? You know he has.'

'I am not saying your father hasn't been a good husband, Jennie. I've never said that,' Janet Tate answered her daughter.

'Well why did you leave him then, why? You weren't rowing. Oh, I don't understand.' Jennie began to sob. 'All this fuss and bother because of what happened to me. I want to go home.'

'Sh, sh,' Janet said. 'There's a car just pulled up at the front.

Sergeant Bradshaw climbed slowly out of the car, slammed the door and walked down the garden path. He pressed the doorbell.

Janet showed him into the sitting room. He looked enquiringly at Jennie.

'Could I speak to you in private?' he asked.

Bradshaw watched Jennie leave the room. Pretty girl Alfie's got, he thought, then mentally amended to 'he had'.

'Mrs Tate.' Janet nodded. 'Well, I—er—well, it's like this, the Chief sent me up. You know who I am?' Janet nodded again. 'I, well, I was sent up to break the news because I know you, I mean I know you slightly.' He looked at Janet. Janet stared back. 'I mean, Mrs Tate . . .'

'It's about Alfred, isn't it?' Janet said quietly.

'Well yes, Mrs Tate, you see . . .'

'Something bad has happened to Alfred.'

It was Bradshaw's turn to nod his head.

'Well, yes, Mrs Tate, something has happened to Alfred.' He felt guilty and asked himself why. Christ, it wasn't my fault, he told himself. I couldn't help it.

'What's happened to my husband, Mr Bradshaw?' Janet asked quietly.

Sgt. Bradshaw stared dumbly for a second or two at Janet.

'He's dead,' he blurted out.

Janet remained silent for what seemed to Bradshaw an eternity.

'How?' she asked at last.

'He was shot. I'm sorry, Mrs Tate. I really am sorry.'

She nodded dumbly, and stared white-faced back at him.

'Why?' she asked at last. 'Why would anyone want to shoot Alfie, why?'

'I don't know, Mrs Tate. We don't know.'

'Thank you for coming all this way, Sergeant Bradshaw.'

'There is nothing you can tell me?' was all he could think of saying.

Janet shook her head.

'You can ring us if you want help.'

She nodded.

'Well, Mrs Tate, there is nothing I can do, is there?' he asked.

'No,' Janet replied, 'nothing.'

'The funeral's tomorrow morning.'

Janet Tate, once more back in her own home, spoke to

Jack Lovel. 'You may come if you wish. Very few people will be there. I'm not allowing Jennie to go. I suppose you know she was assaulted by those thugs that you and Alfred became involved with, and it could happen again.'

'I'll pay my respects, Mrs Tate, but after everyone has left. I don't know if Alfred told you, but in the event of anything happening to him, I was to hand his share over to you.'

Janet Tate looked searchingly at Jack Lovel for a few moments.

'You don't suppose I would touch that money, do you? Alfred died for it,' she continued, 'and my Jennie was savagely assaulted because of it. No, I want no part of that money, and you had best look out for yourself. It is more than likely that they, whoever they are, will be looking for you. Sergeant Bradshaw called and asked questions this morning. I told him nothing, and you can rest assured I never will.'

'Maybe I could put a sum of money in a bank, on behalf of Jennie,' Lovel volunteered.

'Keep away from my daughter,' Janet Tate warned, coldly. 'I don't want you to even as much as speak to Jennie. We want nothing from you.' She looked meaningly at the door.

Lovel ignored the hint. 'Alfred left something in his clothing, it could be dangerous. Have they returned the things he was wearing?'

'Some of them,' Janet answered. 'I should imagine they destroyed the rest. The police delivered some things in a parcel this morning. I haven't opened it.'

Lovel waited while Janet brought in a small neat brown paper parcel from the kitchen. Untying it, he took out the shoes Tate had been wearing. 'Mind if I take these?' he asked.

Janet looked at the familiar black shoes.

'If you wish, I would probably have burnt them,' she answered. Lovel gave an inward shudder at the thought.

He drove to the old quarry, and disposing of the dangerous footwear, made his way to the town centre. Leaving the car next to a parking meter he crossed the market square and entered a florist.

Spotting the E-Type manœuvred into position before the parking meter, Ginger gave his companion a nudge. 'There's Lovel, Tracy.'

They watched him enter the florist's. 'He's buying a wreath for his mate's grave. That's what he's doing. Bet he comes out with a paper parcel,' Ginger said.

They hadn't long to wait. Lovel was scarcely in the shop three minutes. They watched him re-cross the market square.

'That means he's going to the funeral, and that's where we'll take him. What was the name of that village, Tracy?'

They both peered at the small message Janet had had printed in the *Evening News*. 'Best thing would be for us to hide up there and take Lovel, that is, if we get the chance, after the service,' Ginger said, refolding the newspaper and placing it on a wooden bench seat.

Jack Lovel arrived back at his flat, poured himself a large brandy, and sank wearily into an armchair.

He had something definite to go on now, he reflected.

He took his right shoe off and, turning it upside down, examined with interest the explosive heel. 'Now we shall see, Alfie,' he murmured. Removing the shoe from his left foot he placed both shoes carefully beside the chair. No point in tempting fate needlessly.

The thought of taking a blast from Ginger's shot-gun made him shudder. He mentally pictured the gun blasting into his face. Christ! what a bloody weapon to use on a man.

He finished the brandy and poured himself another drink, this time half filling the large glass. Downing most of it, he lit a cigarette. He sat for a long time drinking and chain smoking, his thoughts continually wandering back to the events of the last few days. He finished off the almost full bottle of brandy and started in on a bottle of whisky.

His aching mind now dulled with the effects of the alcohol, he fumbled with the tape recorder. The once so familiar and easy to operate controls now seemed complicated. After several abortive attempts, he managed to get the thing going. Relaxed, Lovel sank once again into the armchair. Lifting the brandy glass, half filled with whisky, he drank half at one go, the other half he spilled down his shirt front. Lovel tossed the now empty glass over to the fireplace, missed the small grate and laughed drunkenly as the glass shattered on the wall. He felt the wet stickiness of the whisky creeping down his neck. He looked down at the stain that was making his shirt front cling wetly to his chest, and laughed.

Looking up, he spied the half-empty whisky bottle. Forgetting that he had thrown the brandy glass away, he began to look for it. 'Bloody funny,' he muttered. He seized the bottle and took a good swig. Suddenly the missing glass seemed to be a very important item. He wanted to drink his whisky from it. 'Must have the glass,' he muttered, 'got to have it.' He lurched to the armchair and lifting the loose cushion, peered underneath.

He took another good pull at the bottle, staggered over to the kitchen and began to search in there. Satisfied the glass was not in there, he returned to the sitting room. Catching sight of his reflection in the wall mirror he swayed drunkenly before it, winked at himself and lifted the bottle again to his lips; most of the whisky spilled down his already wet shirt front.

Suddenly the doorbell shrilled. Lovel looked up with surprise. For several seconds he stood regarding the door with bewilderment. Again it sent out its shrill demand. 'Piss off,' Lovel giggled to himself, 'whoever you are, piss off, leave me alone.'

He stared down at the broken pieces of glass littering the floor, but what they had once been did not now register in Lovel's mind. 'Got to find that bloody glass,' he muttered.

Staggering over to the armchair, he was about to sit down, but seeing his shoes, his interest was suddenly focused on them. Picking the right shoe up he again examined it, this time with drunken curiosity.

'Bloody gelignite heel.' He sniggered. 'Jellied heel, that's what it is. Bloody jellied heel.' Losing interest in the shoe, Lovel dropped it carelessly on to the floor. He returned once more to the mirror and watched as he held the bottle to his lips and began drinking, spilling more of the whisky than he drank.

He watched with fascinated amazement his own reflection as it swayed backward and forward. 'I'm pissed,' he muttered, 'pissed as a bloody newt.'

Suddenly the floor came up, and Lovel felt with surprise its sharp slap. He laughed with drunken amusement as his head rolled uncontrollably off the tiled surround. Within seconds he was snoring.

Glenn Miller played his immaculate best. He played in accompaniment to drunken snores, but Jack Lovel's drink-befuddled mind was far beyond proper appreciation.

Ginger Benett and his partner Tracy hired a car. It was an almost new Hillman Traveller. They had breakfast at the small dingy restaurant which it had, of late, become their custom to frequent.

Ginger had his usual egg and chips, this time with two sausages. Tracy was careful not to make any adverse comment as he watched Ginger enjoying the meal. A bacon sandwich was all he could manage.

Ginger looked up from his plate. 'Be a stone rich man this time tomorrow, Tracy.'

'Think so?' Tracy answered.

'Dead cert,' the small gunman assured. 'Lovel's got the stuff buried somewhere. The only dodgy part is getting him down into that cellar. Won't be sorry myself when this little lot's over,' he continued. 'I've never known a job drag out like it. As I've said before, the old shot-gun raid takes some beating. I ever tell you about that bank we done in Hammersmith?'

He leaned over the table and peered hopefully at Tracy.

Tracy looked back; he gazed with wonder into Ginger's innocent blue eyes, and shuddered.

'Yeah, you already told me Ginge,' he said, mentally adding 'twenty times, at least.'

The cortege passed slowly through the High Street and turned right. Leading the procession, a long black Rolls Royce whispered slowly past the occasional pedestrian. Except for the slight hissing of the vehicle's tyres on the wet road, it made hardly any sound. Here and there a man bared his head in a gesture of respect.

Lovel was awaiting the procession. He sat in his car parked in a lay-by.

The rain, which had suddenly begun to pelt down some twenty minutes earlier, just as suddenly stopped. The wet roads began to steam as the hot September sun once again appeared from behind the clouds.

Lovel watched the leading Rolls Royce quickly pick up speed as it cleared the town and headed out into the open country and the twelve-mile journey, taking Alfred Tate back to the small village, his place of birth.

An almost new Hillman Traveller cut in sharply on the leading Rolls, the driver of which muttered an unholy curse.

The driver of the Hillman had his right elbow out of the side window, his fingers hooked on the edge of the car's roof. Lovel's interest quickened as he noted the unsightly tattoo marks on fingers and wrist of the exposed arm. He made a mental note of the Hillman's number.

Jack Lovel arrived at the village church some ten minutes ahead of the more sedate Rolls Royce procession. He parked his car on the grass verge close to the ancient stone wall.

Forgetting his wreath, he entered the churchyard and approached the gaping six-foot hole which seemed to wait, its clay sides gleaming wetly where the sharp spade had sliced.

Looking down into the grave Lovel cursed bitterly, recalling Janet's grief-stricken face. He tossed the butt of the gold-tipped cigarette he had been smoking into the yawning hole, and watched as the blue smoke spiralled lazily to the top.

Lovel moved back from the grave as the procession drew up. He faintly heard the funeral hymns, played on the church organ. Standing well back and with bowed head, he heard the short graveside sermon.

Janet glanced at the tall, bowed figure, but never once did she see him look up. Lovel heard the first dull clump as the earth was quickly shovelled over the coffin, and suddenly he was alone. He took the few paces necessary to bring him once more beside the flower-massed grave. Plenty of people had sent a wreath, he observed. Just a gesture. A gesture of respect to death. Not to the man they had known as a thief.

Jack Lovel seemed lost in deep meditation, his downcast eyes stared at his black square-toed shoes. He was, in fact, listening with a deep concentration. He knew his enemies were close at hand. After a long pause there was a faint rustle from the yew bushes. They were coming. They were coming to fetch him, at last!

'Now we shall see, Alfie,' he whispered to the silent grave. 'Now we shall see.'

'Haven't placed your wreath yet, Jack.'

Jack Lovel looked up as Ginger spoke. He took in the short barrel of the sawn-off shot-gun, the twin bores of which gaped menacingly at him. The gun was partly concealed by the loose raincoat Ginger was wearing. Ginger Benett also took in the cold, glittering venom that sparkled from Jack Lovel's eyes.

'Now don't try anything silly,' Ginger warned.

Jack Lovel looked directly into Ginger's eyes and smiled coldly.

'Go and get his wreath,' he spoke to Tracy. 'Get his wreath for him, wouldn't be right to leave that. Alfie Tate was his mate; they were "oppoes",' Ginger grinned nervously at Lovel. 'Have a fag if you want, Jack; don't suppose you carry a gun. Wouldn't do you much good if you did, can't miss with one of these.' He gave the shot-gun a jerk.

Reaching in his pocket Jack Lovel took out his cigarettes and lit up.

'Tasty lighter you got there, Jack.' Ginger looked avidly at the gold Dunhill. They both watched as Tracy carefully placed the simple wreath on the grave. At a nod from Ginger, Lovel began to walk from the churchyard, the two men following.

'You get in the Hillman,' Ginger ordered. 'Tracy will bring your car. Don't give me any trouble, Jack; if you do I'll shoot even if it's in the town.'

Lovel climbed into the Hillman, and Ginger slipped smartly into the back seat.

'Now look,' Ginger said as they got under way. 'I ain't bumping you off, Jack. You just have to tell us where Alfie Tate's share of the platinum is. You've still got your own half. Now that ain't asking too much, is it?'

'Why are you taking me back to the house then?' Lovel asked.

'We'll tie you up once you tell us where it is, then if it's the truth you're telling us, we'll come back and turn you loose. Straight up, Jack. I mean it. I won't do you. We were pals in the nick. Alfie Tate got what he asked for. He done the governor, and we were entitled to some of the platinum.'

Lovel watched his own car in the driving mirror. It was tucked in behind.

'Make for Lester Way, Jack. You know your way, you've been there before. Drive right in and pull well over to the right when you enter the drive.'

Lovel grunted a reply, overtook a rattling milk van and parked as he had been directed. The E-Type came to a stop directly behind.

Climbing from the Hillman, Lovel noticed that neither car could be seen from the road owing to tall firs which bordered the garden. Neither could they be seen from the nearest neighbour's front garden. They were in fact isolated from view.

Ginger gave him a nudge with the short barrel of the shot-gun.

'Front door's unlocked. You lead the way, Jack.'

Lovel mounted the stone steps leading to the front door, and entered. His heartbeats quickened as he walked through the short hallway. As his nervous system tensed to meet the deadly danger Lovel suddenly saw with unnatural clarity.

He took in every detail of the dilapidated, old-fashioned hall. The fact that the skirting boards appeared to have wood rot. An unsuccessful attempt by someone to paste wallpaper over the damp patches which were discolouring the ceiling. The smell of stale frying.

'Push the door, and straight down,' Ginger directed as Lovel came to the cellar door. Descending the stairs they entered the cellar. Ginger waved the shot-gun in the direction of the broken-backed chair. 'Sit down,' he said, with a smile.

'Now, which way do you want it, Jack, the hard way or the easy?'

Lovel glanced over at Tracy. He had turned chalk white. 'For Christ sake don't make it hard on yourself, tell him what he wants to know,' Tracy pleaded.

Lovel sat down on the dusty chair. He felt calmer now. In fact he felt almost at ease. 'What guarantee have I got except your word that I'll walk out of here alive if I tell you where the stuff's hidden?' He spoke to Ginger.

'None,' Ginger said, grinning, 'but I'll guarantee that if you don't tell us where that platinum is you won't leave here alive.'

Lovel grinned back. 'You still couldn't find it. I'm more likely to stay in one piece if you don't know where it is. I wouldn't be much use to you dead, now would I?'

'I ain't arguing with you, Jack. We'll find out! The hard way if that's the way you want it.'

He nodded in the direction of the vice, which was fixed to the workshop bench.

'If we have to, we'll put your cobblers in that, and you'll talk . . . you'll talk fast. They all do. You want us to try?'

Lovel looked thoughtfully at the vice for a second or two. 'No,' he replied at last. 'You don't have to. I'll tell you where half of the stuff's hidden. My half. Alfie Tate and I came to an arrangement. Alfred left instructions as to where I would find his stuff hidden if anything happened to him; in which case, I was to take a third of that which belonged to him and the other two-thirds I was to sell and hand the money over to his wife Janet. I also left instructions as to where he would find mine, that is, if anything happened to me. Alfie Tate hollowed out the heel of his shoe, and placed the written instructions inside.'

'Go on, Jack,' Ginger said, 'and where did you put yours?'

'Same place,' Lovel said.

Ginger looked down at the shoes Lovel was wearing. 'Which one, Jack?' he asked softly.

'The right,' Lovel said, holding it up. 'Want to pull it off?'

'No,' Ginger laughed. 'I ain't mug enough to try. You take it off, Jack, and throw it over here.'

Bending down, Lovel slipped off his right shoe and tossed it over to Tracy. Turning the shoe upside down, Tracy glanced at the heel. 'How the hell do I get this off?' he asked.

Ginger peered over Tracy's shoulder.

'It's under the rubber heel,' Lovel said. 'If you look you'll see there have been several slits made around the heel, and also one large slit in the centre. Underneath those slits are screws which hold the rubber heel in place.'

Tracy moved over to the bench and placing the shoe, heel uppermost, tightened the vice.

Picking up a large screwdriver he pushed into the small oblique incision and exposed the head of a small screw.

'Go on, have it off,' Ginger exclaimed impatiently. Tracy inserted the screwdriver into an incision. A few turns of the screwdriver and the screw was out. Within a few seconds he had removed the remaining small screws. He then began prodding the large centre screw.

'Mind if I help myself to a smoke?'

Ginger looked over at Lovel's request.

'No,' he replied, 'but if you're having us on with this

heel, you'd better make the most of it, because that'll be the last smoke you're ever likely to need.'

Lovel lit his cigarette. Both Ginger and Tracy watched as he lit up. As he replaced the cigarettes and lighter they returned their attention to the heel.

Lovel watched as Tracy made three complete turns with the screwdriver, then, beginning to cough, bent down.

Catching the slight movement from the corner of his eye, Ginger casually glanced over at Lovel, then peering over Tracy's shoulder watched with interest the last screw slowly emerge from the rubber heel.

Jack Lovel remembered Alfred Tate's advice. 'Keep your head well down; below the level of the vice and be sure to open your mouth otherwise the blast may burst your ear drums.'

Tracy had removed the large centre screw. The heel had not sprung off immediately as had been intended. With the continuous wear which it had received, the rubber heel had become welded to the heel proper.

Seeing Lovel now bent fully over, Ginger removed his attention from Tracy and thinking Lovel was about to be sick began to make a joking remark at the lack of bottle Lovel was displaying.

Tracy gave a brief glance in Lovel's direction, then inserting the screwdriver into the heel, levered upwards.

There was a terrific crash as the blasting gelatine exploded.

Tracy caught the full blast in the face. It ripped the flesh almost completely from the top half of his face, collapsed his lungs, and hurled him violently backward. His dead body lay spreadeagled not three feet from where Lovel still sat crouched over.

Ginger was luckier. His face had been turned in Lovel's direction, and Tracy's form had shielded him from most of the blast. Nevertheless, part of it caught him, and it was as if he had been struck a violent blow on the shoulder by a very large sledge-hammer. He was spun round and dumped violently against the nearby cellar wall, blood trickling slowly from his burst ear drums. The shot-gun lay close up against the work-bench. For several seconds Ginger Benett sat looking dazedly at Jack Lovel.

Lovel had suffered no permanent injury. The explosion had, however, made his senses reel and he too sat confused for several seconds.

Ginger came to his senses with a jerk. Instantly sizing up the situation, he staggered to his feet and began to lurch towards the shot-gun. For a further second or two Lovel sat and watched, a puzzled expression on his face.

Suddenly a shrill scream of danger seemed to shriek through his confused brain. He came to his feet, and in a sprawling dive he collided with Ginger. The little gunman went down. He began to fight, desperately. He knew that he was fighting for his life.

Ignoring Ginger's flailing arms and feet, Lovel seized him by the lapels of his loose-fitting raincoat, and rising to his feet, hauled his adversary with him. Ginger attempted to bring his feet into play, but it was no use.

Lovel held the little man easily in his grip. For a split second Ginger looked into Lovel's eyes. He saw and recognized death just as surely as if he had looked down the twin barrels of his own shotgun. In desperation, he used the only weapon left him. He butted.

The blow caught Lovel flush on the bridge of the nose, bringing blood and a momentary gush of tears. In the instant he relaxed his grip Ginger wrenched free.

Ginger raced for the door. His clawing hands found the door-knob, but in his frantic haste he had only half turned it when his body hit the still firmly closed door. He never got a second chance. Like a tiger, Lovel was on him, flinging him bodily across the room. Ginger smashed into the wall, and slid down to the ground, while Lovel picked up the discarded shot-gun. Breaking the breach he extracted the two shells, then tossed the weapon on to the work-bench.

Wearily Ginger came to his feet again. He edged slowly and cautiously along the whitewashed brick wall, his eyes darting in different directions, desperately seeking a weapon; desperately seeking a way out.

Lovel brushed his bloody nose with the back of his sleeve. For a second he halted his advance.

Ginger watched his movements with agonized eyes. He had edged himself into a corner. There was no escape for him now without his coming into direct contact with the other.

As Lovel slowly advanced, Ginger shrank tight up against the cellar wall. All strength seemed to leave his limbs. He looked again into Jack's coldly glittering eyes, and it was as if he became hypnotized. What he saw there made him scream: a thin shriek of despair, of utter hopelessness. Lovel reached out and gripped the gunman by the throat, then with a snarling curse he smashed his fist full into his face. The back of Ginger's head came into violent contact with the brick wall, then slowly he sank to the floor.

Lovel lashed out violently with his left foot, catching the man a stunning blow behind the ear. Again and again Lovel's left foot pounded into the now unconscious man's face and temples. He paused. Ginger lay quite still.

Lovel's eyes alighted on the shoes Tracy was wearing. From them his eyes flickered to his own single bloodstained shoe. With trembling hands he removed it and limping slightly, made his way over to the body of Tracy. Quickly taking off the dead man's shoes, he slipped his own feet into them.

Now for the next step. Lovel needed fresh air and time to think. Slowly he made his way up from the cellar and through to the large room at the front of the house. For some time he peered through the bay window and out into the front garden.

Should he leave the bodies where they were or should he clean up the cellar and dump them someplace? As he wondered what to do he noticed the four large concrete slabs of an old disused cesspool. Moving quickly now, he strode over to the cesspool, and heaving one of the slabs out of position, peered inside. The cesspool was almost full. A thick scum covered the surface.

Straightening up, Lovel looked quickly around. No, he could not be seen.

Once again he descended the cellar steps. Heaving the limp body of Tracy over his shoulder he staggered back up, and making his way to the cesspool dumped the body beside it. He tugged and heaved until he had the dead man's legs dangling over the concrete lip, then slowly he slid the body down into the murky depths. He watched the dead man's head gradually submerge. Slowly the scum which floated thickly on the effluent united into a whole.

Lovel rose to his feet. He returned to the cellar for Ginger's body and hauled it up and out to the cesspool. As he neared the edge of the cesspool, Jack Lovel almost let the body drop. He had felt it stiffen and then feebly struggle. He heard a faint gasp, and suddenly Ginger began to moan.

Ginger regained consciousness to find himself lying face upwards on a rough concrete slab. He could hardly see through the puffed and broken flesh that surrounded his eyes. His gaze travelled slowly up to the face of Jack Lovel who seemed to tower above him.

Lovel looked grimly down at Ginger. Raising his right foot he placed it against the injured man's shoulder and heaved. Ginger's unresisting body rolled over, and suddenly he found himself looking into the almost full cesspool. With a superhuman effort he struggled to his knees and attempted to rise. Quickly, Lovel brought his right foot up to rest for an instant on the kneeling man's shoulder, then with one tremendous kick he sent him sprawling, arms flailing wildly, into the gaping hole. There was a splash and flurry as Ginger beat the murky liquid in a desperate attempt to keep afloat. Suddenly his grasping fingers found a leverage; he made a grab at the overhanging concrete lip and secured a grip.

Seeing the fingers suddenly appear on the rim of the cesspool, Lovel first tried to loosen them with the toe of his shoe, but like limpets the fingers clung to the concrete. Losing patience, Lovel brought the heel of his shoe crashing down. Ginger was plunged into the liquid again, to thrash about in a desperate attempt to keep afloat.

Hefting the heavy concrete slab, Lovel quickly dropped it into position. For a second he stood listening to the now subdued splashing. Then came a long low wail of utter despair from the slowly drowning man, and Jack Lovel began to run. He raced for the open kitchen door and down the cellar steps.

Lighting a cigarette, he held his right hand out before him, and grinned weakly to himself at the sight of its trembling.

For some time he sat taking huge mouthfuls of tobacco smoke down deep into his lungs. He would have to clean this cellar up. Wipe it clean of prints; everything he had touched, and that included the Hillman he had driven to this house.

In the kitchen he found a bucket and a large sponge. He set to work, first thoroughly cleaning the cellar, then carefully wiping the door handles of the kitchen and front drawing room. Finally the Hillman, and then as a further precaution, he gave the E-Type a quick sponge down inside and out to erase any fingerprints Tracy might have left. Jack Lovel wanted there to be no way for the police to prove a connection between the two dead men and himself.

He returned the bucket to the kitchen, careful not to touch anything with his ungloved hands.

For some time he peered through the window at the four large concrete slabs covering the cesspool. He wondered if Ginger Benett had finally given up. Even now he might still have a grip on a handhold and could be keeping his head above the fluid. But he could never be able to heave that concrete slab up, Lovel knew.

Next he disposed of the Hillman Traveller, parking it amongst some dozen or so other cars near a large housing estate. Then he returned for his own car.

Wearily he let himself into his flat. He wasn't finished yet. After a quick bath and complete change, he made a bundle of the clothing he had been wearing and disposed of it at the old quarry.

At last Lovel sat in the deep leather-covered armchair and closed his eyes. He felt weariness wash through him. He could relax now, he told himself. But could he? Would he ever again know the full meaning of relaxation?